THE CASE OF THE AMOROUS ASSAILANT

THE CASE OF THE AMOROUS ASSAILANT

Beachtown Detective Agency

Terry Ambrose

THE CASE OF THE AMOROUS ASSAILANT

ISBN: 978-0-9968914-8-6

Copyright © 2022 Terry Ambrose

Cover design by Wicked Smart Designs

BOOKS BY TERRY AMBROSE

Seaside Cove Bed & Breakfast Mysteries
A Treasure to Die For
Clues in the Sand
The Killer Christmas Sweater Club
Secrets of the Treasure King
Treasure Most Deadly
Lies, Spies, and the Baker's Surprise

McKenna Mysteries
Photo Finish
Kauai Temptations
Big Island Blues
Mystery of the Lei Palaoa
Honolulu Hottie
North Shore Nanny
A Damsel for Santa
Maui Magic
The Scent of Waikiki
On the Take in Waikiki
Mystery of the Eight Islands

License to Lie Thrillers
License to Lie
Con Game
Shadows from the Past

Anthologies with Stories
Paradise, Passion, Murder: 10 Tales of Mystery from Hawai'i
Happy Homicides 3: Summertime Crimes
Happy Homicides 4: Fall into Crime

Happy Homicides 5: The Purr-fect Crime

1

MY NAME IS J.D. CAVENDISH. Technically, it's Juliet Delores Cavendish. I don't see myself as a Juliet, Jules, Julie, or any other cutesy nicknames. And I hate the name Delores. Sorry, Great Gramma, but Delores was cool when you were little, not so much anymore. In fourth grade, I decided initials were totally awesome. My friends had other ideas. They felt two syllables were too complicated. Everyone started calling me Jade. Except my ex—ever since I nearly shot him, he's called me Jaded. But we'll come back to that later.

Through a combination of circumstances not under my control, on this particular Monday, I'd become the owner of the Beachtown Detective Agency. Technically, my dad still owned the business. If things went well, I'd be able to pay off the purchase agreement over time. If not, Dad would be coming out of retirement.

But I had high hopes. The agency had put food on our table since I was little, given me my first work experience, and helped send me to UCLA for my degree in Criminal Justice. I hadn't thought about keeping the business after Dad retired, but as the saying goes, plans change.

Outside the front window, strolling tourists and a few locals meandered in search of tchotchkes, cool art, and decadent chocolate. That's Carlsbad for you—an eclectic mix of galleries, gift shops, and restaurants. It had been the same for as long as I could remember. The faces might have changed over the years, but the energy was always dialed up on the laid-back scale. Here, I could surf, run, bike…whatever I wanted. Just not today.

So here I was at ten a.m. on my third cup of mint tea. I was waiting for a client. Any client. Well, almost any client. Dad had given me only one cardinal rule—no divorce cases. Other than that, I was free to run the place as I saw fit. What I hadn't realized when Dad said he'd notified the clients of his retirement was the effect his letter would have on the business. To be polite, let's just say that unless someone walked through the front door soon, the memorial service would be on Saturday.

At eleven-fifteen, just as I was contemplating how I might scare up even a missing pet case, a familiar looking blonde walked in. I'd seen her before, but couldn't place her. Her tailored black top, pants, and beige safari jacket were all high end. We seemed to have the same fashion sense, just not the same budget. I got my tank top for $9.99 on sale at Target. This fashionista's clothes hugged every curve. Mine curved in places they shouldn't—probably from one too many trips through the dryer.

Having only practiced this routine about a dozen times in the past three hours and fifteen minutes, my introduction and invitation to sit came off smooth as butter in July. "How can I help you today?"

Blondie twirled a curly lock and gazed at me. "I want to divorce my husband."

I sighed. One rule. One. Could the universe be anymore twisted?

"I'm sorry, but I don't really handle cases involving marital disputes."

She raised one perfectly plucked and penciled eyebrow and looked me in the eye. "What's your hourly rate, Ms. Cavendish?"

Hourly rate? Without a client, I didn't have one. But what the heck? It would be good practice to actually say the words. I leaned forward, planted my elbows on the desk, and smiled cooly. "One hundred an hour."

Blondie pulled out her checkbook, scribbled out a check for two thousand bucks, and slid it across the desk. "Money is not a problem."

Gawping is so unseemly, but it was the only first check I'd ever receive as an entrepreneur. One rule. That's all Dad had given me. Screw it. This money was all mine—well, mostly mine. Mom and Dad still got their cut.

I picked up the check and read the name on the account—The Rose Investment Trust. I shot a glance at Blondie and blurted, "You're Gina Rose. Excuse me—Darlington."

Blondie grimaced, then let out a heavy sigh. "You were correct the first time. I kept my maiden name."

Holy crap. How had I not recognized her before? She dominated the local tabloids. Ran a financial empire. Was a fashion icon. Supported a gazillion charities for kids, families, trees. You name it, she was there. And she'd zipped through her Ivy League education while I was juggling part-time jobs, filing scholarship applications, and using my parents' contributions to help me through UCLA. We might be the same age, but we were from different worlds.

The heat began in my neck and spread into my cheeks, which now felt like they were glowing scarlet. "Sorry. I didn't mean to go all fangirl on you. My mom always told me I blush because I have an overactive sympathetic nervous system. Oh, gawd, I'm rambling. Sorry."

She smiled again and nodded. "Don't worry, everybody does it. Look, call me Gina. I hate formalities. You don't mind if I call you Jade, do you?"

I had no idea what the etiquette was for when a twenty-six-year-old heiress who had been born and bred to run her father's real-estate empire plopped herself down in your guest chair. "No problem…Gina." I did my best to hide the fact that I was totally gobsmacked. "We're talking about Bert. Right? You two have been married for…what…a year or so?"

"Two-hundred-seventy days."

Okay. Who was I to judge? My long-term relationship with Jason Taylor—the ex who, in my defense, deserved to be shot—cratered before I made it to the altar. "How long have you two been having problems?"

"We're not."

"Excuse me? Then why do you want a divorce?" Okay, I was gawking again.

"Because he's been stealing money from me. I've suspected something for about eight months."

And they'd been married for nine? I didn't feel like such a loser now, but it didn't erase the overwhelming urge I had to ram my fist into Jason's jaw. I know, next to the involuntary blushing, my anger over his betrayal ranked right near the top of my must-fix personality defects. After all, I owned a Taser and a gun and my biggest fantasy was still inflicting bodily damage on him in a very personal manner. But I was now an entrepreneur. A grownup. Someone with responsibilities. I pushed down my anger and focused on my new client.

"If my math is correct, that means you first noticed the problem in August of last year?"

"Jade? Are you okay? Your face is all red and you're carrying a lot of tension in your voice."

I forced a smile. There was no need to burden her with my personal baggage. She wasn't my emotional porter. She was Gina Rose. *The Gina Rose.* And this was supposed to be a business transaction. Right? So I lied. "It's nothing. I broke up with my ex recently, but I'm working through it."

Gina sat up straight, the fine lines of her face now hardened by anger. "Was he cheating on you?"

Cheating? What a nice way to say I caught him screwing another woman in our bed. "We'd been together for five years and I was expecting a ring. Apparently, I didn't know him as well as I thought."

"So you caught him *in flagrante delicto?*" Gina nodded knowingly.

In the back of my head, I could hear Dad telling me to stop baring my soul to a perfect stranger or a client. Dad was right. Soul-baring was not a way to impress clients. "Let's just say I had no idea he was so creative," I said casually.

We were both silent while I grappled with the gravity of this moment. Gina was what my dad always called his dream client —she had the money to pay the bill, a desire to get things done, and a problem she needed fixed. It was basically the same thing as the means, motive, and opportunity test the cops used, but in our case it meant we—correction, I—could pay the rent. Dad had spent years learning how to handle this type of client. I had, what, ten minutes?

"Do you want to talk about it?" Gina asked.

My jaw dropped. It? Which part? The Jason part? The still living at home part? The I-hadn't-prepared-myself-to-be-a-grownup part?

"I like you, Jade. We girls have to stick together. What happened?"

"You don't want…"

"Of course I do. I told you. I like you. I think we could be friends."

Friends? With Gina Rose? Since when did the hoity-toity make nice with the hired help?

"Do you surf?" she asked. "You look like you do."

"What kid who grew up here doesn't? Right?"

"Me," Gina said. "Daddy would never let me. He said it was too dangerous." She glanced over her shoulder toward the front window. "I'll bet your ex was one of those guys who loves his surfboard more than anything. Daddy always said they were heartbreakers."

Was this let's-be-friends thing some sort of nouveau business tactic? Make the hired help feel comfortable so they'll work harder? Or maybe this was some other kind of game…either way, I was intrigued. Gina definitely had my curiosity up.

"It wasn't one of them," I said. "His name was Jason, and I thought we were happy. I'd been to Fredericks of Hollywood and spent a bundle."

"You wanted to make him realize you were sexy," Gina added. "I know. I did the same thing with Bert at first." She leaned forward in her chair and peered at me. "How'd you catch him?"

Nope. Not going there. I needed to get this back on track. "Let's talk about Bert. Okay? Why do you suspect he's stealing money from you?"

Gina stiffened as though she'd been slapped. "Jade, I need to make sure we're simpatico. That means I need to understand you as a person. I see this as a potentially long-term relationship. If you don't want that…"

The way she let the last words hang in the air, her intent was obvious. My first client could easily become my last. There was only one thing I could do. Go with what Dad told me right before my first karate match when I was seven. I'd been petrified because my opponent was a year older. But Dad had given me sage advice when he said, "Sometimes, honey, you just gotta poke the bear."

2

THE TROUBLE WITH GIVING A seven-year-old sage advice is that they can become highly enthusiastic even though they're woefully unprepared. Yes, I got my butt kicked in that first karate match. And yes, Mom had spent days soothing me and telling me I was a winner despite the loss. To this day, the thought of losing still irritated me to no end. It was probably that competitive spirit— along with my growing curiosity—that drove me forward. It was time to find out if Gina Rose and I were, as she put it, simpatico.

"I moved back here to live with Jason after I graduated. We had big plans. He wanted to open a self-defense studio. Even though I was working, I agreed to help him get it up and running."

Gina nodded knowingly. "I did the same thing with Bert. Tried to help him out. Did you get the business going?"

"The opening was a huge success. It was like we'd achieved everything we wanted as a couple. I'd just gotten paid, had the afternoon off, and even had a little extra money, so that's when I went to Fredericks."

"Did it do the trick?"

"Not the way I planned. I drove straight from the mall to our apartment. You know, I wanted to surprise him. I surprised him, all right. He was with a bleached-blonde yoga instructor. They were right there in our bed."

"Infidelity has not been one of Bert's problems. At least, not in that sense."

"My situation was way less complex than yours, Gina. All I had to do was grab my stuff and walk out." Well, that wasn't exactly what happened. "Did you two sign a prenup?"

"My attorney had a fit because I didn't want to make Bert feel like I didn't trust him."

My insides cringed. All that money and they had no prenup? So much for an easy divorce. "That will make things more complicated, but we can work through it. How'd you meet?"

"At a party down in San Diego. He came up to me and I could just feel the connection. You know? He had this mysterious vibe I couldn't resist. He wanted to do all these super dangerous things like skydiving and car racing. He told me he was a venture capitalist. Said he had all these projects in the works. We talked about doing some philanthropy together. It seemed like I'd finally met someone who was—well, my equal. God, that sounds awful."

"Not at all." I lied. "He had resources and his own income. You figured he wasn't after you for money."

"Exactly. I didn't find out his real situation until after we were married. All of a sudden, I realized he'd been borrowing heavily to support the lifestyle."

"Do you think he was doing all this borrowing because he had no money sense or because he was trying to impress you?"

Gina sighed and stared at the remains of a potted plant in the corner of the office. Dad had used it as a coffee toilet a few too many times, but I was determined to bring it back from the brink. Assuming I was in business that long. When she didn't answer, I made eye contact and summoned a reassuring voice. "Gina?"

"Bert told me he was in debt because he'd gotten swindled by a man whose company declared bankruptcy. He'd invested a few million dollars in a tech company, but as soon as the deal was done, the owner skipped the country. Bert had all this documentation. It looked to me like he'd been swindled, but my attorney told me I needed to perform more due diligence before I gave him anything."

"Your attorney gave you excellent advice. What did you find?"

"I didn't do what he said. Bert was my husband. I still believed I could trust him. You know?"

At last, we were finally getting somewhere. I felt confident that I was now in control and, given the arrangement between Dad and me, that I might eventually work my way out of the financial sinkhole I currently lived in. Assuming I didn't blow the whole deal by trying to become BFFs with the likes of Gina Rose.

"I understand. It's hard not to believe in them when they're still in that cute stage. Right?"

"Exactly." Gina flashed a perfect, white smile, but it disappeared a heartbeat later. She nodded absently as she fingered a black pearl pendant hanging from a gold chain around her neck. The piece was stunning. Ocean waves made of gold and diamonds curled over a single pearl. That one piece had to cost more than the check she'd just written.

I waited silently, hoping she'd grown comfortable enough to tell me more. It didn't take long.

"We'd only been married a couple of months when this happened," she said. "At the time, it felt like I was prying the bad news out of him. The truth is, I was still madly in love and hated to see him so unhappy. He agreed to accept a loan—he insisted I couldn't just give him the money."

"Has he made any attempt to pay you back?"

"His company has lost money for eight months in a row."

I'd take that as a no. I studied Gina's face, noting that she looked everywhere but at me. Who would have thought that a woman with her business training could be blinded by love so easily? "Eight months is a long time."

She grimaced and threw me a weak smile. "I started giving him deadlines. They came and went. I had to loan him more money to keep the business afloat. The last deadline was March 31." She rolled her eyes. "The next day, he took me out to breakfast and told me he needed another loan."

"April Fools," I muttered.

"Exactly."

Gina brushed away a strand of hair that had fallen forward, leaned back in the chair, and wrapped her arms around herself.

"Let me make a few quick notes." I pulled a yellow notepad from the top desk drawer and jotted down key phrases to trigger my memory—*husband stealing?, client angry, surveillance starts tomorrow, lost money for eight months in a row*. I made a dollar sign on the page and put a question mark behind it. The number had to be significantly larger than anything I'd loaned Jason. What were we talking? Four figures? Five, tops? "So how much does Bert owe you?"

Her jaw tightened, and she glanced out the window. When she looked back, she bit her lower lip. "I loaned him ten thousand." She paused for a few seconds and added, "Each time."

The math was easy, straight out of third grade. Eight times ten. It was the total amount that made me wish I'd asked for a larger retainer. "He owes you eighty thousand…dollars?"

Gina squared her shoulders and sat up straight. "Not exactly," she snapped.

"I'm sorry. I shouldn't have said it that way." Obviously, she was not used to having her choices criticized. Or I was being manipulated. I might have only been in this business for three hours, but I knew from experience how people bent the truth to meet their personal needs. "It's a lot of money. That's all."

She winced, then shook her head. "Who am I kidding? It's more than eighty thousand. He said he wants to have breakfast again next Tuesday. He even had the gall to tell me he had all the problems figured out."

"And you think breakfast means another loan?"

"Yes."

I rested my elbows on the desk and slipped back into be-the-supportive-friend mode. "I can see why you're upset. So what is the total amount we're talking about?"

"More than half a million."

It took a few seconds for the number to register. When it did, I wondered why in the world she'd come to me. "I'm sorry, Gina, but I don't think I'm the right person to do this job. You need someone who's an expert in forensic accounting."

"No, Jade, I need you. The type of person you're talking about isn't going to tell me everything I want to know. A private investigator can do what I want."

"And what exactly is that?"

"I not only want the proof he's been using my money for his personal gain, but I also want to put the spotlight on his lies. In a sense, he's been cheating on me financially for eight months. I want him to pay for what he's done. I want to send him to jail for fraud, but I want my money back first." Gina leaned forward. Her eyes burned with an intensity I hadn't seen before. "He's made a fool of me for the last time. I intend to pay him back a hundred times over."

3

WITH GINA GONE, I SPENT about thirty minutes writing up my
notes and doing a little background on Bert Darlington's
business activities. The moment I discovered Bert had properties
in San Diego County, my inner butterfly took over. I so wanted
to get out of the office. Time for my very first office field trip.

Ever the optimistic overachiever, however, I reminded
myself I now had a client who'd paid me for twenty hours of
work. Gina promised to send me an accounting of the amounts
she'd given to Bert. My personal opinion, the one I'd kept to
myself, was that Bert had a second household. Assuming I was
right, it should take me no more than a few hours to follow him
to his mistress and their little love nest.

Twenty hours minus the few it would take to unveil Bert's
charade was still a bunch of hours. So as long as I kept track, it
should be no problem to indulge flitting urges.

I grabbed my go bag, which I'd inherited along with the
agency, and headed for the front door. The bag contained a
camera with a telephoto lens, a monopod, and a tape recorder
that had come from Dad. I'd added a small crossbody bag, a hat,

a shirt, and a bottle of water—everything I needed for a few hours of surveillance.

I could pick up a sandwich, deposit Gina's check, then drive to Bert's closest investment property for some background research. Easy peasy—except that my dad was now standing out front talking to Delbert Dodge, the owner of the pizza place next door. Mr. Dodge's grandson, Delbert III, was a prime example of why I had a love-hate relationship with Carlsbad. Delbert III and I went to the same high school, dated exactly once, and that's when I'd realized Dodger, as we called him, was an underachiever. Too few ambitions. Too many hormones. And no desire to leave home. Ever. Need I say more?

With a sigh, I dropped my bag on the desk and waited. The big problem with me joining the conversation out front was that Mr. Dodge would probably again try to hook me up with his grandson. If Mr. Dodge wasn't such a sweet old guy, it would be much easier to tell him I was not going out with a thirty-something man who still lived at home and had his grandmother do his laundry.

The conversation ended after a few minutes. Mr. Dodge tottered back to his business, and Dad entered through what was now my front door.

"Hey, Jade. How's it going?"

I forced a smile. "Good."

"Something's wrong. I can see it on your face."

"No. Nothing…" Why lie? This was the man who'd known the night I let Bobby Kaminski get to second base in the movies. I couldn't win, but maybe I could delay the inevitable. "Dad, I thought we agreed you didn't need to be here every second."

"Just checking up on my girl. That's all." He glanced around the office, stuffed his hands in his pockets, and gave me a sheepish grin. "I thought I might take you to lunch. You know, maybe we could have a little father-daughter time."

What had I done to screw up my karma this much? Lunch meant we would talk shop. He'd give me pointers. Offer encouragement. Oh gawd. It was better to just confess and get this over with. "I broke the rule."

"Excuse me?"

"You know. You gave me one rule—no divorce cases."

"Oh. That."

"I have my first case, Dad. And it's probably a philandering husband." I held my breath, expecting anything from a mild rebuke all the way up the ladder to having Dad rip up our agreement.

He nodded. Smiled. "I'm proud of you, Jade. Do you know how long it took me to get my first client? A long time. I hope you got a retainer."

"Wait. You're not mad? You said no divorce cases."

"When did I say that?"

"Um, last week. Friday, dinner, over roasted chicken and mashed potatoes, to be exact."

He pursed his lips and nodded, then winked. "I love your mom's roasted chicken." A moment later, he reached out, put a hand on my shoulder, and gave it a gentle squeeze. "I was just angry over what Jason did to you. The truth is, I shouldn't be laying down those types of rules—you're not a child anymore. You need to be true to yourself. Take the cases you want. Whatever you do, remember there are two sides to every story— and always seek the truth."

"I do, Dad. You taught me that when I was little. See? I really do listen."

"I know, honey." A faint smile crossed his lips, and he pointed at the bag on the desk. "I see you're on your way out. I guess that means lunch is out." He chuckled, then let out a wistful sigh. "Look at me, first day of retirement, and already I'm missing things. I'll let you get on with your case."

He started to turn away, but I stopped him with a hand on his arm. I put my arms around his neck and gave him a hug. "I love you, Dad."

"I love you, too, honey." When he pulled away, he took me by the shoulders and held my gaze. "Come to think of it, there really is one rule I never want you to break. Don't get hurt."

As I locked the front door behind us, I saw a sadness in his eyes. Was he already regretting his decision to retire? He was the one who'd said he wanted to pursue other interests. Mom and I called it a midlife crisis. Either way, now that a client had dangled cash money in front of me, I wasn't about to go backwards.

"See you tonight at dinner?" he asked, his eyebrows raised expectantly.

"Of course." I winked at him, told him we could catch up tonight, and left.

With lunch in a paper sack and Gina's check in the bank, I tackled the drive to another of Bert's investments, a shopping mall called "The Rose of Nestor." Fun Fact #1 was that even though I'd lived in north San Diego County all my life, I'd barely heard of Nestor, which it turns out is a bedroom community consisting of apartments, condos, and older single-family homes. Fun Fact #2, apparently Bert's company had named the center in honor of his wife. Apparently, the act of lending someone a half-million bucks brought with it certain perks.

The GPS guided me right to the mall's main entrance. A street monument, an oversized stucco-and-neon eyesore visible from two blocks away, proudly proclaimed The Rose to be "Nestor's Finest Shopping Destination." Eyesore that the monument was, I had to admit Bert's company must have spent a ton of money on it. It even had a fancy red decoration in the background that was supposed to resemble, well, a rose.

I counted a dozen empty storefronts while I waited at the left-turn signal. The only businesses open were a liquor store, an off-brand cell phone outlet, and a dry cleaner. Security bars lined the front of each store and the windows of what had been the anchor tenant were boarded over with four-by-eight sheets of plywood. Yellowed pieces of paper flapped in the afternoon breeze, clinging to the weathered plywood by thin strips of silver duct tape.

The light changed. I made my left and snuck a final peek at the monument. As ugly as that thing might be, it shined like a jewel in an oasis of regret.

I parked in front of the liquor store and scanned the empty storefronts, then crossed the lot to the anchor store. I pinned one of the tattered sheets of paper to the plywood with my fingers. It was an announcement for an unnamed new tenant. Unless San Diego was going to throw some serious redevelopment dollars at this location—a new tenant was, in my opinion, totally unlikely. The only prospective tenant I could envision might be a Salvation Army soup kitchen.

The pungent scent of marijuana drifted out of the entrance of the liquor store. My shoulders tensed as I warned myself not to breathe. An alarm cling-clanged as I walked through the open door. The clerk glanced up from his phone, raised his bushy eyebrows, and shrugged. It was totally unfair to stereotype the guy, but with an outgoing personality, dark hair, and scraggly goatee, Mr. Congeniality definitely ranked below Delbert Dodge on my willing-to-date list.

"Hey," I said.

He sighed and barely looked at me. "You lost, lady?"

I shook my head and smiled. "Soft drinks?"

"Back wall." He raised his chin to indicate a refrigerator case to my left, then returned his attention to his cellphone, which sounded like he was playing some sort of swords-and-sorcerers game.

On my way to the display he'd pointed out, I snagged a bag of chips. Checked the date. They'd only expired two weeks ago. What the heck? Expiration dates were just a suggestion. Right? And for all I knew, this might be the big sale of the day. Based on inventory, beer and wine were the obvious top sellers.

It sounded like a hundred guys died in the melee playing out on Mr. Congeniality's cell in the time it took me to collect my measly two items. And in that time, he never once looked up. With items in hand, I approached the register.

After about ten seconds of being ignored, my temper started to rise. For real? I took second place to a video game? Since when had I stopped turning heads? I crossed my arms over my chest.

Still no reaction. I'll bet he wouldn't ignore Gina. Come to think of it, what would she do? Got it. I licked my lips, laid my two items down, and planted both elbows on the counter.

"You ready?" He made some sort of do-I-have-to-do-this? face thing and glanced up. His jaw dropped. He did a double take and swallowed hard, then jammed the phone into his back pocket. Stepping forward, he picked up my bag of chips and leered down the front of my scooped neckline.

A little surge of satisfaction coursed through me. Take that, swords-and-sorcerers. Take that, Jason Taylor. "What's your name?" I asked.

"Donny. What's yours?" He craned his neck to one side and stroked his lips with his fingers.

The heat began in my chest. Oh gawd, not now. The blush continued up my neck and rose into my cheeks. I stood up straight and gave the bottom of my shirt a self-conscious tug. "I'm Jade. Are you the manager?"

"Nah. I just work here part-time." He licked his lips and eyed me. "You ain't looking for a job or nothing like that? Right?"

"No. I work for an investor who might be interested in buying the mall. They'd like to do a lot of upgrades. Sort of a revitalization project."

Donny did a double take, scrunched up his cheeks, and craned his neck forward, a clear look of confusion on his face. "Why?"

"Why what?"

"Why would anyone want to throw money at this place? Nobody shops at this dump."

I looked out the front windows at the parking lot. A half dozen cars. "Good point. But that's usually the idea behind redevelopment. The investment is supposed to bring in more business."

"Lady, you can't make a silk purse out of a sow's ear. They already tried and look what happened." He reached down below the counter, pulled out a joint, and held it up. "You want a hit?"

"You're allowed to smoke weed in a liquor store?" I blurted. Oh gawd. I sounded like a total rube.

"Purely medicinal. That a no?"

"Good guess. Where'd you hear the expression about the silk purse, anyway?"

Donny grabbed a lighter off the counter, flicked it, and stuck the joint in his mouth. He inhaled, held his breath, then closed his eyes and blew smoke toward the ceiling. "My grandma. She always used to say, 'Donny, you can't…'"

"Got it." I waved my hand in front of my face to cut Donny off. "You ever see the landlord?"

"Nah. And the owner only comes in to open. Mr. Chung-whatever next door runs the cleaners. He might."

I pointed at my two items. "How much?"

Donny took another hit off the joint, leered again at my neckline, and shrugged. I did my best not to breathe while he scanned my two items, then hurried out the door.

4

I TOOK SEVERAL DEEP BREATHS to clear my head as I walked slowly to the dry cleaners. Thank goodness the rush of heat that had overcome me was now gone. I dawdled near the door as a stout woman carrying clothes protected by clear plastic bags exited. The odor of cleaning products wafted behind her. She was dressed professionally in a white blouse and peach slacks. A rush of panic washed over me when she glanced in my direction and gave me a curt nod. Was the scent of marijuana following me around? I hoped not as I entered the store.

Like most cleaners, this one also performed alterations. On the right side of the store, just inside the entrance, stood a small sewing desk with an old Singer at the ready. Spools of thread in a rainbow of colors lined a rack above the desk. A man's blue blazer lay next to the sewing machine. The stitching on one of the cuffs had been taken out, leaving the seam unfinished. The garment conveyor running around the perimeter of the store was filled with hanging clothes. Unlike the liquor store, it appeared the cleaners actually had customers.

A small man with thinning hair emerged from the back of the store. His smile was ready and welcoming, and he nodded agreeably as he approached.

"Welcome, Miss. Are you picking up?"

"I was hoping to speak with the owner."

"I am the owner. My name is Mr. Chang. How may I assist you?"

Smart move on my part to not trust Donny's ability to retain names—or anything else, for that matter. "Marsha Cavanaugh. I'm a reporter working on a story about redevelopment projects. Would you have a few minutes to answer some questions?"

The man grimaced as he slipped by me and laid a silky, flowered print dress on the stand next to the old Singer. "What do you want to know?"

"Business here at this shopping center appears to be very slow. Has it been that way for long?"

"Yes. For some time now. My business is good. We have loyal clients. Other businesses—" He stopped and shrugged. "They come and go. Most are not the right type of store for this center."

"What was the anchor tenant before?"

"Before what?"

"Before they moved out."

"They did not move out. They never moved in. We were supposed to get some kind of market, but it never happened."

"Have the landlords done any renovations? Anything to revitalize the mall?"

"A new company bought the property a few months ago. They came in with big ideas and put that monstrosity out front." He gestured at The Rose of Nestor monument.

I glanced back toward the mall entrance. "I see. What else did they do?"

"Nothing. They said they had spent so much money on buying the property and marketing that they needed to raise the rent. The old landlord was very good. This company is not friendly to its tenants."

"I'm sorry. Do you hear from them very often?"

"Only when the rent is due or they want to bring bad news."

"When was the last time they contacted you?"

"Two weeks ago." Chang's voice rose in pitch as he continued. "I cannot afford their clumsy management. They claim that when they purchased the property, my lease became void. Rather than go to court, I agreed to go on month-to-month. I also told them I wanted a lease and guaranteed rent for two years. I am sure when they come back, I will not be able to meet their terms."

"I'm sorry, Mr. Chang. I didn't mean to upset you. It sounds like your landlord doesn't do much other than hold their hands out for money."

Chang crossed his arms over his chest and glared at me. "Ever since this new company took over, things have not been good. They pretend to be some big outfit, but they have no idea what they are doing. They cannot agree on anything."

"What do you mean?"

"You are a reporter?" Chang licked his lips and shook his head. "I should not be telling you all this."

"We can be off the record, if you'd like. I'll only use the information you give me as background. I will not print anything you tell me in the article."

I waited as Chang ran his fingers over the worn wood of the sewing machine table and gazed out the front door. Finally, he gave me a curt nod. "Very well. Off the record. The center manager came by to deliver the news. She is disgusted with their whole setup. She said the owners contacted her to tell her if they could not get more money out of the tenants, one of the partners wanted to sell. But the other one wanted to put more money in. She said they do not get along."

"Really? The center manager told you all that?"

"She is a cousin. And she hates her job."

"I see. Do the partners themselves ever come here?"

"No." Chang shook his head and looked around. "If they did, the tenants who are left would tell them what we think of them. They are afraid to come here."

"What about your cousin? She's not afraid of the other tenants?"

"We all know she has no power. What is the point in killing the messenger?"

"Of course. If they were to decide to do more work on the center, what would they do?"

"I have no idea. Neither do they. According to my cousin, those two fight like cats and dogs. Their disagreements are getting worse all the time."

"Would your cousin talk to me, Mr. Chang?"

"I doubt it. Her husband is a lawyer, so he is very suspicious. I do not know that she would tell you anything new."

"What was the outcome of your cousin's visit?"

"Stalemate—for now. They will be back because they will want to raise the rent. According to my cousin, unless they want to let this center go into bankruptcy, they have to sell it to a company with deeper pockets."

A man dressed in a tee shirt, shorts, and flip flops walked in carrying a suit and a couple of women's sweaters. He nodded at us and laid the items on the counter. My conversation with Mr. Chang felt like it had run its course, so I thanked him and went to the cellphone store. From the moment I entered, it was obvious the girl behind the counter was clueless.

She couldn't have been more than eighteen and did her best to ignore me, just like Donny had initially. I was pretty sure the same trick wasn't going to work on her, so I asked when the owner would be in.

The question earned me a blank stare, followed by a shrug and a quick, "I dunno."

I sighed, thanked her, and walked out the door. She might be a waste of time, but I'd learned three things here at The Rose of Nestor. First, Bert Darlington had a business partner. Second, the two men didn't get along. And third, they needed money. Perhaps I'd been wrong about Bert. If his business decisions included buying properties like this one, Gina's case might have nothing to do with another woman. The only way to prove that would be to follow him.

Back in my car, I jotted down notes from my conversation with Mr. Chang and what I'd learned. I also wrote down a question—*why didn't Gina tell me Bert had a business partner?* I quickly added another—*does Bert want to talk to Gina about more money for the Nestor project?*

Gina had probably never even been here. Or maybe she had, and that's why she wanted her money back. Either way, I gave the tired storefronts one final look, opened my bag of chips, and popped the top on my soft drink. It was time to leave The Rose of Nestor where it belonged. Behind me.

5

THE TRAFFIC HOME WAS THE usual San Diego slow-and-go—
except where it was stop-and-no-go. By the time I arrived, I was
whipped. As much as I hated to admit it, I needed to talk to Dad
—without Mom around. I found them both in the kitchen and
wondered if this might be the new normal now that Dad was
officially retired. Rather than even attempting to exclude Mom
from the conversation—an impossible task—I slipped up to my
room to do more research on Bert and Gina.

Mom announced dinner was ready around six. Dad had
barbecued something resembling fish. To be fair, he'd never
gotten much practice in the art of barbecuing when he was
working. I said a small prayer to the barbecue gods that if my
dad was going to be delving into the dark art of grilling, they'd
allow his inner grillmaster to surface.

Sadly, tonight was not a night to celebrate success. We were
all picking at the crispy critters on our plates when Dad
grimaced and set down his fork. "Guess I got it a bit on the
overdone side."

I speared a blackened chunk. It skittered from beneath the tines of my fork, leaving a trail of charbroiled fragments behind. "Just a touch," I said.

Dad pushed his plate away and leaned his elbows on the table. "Who wants pizza?"

Mom and I exchanged a look. We sighed in unison and raised our hands. Clearly, the barbecue gods needed to provide more guidance to their newest student. But, what Dad lacked in grilling skills, he made up for in pizza ordering. The moment he set down the phone, he said, "Thirty minutes. How'd your day go, Jade?"

"Who wants more wine?" Mom picked up the bottle, topped off her glass, then looked at me. "Jade?"

She didn't wait for an answer, but immediately began to pour. Apparently, Mom and I were going to get our dinner calories from alcohol.

I had to accept the fact that a talk alone with Dad wasn't going to happen. That meant wine was fine by me. I took a healthy gulp from my glass and sighed. "It was good."

"Just good?" Dad peered at Mom with raised eyebrows and smiled. "Her first day as her own boss, and she says it was just a good day. What will she be like in twenty years?"

"You're prying, Thomas. Jade will tell you when she's ready." Mom took a sip from her glass and fixed me with a you-will-do-this-now stare. "Won't you, Jade?"

I eyed the bottle. There wasn't enough alcohol left to make this work. "I will be happy to share, Dad. Once I have something to tell."

"How could there be nothing to tell us about? You got a case. Your very first one."

Mom did a double take, took a larger sip, then gawped at me as I had Gina Rose. "You got a case?"

"Dad didn't tell you?"

"You went to the office, Thomas?" Mom glared at Dad. "I thought you were taking a walk."

"I did."

"Wait—you lied to Mom about where you were going?"

"It wasn't a lie. And why are you so tightlipped about your new case?"

"I'm not being tightlipped—it's complicated."

"What's complicated?" they asked in unison.

Oh, gawd. Why me? "Okay." I raised both hands in surrender. "My case involves Gina Rose's husband. She believes he's been stealing money from her." I proceeded to describe my trip to Nestor. There was no point in leaving anything important out. I'd been through enough of these inquisitions all the way back to that infamous date with Bobby Kaminsky in eighth grade—the one where he got to second base.

But the Bobby Kaminski episode had taught me a valuable lesson. A successful outcome in this type of conversation was all about the details. The ones I left out. Yes, it was one of my top 'surviving Mom' rules—too much information was too much trouble. The interaction at the liquor store—from the marijuana episode to letting Donny leer down my blouse—fell into the category of oversharing as far as I was concerned. Mom and Dad were not on the need-to-know list for today's embarrassing encounter. I just wish I'd known this lesson the night I confessed and told them exactly where Bobby Kaminski's hand had been during the last half of the movie.

Dad scratched his chin, then turned his attention from me to Mom. "Can I give her some advice?"

Mom eyed him closely. "Are you doing this as her mentor or her father, Thomas?" She turned to me. "It's up to you, honey. If you want your dad's advice, that's one thing. I just don't want him getting so involved he takes over. You know how he is."

"I do, Mom."

"I'm right here," Dad said.

"We know," Mom and I said together.

"I'm not that bad," Dad grumbled.

Mom and I both fixed him with a deliberate stare. "You are."

He planted his elbows on the table and massaged his temples with his fingertips. After a few seconds, he sighed. "Okay. You can give me a status report when you're ready, Jade. If you want help, I'm here for you. Otherwise, I will mind my own business." He picked up his glass, grimaced, then set it down.

Why is it when you get your way, you suddenly realize it may not really be what you really want? "Dad, I'm sorry. I didn't mean to cut you out. And actually, you can help me with something—as long as you maintain some emotional distance."

"Fair enough," he said.

I turned to Mom, took a deep breath, and blurted, "You need to keep some distance, too. This is strictly business, Mom."

She started to say something, huffed, then nodded. "Okay. This is between the two of you."

I described what I'd learned about Bert Darlington—his poor business sense, his disagreements with his business partner, and even my suspicions that this case might be more than just following a philandering husband. When I was done, Dad gazed at me, then turned to Mom.

"The Case of the Three Eggs," Dad said.

"You would bring that up." Mom rolled her eyes and shook her head.

"Excuse me?" I'd heard about a lot of the agency's cases, but not this one.

"Contrary to popular belief, Jade, I am not going to tell you what to do. But I am going to tell you how I learned the importance of perseverance and resourcefulness. A long time ago, when I was just starting out, I asked this pretty girl out for dinner."

He stopped and winked at Mom. She did the same thing I would and blushed bright pink. "I still can't believe you pulled something like this on our first date."

"Anyway, I was working a case with my boss. We were doing the same thing you are. Following what we were sure was a cheating husband. We tailed him for a couple of weeks. We'd become convinced our client's husband was playing house with his girlfriend. But we needed proof."

I sipped from my glass and waited eagerly. I'd never heard about Mom and Dad working together. And judging by the way they were smiling at each other, this had to be good. Turning to Dad, I asked, "Did you get the proof?"

"That's where it got tricky. My boss and I tailed the husband after work, but something happened each time and we lost him. On this particular night, we got lucky. We followed him to a large complex. Unfortunately, a moving truck got in the way, so we lost him again. This place was huge. There were multiple buildings, and we didn't even know which one he might be in."

"Why wouldn't you just drive the parking lots and get the number off his space?"

"The spaces weren't assigned. But we did finally find his car. We decided to try the closest building. So my boss had me go door-to-door. I knocked on this one door and I found myself face-to-face with the guy."

"Awesome. You had him."

"No, I didn't. There were no names on the mailboxes or on the apartments. All I had was our guy in an apartment. Not exactly strong proof he was living with someone. Still, I figured all I had to do was work my way in and I could do a little reconnaissance. So I asked him if I could borrow an egg."

"An egg?"

"Yes. I said I had just moved into the unit a few doors down and was in the process of baking a cake when I discovered I didn't have any eggs. It seemed like a pretty good story until the guy tells me to wait and closes the door in my face. He comes back a minute later with an egg."

Mom laughed and patted Dad's hand. "You have to admit, it wasn't a particularly clever excuse, Thomas. Who moves into a new place and starts baking? And if they do, they're not going to do it without checking their ingredients first."

"It seemed like a good idea at the time." Dad scrunched up his face, then continued. "So, I went back to my boss, who was waiting in the car, and told him what happened. He chewed me out and told me to try again. I didn't know what else to say, so I went back and told the guy I needed another egg. I asked him if I could wait inside while he got it, and he said no. By this time, he was a bit annoyed, but he did the same thing. He got me another egg and sent me on my way.

"You have to realize this was one of my first cases, so I was completely dejected when I got back to the car. My boss chewed me out again and told me to go back up there and get the proof. I asked him what recipe called for three eggs, and he said to tell the guy I broke the last one."

I frowned and looked from Dad to Mom. "Where do you come into this, Mom?"

"Later. Your dad went back and tried again, but all he got was a third egg. He and his boss gave up. Your dad rushed across town to pick me up. He was late, and he was terribly grumpy. When I asked him what was wrong, he told me the story. I suggested we go back with a cake."

"Okay. Didn't see that one coming."

Mom winked at me. "Resourcefulness, honey."

Dad glanced at Mom, smiled, then turned to me. "So we went to the market and bought a cake. We thought we could just move it onto a plate, but we couldn't get it off the plastic tray without destroying it. We didn't know what else to do, so we left the cake in its original packaging and went back together. I knocked on the door. This time, the guy opens the door, and he looks like he's going to call the cops when your mother steps in and says, 'The cake fell.'

"The guy burst out laughing, so I went into this story about how nice he was to loan me the three eggs, and how terrible I felt for having taken his eggs, and he got nothing in return. I told him your mother insisted we go to the store, buy the cake, and bring it to him."

Mom said, "So he invited us in. He went and got his girlfriend, introduced her to us. They told us they'd moved in the month before and were planning on getting married. All they were waiting for was his divorce to become final."

"Of course, the guy hadn't filed for divorce at this point. I'm not sure he ever had any intention to. So I ended up with the proof. I had his name, his girlfriend's name, and their admission that they'd been living together. My boss was so happy he gave me a raise."

"So you're saying I should give Bert Darlington a cake?"

"I'm saying you should think outside the box. Don't be afraid to keep trying—even if you have to do something crazy. It might just pay off."

As the night wore on, I kept thinking about tomorrow morning. It would be my first surveillance. The first time I might have to come up with a Plan B on the fly. I wasn't yet sure what Plan B might be, but unless I was sorely mistaken, it would have nothing to do with the Rose of Nestor. Or baking a cake.

6

I AWOKE AT FIVE ON Tuesday morning feeling ready to tackle the day. At this hour, I expected to have the kitchen to myself, but the moment I opened my door, the heavenly aroma of freshly brewed coffee filled my senses. The good news was that I'd soon be getting my little morning buzz. The bad? Mom or Dad, maybe both, were already up.

Mom looked up from her laptop when I walked into the kitchen. She'd parked herself at the island and was halfway through her mug of coffee. "Morning, honey. How'd you sleep?"

"Okay. You're up early."

She shrugged. "It's an old habit. Whenever your dad had a stakeout, I was up early to make him a snack and a thermos of coffee."

"I remember when I was little you'd give me hot chocolate and tell me it was what Daddy drank. I can't believe I fell for that."

"You were very trusting." Mom smiled and tilted her head to one side. The brand new thermos and the purple, insulated lunchbox she'd given me over the weekend were already on the counter.

"You're all set. Hey, have you seen this?" She turned her laptop so the screen faced me. "This is the kind of perseverance your dad and I were talking about last night."

A little chill ran down my spine. So much for getting out of the house sans parental advice. I read the headline and rolled my eyes. "This woman needs spelling lessons."

"I agree she's not going to win a Pulitzer, but she's been following the Amorous Assailant since the first attack. This is her report on the third attack."

"Really, Mom? The Amorous Assailant? She gave him a name?"

"Well, he ties up his victim with red silk, kisses her on her cheek, and leaves a red rose at her side. All I'm saying, honey, is you need to have this kind of stick-to-it-tiveness to succeed."

"I'll work on that," I muttered. Coffee. I definitely needed coffee to get through this.

"I'm sorry, honey, I've upset you."

"No. It's not your fault. It's me. I'm just being cranky. What I need is some caffeine, a shower, and to hit the road."

"We'll talk later. I'll let you get to it." Mom turned the laptop around and continued reading. Almost immediately, her eyebrows went up, and she pursed her lips.

After taking the fastest shower in history and packing a makeup case so I could finish making myself presentable during the stakeout, I made it out the door within forty-five minutes. I arrived at the Rose residence before the sun was up. The morning sky was a deep blue, streaked with wisps of pink and gray clouds. The house was located near the top of what Mom and Dad call the Hills of Money. This quiet residential street was like any other in north San Diego County, except that the homes went for millions more and had ocean views galore.

Bert Darlington pulled out of his driveway at twenty-two minutes after six, precisely as the first rays of sun radiated across the sky. He stuck to the side roads where there were few cars out and about. It made the job of following him easy, and the job of staying undetected a major challenge. But I must have been successful because he never made an abrupt turn or changed speed. He drove straight to the parking lot at the end of Ocean Street, grabbed one of the spots facing the ocean, and strolled toward the sea wall.

If Bert had been wearing sweats or shorts, I would have assumed he was going for a run, but he was wearing business casual. Maybe a walk along the sea wall before he went to work? I parked hastily and watched as he turned left at the end of the lot. I grabbed my camera from my go bag, put on a hat and a light jacket, and went to the end of the parking lot, where I pretended to take photos of the scenery.

A gentle breeze blowing in off the ocean caressed my face. For the briefest of moments, I let myself soak in the moist, cool air. After taking two photos of the shoreline, I turned to look behind me. There was Bert, sitting on the patio of Java Joe's.

The first time I could remember being at Joe's was when I was five. Mom and Dad brought me in for hot chocolate. Yes, I was big on hot chocolate in those days. Come to think of it, that hadn't changed. My parents liked Joe's because they made their coffee strong and had outdoor seating. The combination made the place a landmark in the Village and a popular hangout for locals and tourists.

For the next thirty-plus minutes, Bert, the subject, sat at one of the outdoor tables being preoccupied with his phone, drinking coffee, and shooting an occasional glance at the ocean while I meandered, sat, and occupied myself with sneaking an occasional photo. I found it hard to believe this was the routine of a man who'd pocketed more than half a million dollars of his wife's money. This was the routine of someone who didn't clock long hours in the office, but also didn't spend frivolously.

It wasn't the first time I wondered if Gina might be manipulating me for some other purpose.

At six-fifty, the subject stood, threw his paper cup in the trash, and strolled nonchalantly back to his car. I tailed him to a swanky commercial building about five miles inland. He parked near the expansive glass front of the building, locked his car, and meandered inside.

Wow. Was that all there was? I hoped not. This was only the first morning. Dad had tailed the three-eggs guy for weeks. Maybe Mom was right. I'd need to have the same kind of patience and determination as that blogger person she talked about. What was her name? Zoe something-or-other.

I opened the thermos, poured myself some of Mom's brew, and waited.

By nine, I was bored and needed a restroom. I'd have to ask Dad how he survived long hours of surveillance after drinking so much coffee. Even though Gina had been giving Bert money for his business, I had the feeling Bert did not own this building. If I was correct, he was renting office space here. The problem was that I could hear my dad warning me to never go into a situation without all the facts.

I pulled out my phone and did a quick search for the address. To my surprise, the building was operated by Xander Professional Virtual and Private Offices. I'd heard of virtual office spaces before, but never did I suspect the business Gina's husband operated would be in a place like this. Did this mean Bert didn't even have a real office?

With my curiosity in high gear and bladder near the breaking point, I got out of my car and entered through the front door. A receptionist by the name of Meghan pointed out the restroom. I thanked her, went and used the facilities, then returned, hoping I could get a few questions answered.

"Thanks again for letting me use the restroom," I said as I approached.

Meghan was a middle-aged, heavyset woman, and had a friendly smile. Tiny crow's feet around her dark brown eyes crinkled as she shook her head. "No problem. I understand. Who are you here to see?"

"Bert Darlington. I'm Jade, by the way."

"Nice to meet you Jade. Do you know which office you're going to?"

"I left my note at home. Can you tell me where to find him?"

"Let me check for you." Meghan consulted her computer monitor. After a few seconds, she nodded. "Mr. Darlington is in Suite 204. You go up that elevator and turn right. It will be the second office on the left."

Now what? Meghan expected me to get in that elevator. I didn't need to blow my surveillance by walking into my subject's office. "Thanks, but you know what? I was in such a hurry to find a bathroom that I left my laptop in the car."

As Meghan and I waved goodbye to each other, I congratulated myself on the neat-and-tidy excuse. Bert's car was still parked in the same spot, so I crossed the lot to my car and opened the door to vent the hot air that had probably built up in the ten minutes I'd been gone. While standing there, I dialed Gina's number. We exchanged pleasantries, then I gave her a short update on what had happened this morning. When I said I thought Bert might not be going anywhere for the rest of the day, there was a long silence.

"Maybe I was wrong, Jade."

"Wrong about what?"

"You," she snapped. "I thought you were stronger. Maybe I should look at a different agency. Someone who will do a proper surveillance and not give up after a few hours."

I swallowed hard and took a deep breath. Mom and Dad would not be pleased if I got fired by my first client on my first real day. For that matter, neither would I.

"No, Gina. I wasn't giving up. I just thought you should know what I'd found out. I'll stick with Bert and give you an update at the end of the week."

There was a pause, during which my heart thudded in my chest—don't fire me, don't fire me, don't…

"Okay, Jade. Let's give it another few days. Let me know what you find out at midday on Wednesday. That's when your retainer will run out. Right?"

"Two-and-a-half days. Yes. I'll be in touch…"

But she never heard me. The line was dead.

"Wednesday," I murmured to myself. "We'll talk…then."

Okay. Different Gina. This was the Gina I'd heard about. The hard-nosed businesswoman, not the BFF-seeking anachronism who'd walked into the agency. Needless to say, I spent the next four plus hours watching Bert's car do nothing while I also tried to figure out what was going on with Gina.

At one-thirty, Bert exited the building. He went to his car and drove to a nearby taco shop, where he ordered two tacos, a churro, and a soft drink. While he ate, my stomach grumbled that I was stuck with a cold snack while he was scarfing down a hot lunch. After lunch, he drove home and parked in the garage. Once again, my stomach reprimanded me for not being brave enough to have grabbed a couple of tacos for myself. I watched him enter the house at two-thirty-four p.m.

Now what? Did I stay with him or give up for the day? There was no way Bert could be spending all of Gina's money at taco stands and coffee shops. Whatever he was doing, it didn't involve food. He did have office expenses, but it couldn't possibly be ten grand a month.

Heading home at this hour would be a major mistake. So would going to the office if I wanted to avoid spending a small fortune at one of the local restaurants. Besides, I'd gotten this far. I could skip lunch. And being hired had made me realize I didn't have another job lined up after this one. Bottom line? I had to get my life together. Fast.

Given my present state of mind, I'd be better off burning calories than consuming them. It was time to turn to my drug of choice for days like this, punching out the heavy bag at X Factor Self Defense. It helped me focus on one thing—destroying my opponent. I drove to the gym, opened my locker, and changed. Then I took out a photocopy of Jason's picture and applied a piece of tape to the top.

"This workout's for you," I said as I carried the paper into the gym.

I took the photocopy of Jason's face, attached it to the heavy bag, and drove my fist into it.

Life was better already.

7

I WAS UP AT FIVE o'clock again the following morning. Mom was in the kitchen, laptop in front of her. She finger waved as I walked in.

"How'd you sleep, honey?"

"Good. Really good. Mom, you don't have to make coffee and a snack for me each day."

"Old habits die hard. I didn't do this for your father all those years because I hated it. It makes me feel like I'm contributing." She pointed at the thermos and lunch bag. "So, there you are. You didn't say much about your surveillance last night."

"There wasn't much to report. It was just a dull day. I've already had a shower and I'm heading out. See you tonight."

Mom gave me a hug on my way out the door and told me to stay safe. I imagined it was the same thing she told Dad each day he went to work.

I was in front of the Rose mansion in plenty of time to watch Bert leave. We followed the same routine as the day before—coffee and breakfast at Joe's, leisurely drive to work, park, wait.

By ten-thirty I was bored and tired of my little inner demons berating me. I needed to do something productive and not just sit here waiting for Bert to drive to the nearest casino or his girlfriend's apartment. To pass the time, I looked over my notes from my visit to Nestor.

Mr. Chang had told me Bert and his partner couldn't agree on anything and were thinking of selling the investment. He'd also said they might be running out of money. Was that Mr. Chang's opinion or something more concrete? Dad had always compared people to leopards. He was a firm believer that leopards couldn't change their spots, and people couldn't change what made them tick. From what Gina had told me, money made Bert tick. So how did a businessman burn through so much money in so little time? Unless he hadn't.

According to Gina, who'd gotten her information from Bert, his company was losing money every month. The more I thought about that source of information, the more I could hear my dad clucking over my shoulder—honey, you know third-hand information is unreliable. Right. What I needed was rock-solid proof that Bert's company really was in such bad straits. And if it was, what did those losses mean for his other investments? If they were anything like the Rose of Nestor, that could explain a lot.

Bert's next closest investment was at the Carlsbad Business Park. It was only a few miles from here. And I was curious. I bit my lower lip, checked the clock, and debated. Go? Or stay? Screw it. Bert would be at work for a few more hours, so why not give Gina her money's worth?

I plugged the address into my phone and got directions to the property. "Lead on, Siri," I said as I pulled out.

My route took me along El Camino Real. Even though the City of Carlsbad had transformed the major thoroughfare only a few years ago with a couple of new lanes and a beautifully landscaped median, maintenance crews were hard at work. Oh well, that was life in a city where the industrial and commercial tax base let the city support a lot of projects.

The GPS routed me onto Faraday, another road that had undergone recent major upgrades, then onto a side street. When Siri proudly announced that I'd arrived at my destination, I found myself in front a sign advertising a new addition to the Carlsbad Business Park.

"Hey, Siri. What is this? A joke?"

"I'm not sure I understand," my phone replied.

"That makes two of us," I grumbled.

The only improvements that had been made to this pile of dirt were the driveway, a small parking lot, and this big mother of a sign. Apparently, Bert's company was big on signage.

No wonder Bert was losing money. He had no tenants. No buildings. There was nothing here but dirt…and the sign. I read through the sign again, jotted down the name and number of the contact, and made the call.

"Eric Andrews." The man had answered so quickly that I wondered if he had anything else to do.

"Is this D&A Investments?" I asked sweetly.

"Yes."

"I'm interested in learning more about the building you're planning here in the business park. Your sign says to call for information. Would you have time to talk?"

There was a moment of silence, then he blurted, "You're here? Now?"

"Reading the big sign on the vacant lot." I tried to sound casual, but it came out more like I was being catty. I winced and waited.

"No problem. Let me give you the address of my office. It's only a few blocks away. We can talk."

Andrews gave me the information, and I let Siri do the heavy lifting. Ten minutes later, I was meeting and greeting the 'A' half of D&A Investments. If I'd have been wearing heels, Andrews and I would be the same height. He had a few inches on me, was stocky and not overly handsome, but enough so that he'd probably never had a shortage of dates.

He guided me to an office done up in modern cheap. There was plenty of glass and stainless steel, but everything looked more warehouse than upscale. In fact, I wondered if the furniture might be rented.

"Have a seat at the table," Andrews said as he went to a coffee pot in the corner. "Would you care for some? Or are you a tea drinker?"

"I'm fine, thanks. I've had too much caffeine today, anyway." Boy, had I.

He poured himself a large mug of coffee and set it down on the table.

"I'm guessing you go through a lot each day," I said as he sat.

Andrews picked up his mug and raised it to his lips. He took a long sip, but continued to watch me. "How'd you guess?"

"The rim of your mug is stained, the carafe for the coffee maker is generic, indicating you had to replace it at some point, and the scent in the room is strong."

He held my gaze, then smiled ever-so-slightly. "You're a regular Sherlock Holmes, aren't you?"

I returned the smile. No ring on his finger. I'd put him around five years older than Jason. Oh, gawd. How pathetic could I get? Now I was shopping the rebound aisle in the men's department. I had to be on a quest to prove I was still attractive. "Well…since you mention it. I do love a good mystery."

He took a long, slow sip of coffee, then set the mug on the table. "And you're wondering about the mysterious vacant lot?"

"Amongst other things."

He cleared his throat. "Such as?"

"Well…" I dragged out my response. Held eye contact.

A piercing ring shattered the mood. He pulled out his cell phone, took one look at the screen, and muttered something under his breath.

"This isn't a good time," he snapped when he answered.

Andrews might be unhappy about the interruption, but I wasn't. It didn't bother me in the least that the PI gods had intervened at precisely the perfect moment. I suspected he was ready and willing, and he thought I was the same. We could leave those impressions right where they were and move on.

"No. I can't…fine. I'll pick her up at six."

Andrews glared at the screen as he jabbed the button harder than necessary to end the call.

"That doesn't sound good," I said.

"My ex. She needs me to pick up my daughter tonight."

"Kids? I didn't see you as the dad type."

"Don't know what you're missing." He pointed to a photo on his desk. A young girl, not much more than a toddler, wore a bright pink-and-purple dress and a matching flowered hat. She sat in an oversized Adirondack chair, smiling for the camera. "Melissa Nicole. The only good thing to come out of my marriage."

Aha, he had an ex. Common ground. "She's adorable." I sighed. "I just went through a nasty breakup, too. You seem like a much nicer guy than my ex. How old is she?"

"She's three. The love of my life." He laughed as he continued to gaze at the photo. "Already I'm thinking about everything from preschool to a college fund."

"So what caused the divorce?"

44

Andrews snatched up his mug and nearly spilled coffee, then pointed at an artist's rendering on the wall and rolled his eyes. "The missing building."

"Excuse me?"

"Look…wait, what's your name? You never said."

"Mandy."

"And you're working for…"

"Confidential, so far. If things go to the next level, you'll be brought into the loop. How is the missing building responsible for your divorce?"

"I'm the kind of guy who, when he's in, is all in. You know what I mean?"

"I think so. Let me guess, you're the nuts-and-bolts guy in the partnership. Your partner is more blue sky."

Andrews seemed to be weighing possibilities. Thinking about me in terms of romance, not business? If I'd played my cards right, he'd be stuck on that dilemma while I got him to give me information. As far as I was concerned, dilemmas were good. For him, not for me. Just in case, it was time to move the needle a bit.

I pulled on a strand of hair, wrapped it around my fingers, and gave him a slight smile. "I really like you, Eric."

His eyes widened and the corners of his mouth curled up slightly. He bit his lower lip, and it looked like he was letting his intellect and his libido battle it out. "You do?"

Good. Libido won. I continued to twirl the hair around my finger, then smiled and nodded once.

He leaned forward and motioned back-and-forth with one hand. "Is it just me, or do we have some sort of connection going on here?"

"You feel it, too?" My cheeks warmed and for once in my life, I felt like that reaction was working to my advantage.

For a moment, I thought he might jump across the table, but he suddenly frowned and gazed at me. "I'm serious, Mandy. I really like you."

Wow. Five minutes and the guy was ready to propose? "It's too soon after my breakup to be thinking about a relationship, but…"

The word hung in the air like a fly-fisher's line, and Andrews leapt out of the water to snag the lure.

He tugged on his collar. Did the eyebrow quirking thing. He even gave me a devil-may-care smile. "Right. I get it. Look, Mandy, I think we could have something solid. You know? That's why I can't in good conscience lead you on. Nothing's going to happen on that lot. We don't have a way to make it happen."

"Cash flow problems?" I pressed.

"Big time. My partner's got all these grand ideas, but he's got no focus. He's always talking about paying it forward, but he doesn't walk the walk."

"If it's such a bad match, why are you in business with him?"

"We knew each other in college."

There were plenty of people I'd met in college, but that didn't mean I ever wanted to see them again. There had to be a lot more to the story. "What did you do, meet on the track team or something?"

"Are you kidding? No." A moment later, he chuckled. "It was soccer."

"Really? You guys go that far back? What did you study?"

"Law, for me. Bert majored in girls. He was the guy who had a different one every night. During the last semester, he was dating this rich girl, and he got a pile of money from her father to break off the relationship."

Aha. Gina wasn't the first. "So he had cash and wanted a partner and turned to one of his school buddies."

Andrews rubbed his jaw and nodded. "It was a lot of money."

"Must have been. So what was the plan? Leverage the cash and make a killing in real estate?"

"Something like that. Bert had the money to attract more, and I had the legal expertise. We started D&A. That's when I gave up my career in law to do this."

"Were you with a big firm?"

Andrews winced. "Very. I was on track to make partner in, oh, ten years or so."

"Ten years is a long time."

"You got it. And Bert was always a good sales guy. He made this sound like a sure thing."

"What went wrong?"

"What didn't? Bert started wanting to do more and more. Not long ago, we bought a dog of a shopping center in Nestor. Are you kidding me? Nestor? Who goes there to shop?"

"What's a Nestor?" I asked with a smile.

"Exactly." He laughed. "Wow. I can't believe this is happening."

I held his gaze, licked my lips, and his breathing quickened. Now, who was looking pathetic? "So you had too many projects and not enough cash to go around. That's the problem?"

"I keep trying to tell Bert to stop spending, but he won't listen. We're bleeding money." Andrews closed his eyes and rubbed his face with his hands.

It sounded like I had one of my answers—Andrews was in a financial bind, too. The guy had given up the world of thousand-dollar suits for a position selling dirt to strangers. But I wasn't his therapist—I was here to dig out the truth, and the more I could get out of him, the better.

"Let me guess. I'm betting the missing building isn't the only reason your wife is divorcing you."

"No," he grumbled. "My wife claims I'm an unfit parent."

8

I HELD ERIC'S GAZE WHILE I struggled to process what he'd said. Judging by how quickly he'd discovered our love connection, I had a feeling women were part of the problem. But if I truly felt the way I'd been acting, I'd be willing to overlook that. Solution found.

"Your wife divorced you because you're a bad dad?"

"According to her. She's got mental problems. It's all bogus. When it went to court, I got shared custody out of the deal. If I'd have wanted, I probably could have gotten full custody, but I didn't want my daughter growing up and not knowing her mother."

Sure. I believe you. "Sounds like you two had irreconcilable differences—with a little girl caught in the middle."

"It got ugly. Let's just leave it there. This is not first-date material."

"I didn't realize we were on a date."

He shrugged, picked up his mug, and sipped. "Technically, we're not. But we could fix that very easily."

"Hold that thought. I have a question about the business."

His cheeks tightened, and he sat back in his chair. "Okay. Shoot."

"You said your partner was Bert Darlington?"

"Yes."

"His wife is Gina Rose? Right?"

Andrews did a double take. "You've heard of her?"

"She's an icon. And the reason I ask is my employer is… well, we're big on family values. Your divorce could be problematic, but we might be able to overlook that if Bert's marriage is solid."

"Bert was and is totally committed to Gina. Those two are soulmates." He paused, then peered at me. "This is getting pretty far afield from a business investment."

"Not really. We're big on family values. We don't want anything tarnishing our reputation, but we also know the value of stability. And Eric, we are talking about a substantial investment." I winked. "And a potential long-term relationship. So I guess I have a bit of a personal interest here, too."

His smile returned and his attention flitted between the photo of his daughter, the artist's rendering on the wall, and my face. Suddenly, he stood and went to the drawing. "This is what we intend to build, Mandy. Everything is state-of-the-art. It meets the highest energy-efficiency standards. Our goal is to make this a model for future generations."

"Look at you! Doing an impromptu sales promo." I winked at him. His smile broadened, and he stood a little straighter.

"It's a good project, Mandy. We just need focus."

"Sounds awesome. Let me talk to my boss and see if we want to look further. As I said, we're in the preliminary stages."

He came back to the table, took his seat, and then tilted his head in the direction of the rendering. "It's getting close to noon. Let me buy you lunch. I know a great place right on the water. We can go there now, have a drink, then order something obscenely expensive. We can talk about this project the rest of the day if you want."

That was so not happening. I had no desire to spend my afternoon fending off advances from a wolf in bad-dad clothing. Besides, I needed to get out before I started tripping over my own lies. "You do know how to turn on the charm, don't you? Tell you what. Let me take a raincheck. I believe you have to go get your daughter."

"That won't be until this evening."

"Sorry. I have obligations."

"What's your number?"

"I'll be in touch." He started to protest, but I raised my hand with my fingers splayed. "We're in a good place right now, Eric. Don't blow it by pushing too hard."

He nodded, we said our goodbyes, and I left. What I couldn't figure out was whether Eric Andrews was really a good guy with a bad friend or a deadbeat dad with a good lawyer.

It wasn't even five minutes into my drive when I realized my retainer had run out. After two-and-a-half days of looking into Bert Darlington's life, all I had were more questions. I was especially curious about the comment Andrews had made about Bert being devoted to Gina. I couldn't imagine she was going to be happy with me at all. My phone rang and, without thinking, I picked up. I fully expected it to be Gina. Instead, it was a deep, melodic male voice I recognized immediately.

"Hey, Jade. How've you been?"

"What do you want, Jason?" I snapped.

"Can I start with an apology? I'm sorry. I really am. I didn't mean to hurt you."

Right. What he really meant was he didn't intend to get caught. "What do you want?"

"I know things are tight for you right now, so I thought I'd offer you a chance to help me teach a women's self-defense class. You were one of my best students and…"

"Too bad you didn't feel that way when we were together, Jason. Why are you doing this?"

"I just wanted to help you out. That's all. I've changed, Jade. I was stupid, and I thought maybe this could be the first step to mend the rift between us."

Under my breath, I muttered, "What a load of crap."

"What was that, Jade?"

I had to give Jason one thing. He always was smooth. The same as Bert and, quite possibly, Eric Andrews. He was right about the money, but Jason always had an ulterior motive. "What's the catch?"

"Besides the fact that you were one of my best students?"

"You already said that. And I wasn't 'one of,' I was the best."

"You were. That's why I think we'd be a perfect team."

No matter how I felt about Jason, my sole source of income was about to dry up. "I'm on the road right now. I can't talk."

"Of course. No problem. But I want to pay you for your time."

I could think of three crappy reasons to say yes. I had no other clients on the horizon. I could manage my emotions. Well, most of the time. And I really did want to stop living with Mom and Dad, eventually. "How much?"

"Fifty bucks. Cash."

"No way. I helped you get that business started, Jason. I know how profitable those classes are. I want half. We split the proceeds fifty-fifty."

He paused, then asked, "After expenses?"

"How many are enrolled?"

"Twenty right now. There's a couple more who said they might walk in."

"It's a deal. And Jason? If you screw with me, I swear I'll go get my gun and shoot you dead. Text me the details." I disconnected the call and glared at the road.

For the next few minutes, I debated whether to call back and tell Jason to forget the whole thing or suck it up and work with my slimy ex. The truth was, I couldn't bring myself to shoot him for two reasons. First, I didn't want to spend my life in an orange jumpsuit—I look terrible in fall colors.

The bigger reason was how my heart had leapt at the sound of his voice. As much as I hated to admit it, I didn't know if I was really over Jason Taylor.

I had to find out.

9

I WALKED INTO SANDY'S WICHES shortly after noon in search of sustenance and advice. All the customers got the first part, but seldom did they qualify for the second. I was special because my best friend, Charlotte Harper, owned and managed Sandy's. Right after my breakup with Jason, Charlie had single-handedly managed to put me back on the track to recovery.

Charlie smiled and waved to me from behind the counter. As she usually did when she worked, she had her hair pulled back in a ponytail and wore her trademark Sandy's Wiches' T-shirt over a pair of black shorts. The man ordering from her was one of at least a dozen of Charlie's regulars who popped in for lunch. From his tussled sandy hair down to his tanned legs and flip-flops, this particular one had the laid-back surfer look down to a science. Like her other male regulars, the surfer guy was flirting with Charlie—a not uncommon occurrence when you're a smoking hot blue-eyed blonde with fine cheekbones and the body to match.

I grabbed my usual table in the back of the shop. This one wasn't popular with tourists due to its proximity to the restrooms. I liked it because it gave me a view of the entire store and the opportunity to people watch. Since Charlie was busy with the surfer dude, I called Gina's number. I might as well get my termination over with. Unfortunately, her assistant told me she was in an important meeting. I pocketed my phone just as Charlie plopped herself down in front of me.

"You look like crap, Jade. What's up?"

"I think I lost my client."

"Already? Is that even possible? Didn't you start, like, what? Two days ago? Did you get fired?"

"It's been two-and-a-half. And she told me to follow her husband, but I've spent more time chasing his finances than I have tailing him. She'll fire me for bad judgement… incompetence…bad hair. I don't know. Actually, she doesn't even have to fire me. She can just not renew my contract."

"Wow. You are down. Don't worry, you'll get another client. It wasn't easy for me when I took over the shop, but I got by. You'll be fine."

"And Jason's back."

Charlie winced. "Oh. Now I get it." She reached out and took my hand. "Are you okay? Did you tell him to get lost?"

"He wants me to teach a class with him—tonight."

"You told him no. Right?"

"Wrong."

"What? Are you…"

"Yes, Charlie. I'm certifiable."

"This is going to take some time. Wait here. Your usual?"

I nodded and waited while Charlie went behind the counter and worked her magic. To pass the time, I planted my arms one over the other on the table, rested my chin on top, and puppy-gazed at Charlie as she gave instructions to her staff. She was a take-charge woman, much like Gina in many respects. Except that with Charlie, I never doubted her dead-on honesty. That was not something I could say about Gina.

Charlie returned a few minutes later with a pair of sandwiches, two bags of chips, and soft drinks. She pushed one of the sandwiches and a bag of chips at me as she sat. "Eat. You look like you're going to waste away."

"Look who's talking." I unwrapped the sandwich and said, "You can't afford to feed me forever, Charlie."

"Oh please. Someday I'm going to need a big ask from you. If you turn me down, I'll totally remind you of all the free food you've gotten here."

"I'd never turn you down. You know that."

"You wouldn't dare." She winked. "Now, what's the deal with Jason?"

I told her about the call. Charlie did a lot of eye rolling at the details, but the bottom line was I needed to make a decision this afternoon because the class was tonight.

"I should call him back and tell him to buzz off. Right?"

"You need to be strong, Jade. Don't let that guy jerk you around."

"Okay. I'll call him. Deal's off."

"What? No way. I've got a better idea. You go to the class. You take his money. And when he tries to come onto you, that's when you tell him he's lost a good thing."

Another one of Charlie's regulars walked in—a tall, black man wearing a custom-tailored suit. He smiled and waved. When I returned the gesture, Charlie turned. She gave him a little finger wave. He smiled and winked at her.

I whispered, "How many guys are you stringing along, Charlie?"

She pursed her lips and thought for a moment, then shrugged. "We're not discussing my love life. This is about you.

Hey, do you want me to introduce you? Roger's a really nice guy."

"You want to hand-me-down one of your boyfriends? Am I that pathetic? Oh, gawd."

Charlie took my hand again and shook her head. "There's nothing going on between me and Roger—well, not now, anyway."

"But there was."

"We went out a few times."

"How do you do it, Charlie? You slip in and out of relationships faster than I can change jeans."

For the first time in a long time, Charlie's smile fell. She frowned and bit her lower lip. Roger appeared at the side of our table carrying a Sandy's Wiches bag. He waited until Charlie looked up at him, then laid a hand on her shoulder.

"You okay, Cee?"

Charlie nodded and gave him a weak smile. "See you next time?"

"You got it." He squeezed her shoulder and strolled out the front door.

"I'm sorry," I said. "I didn't mean to remind you."

"I was too young to become a widow, Jade." She closed her eyes, sucked in a breath, then said, "It's been four years, and I still miss Shawn every single day, but he's gone. Permanently. The hurt's always there, but it gets easier to cope." Charlie rubbed her cheeks and sniffled. She took a slow breath, let it out, and wagged a finger in my face. "If I can struggle through night classes to get my degree in hotel and restaurant management, you can go teach self-defense. You kick butt. And don't let that worm mess with you again."

I walked out of Sandy's Wiches feeling strong and empowered. If Charlie could survive the sudden death of her husband, I could survive my little trials—whether we were talking about the drama Gina and Bert called their lives or Jason's betrayal—it was all minor compared to the life-changing disaster she'd suffered. I'd intended to return to the office, but really needed to clear my head. Doing an about face, I walked toward the one place I could count on to do that—the ocean.

It was only a few blocks to the boardwalk. The closer I got, the stronger the scent of sea air became. After crossing diagonally with the light at Carlsbad Blvd., I passed Java Joe's. It struck me as ironic that 'my happy place' was almost the same as Bert Darlington's. The difference was that he came here for his morning coffee, but I visited whenever I needed to clear my head.

Over my shoulder, a voice called, "Hey, Jade!"

I turned just as a guy I'd known since high school weaved by me on his skateboard. "Hey, Whistler!" I called after him, but he'd already passed two more people. Whistler was actually his last name, but just as I'd been tagged with Jade, Jerome became Whistler after a few friends decided that was more cool than his first name. And just for the record, no, I'd never gone out with him. Any guy whose only form of transportation was a skateboard qualified as friend material and nothing more.

A couple ahead walked arm-in-arm, weaving like drunken sailors as they sidestepped gawkers and walkers coming toward them. When the breeze shifted direction, I caught the faint odor of marijuana. From their carefree attitudes, I took them to be tourists. And a grand vacation they were having.

The boardwalk almost always teemed with activity. The people around me, whether they were here to visit, hang out, or simply forget their troubles, all had one thing in common. They were on a temporary escape from reality. I found an empty bench, parked myself, and gazed out at the hazy blue horizon.

Closing my eyes for a moment, I breathed in the salty air. Jason's call had dredged up bittersweet memories. I'd thought we were in love. At least I'd been planning on getting married. Raising our own kids. But now, all I wanted to do was get over him. Really get over him.

I let out a deep sigh. Tonight's class was five hours away. Terrific. I didn't dare go home. Gina hadn't called me back yet. And I definitely did not want to spend the afternoon thinking about Jason. What I needed to do was show Gina my mettle and keep working, even though my retainer had run out. Yes. I could bury myself in work, move on from Jason, and get my life together.

Retracing my path, I went into the office and emailed a quick summary of what I'd discovered to Gina. After that, I grabbed my go bag and drove to Bert's office. On my two previous days of surveillance, Bert hadn't left work until mid afternoon. It was time to see if he again went home or if he took a different route. The streets on the way to his office were clogged with afternoon traffic. It took thirty minutes to make the drive, so it was almost one-thirty when I pulled into the parking lot and cruised by his spot.

I slammed on the brakes and stared at the empty space.

Bert was gone.

There was no question.

Gina was going to fire me for sure.

10

I HAD A MILLION REASONS to bail on Jason, but if I was ever to look Charlie—or myself—in the eye again, skipping out on class was not an option. Gina still hadn't called me back, and by four-thirty I was convinced silence could only mean I'd lost my first client. All the more reason to be here.

Jason was doing what Jason did. Posturing for all the women ogling him. If I didn't need the money so much, I'd just walk out. But then again, he'd paid me in cash when he closed down registration and I was not giving the money back under any circumstances.

"This is my assistant, everyone. Her name is Jade. Everyone say hi."

All the women dutifully said some version of, "Hi Jade." It sounded very much like the introductions you hear about at AA meetings. A couple of the women looked familiar, and one I definitely recognized from high school. We'd run in different circles in those days, but she smiled at me and mouthed, "I remember you."

I nodded and waved to the others in the room. "Hi, everyone. This is a large group. Can I ask why you're all here?"

"I'm worried about all these attacks…"

"I wanted to learn to protect myself…"

As the comments continued, I realized most of the women had signed up for this class as a direct result of the Amorous Assailant. I must confess, the assaults consumed my afternoon, too. After the shock of seeing Bert's empty parking place wore off, I drove by the house. There had been no sign of his car, so I'd given up, gone to the office to wait for Gina's call, and read up on the attacks.

Very quickly, it became obvious the woman who had written the blog posts had a flair for the dramatic, matched only by her passion for taking down the man she claimed was "stalking our town." I could see why Mom had become fascinated with the stories. They were a cross between a wrestling match and an old soap opera—lots of bluster balanced with redundant prose.

"I heard from my girlfriend that the instructor was hot."

Of course, the comment had come from a five-foot-four brunette with doe eyes and excellent posture. She'd introduced herself earlier as Valerie. Her outfit had more crisscrossing straps than the Golden Gate bridge and revealed more than it hid. Most of the group laughed nervously, raised their eyebrows, and ogled Jason again.

"Now, now, ladies," Jason said. "We're here to learn self-defense. This isn't the dating game."

But even as he spoke, he and Valerie had their eyes locked on each other. Now that Valerie had made her intentions clear, I figured they both had plans for after class. During the first half hour, Valerie continued to flirt with Jason, and he reciprocated. I cautioned myself against getting angry. I was done with my dirtbag ex-boyfriend. I'd been paid, too. What they did was none of my business. Except that just seeing Jason play his little seduction game totally pressed all my buttons. When he spoke to me and asked if I would help, I realized I'd been glaring daggers at him.

Taking a deep breath and adopting a chirpy tone for the crowd of onlookers, I said, "Sure. What are we doing?"

"We're going to begin by demonstrating how to break a two-handed front choke hold."

"Of course. Let's do this."

Jason gestured for me to stand facing him. I let him lightly wrap his hands around my neck. He scanned the room, but the heat rose in my chest and neck when he exchanged another flirtatious smile with Valerie. Really? He had his hands around my neck and was using me to pick up his next conquest?

"To break a two-handed choke hold…" Jason paused for effect, tightened his grip around my neck, and let his gaze lock onto Valerie's. I could almost feel the sexual tension between them.

My breath sped up as Charlie's voice echoed in my head. *Don't let that worm mess with you again. Don't let…*

"You first want to drop your chin," he said.

"Jason, how far down should you go?" Valerie winked at him as though they were the only two in the room who understood her meaning.

Don't let that worm…

"Well, Val, in this situation, you're only making sure the attacker stops choking you." Jason stared straight at her and winked back.

Don't let… "Screw you!"

I seized Jason's wrists. Pulled down hard. Then I rammed my knee into his groin. He crumpled to the floor and lay there doubled over, gasping for breath. All except one of the women gaped at me. The exception was Valerie, who rushed to Jason's side and fawned over him while we all watched.

But Jason didn't matter anymore. With one quick action, I'd vanquished all my anxieties. Jason was a two-timing slime and always would be. Charlie was so right—I was better off without him. Forget him. Forget Val. I straightened up, took a deep breath, and looked around the room. "That, ladies, is how you break a frontal choke hold. I'm sure Jason will want to continue the class once he—catches his breath. Now, if you'll excuse me. I'm done here."

I held my head high as I walked toward my bag. I kept my back to the group to avoid their stares. I might have regained my self-respect, but didn't want to face a roomful of women ready to lynch me because I'd crippled the hot instructor.

As I was pulling on my sweatshirt, someone tapped me on the shoulder. I closed my eyes, took a breath, and turned around. To my surprise, the woman facing me wasn't Valerie. I'd fully expected her to want to chew me out for being so mean to Jason.

The woman I faced had long dark hair pulled back into a ponytail, which she'd secured with a silver scrunchy. Her eyes were intense, but her smile was definitely friendly. "Hey, you did a real number on him."

"Yeah. About that…I might have gone a little overboard."

"No way. I'm Zoe." She stuck out her hand. "We were just talking about it and thought you should know we all agree he had it coming."

"We?" I asked as I shook her hand.

"Me and the other girls."

She turned and gestured at two women standing off to the side giggling while they shot sideways glances at Jason and Valerie, who'd taken on the role of doting nurse.

The two women approached, and the taller said, "I'm Alyssa. This is my friend, Gail."

Gail was a petite Asian who smiled quickly and easily. She extended her hand, and when she spoke, her voice was soft and melodic. "I'm happy to meet a strong role model. You were awesome. We're all here because of that stupid Amorous Assailant. He's got all my friends spooked. I've got like ten friends who wanted to be here, but couldn't make it."

"This isn't an ambush, then?" I gaped at Zoe first, then Alyssa, then Gail.

"Ambush? No way," Zoe laughed. "He so had it coming. I just don't get what Valerie sees in him."

"To each her own," I said, then smiled.

"You totally have history with him, don't you?" Alyssa said.

I felt the blush coming on fast. "That's a nice way to put it. Look, I really should be going. I'm sure Jason will want to continue class."

Gail snickered. "Once he recovers."

Alyssa and Zoe both laughed. I couldn't help myself from joining them as I looked past Zoe to where Valerie had coaxed Jason to a sitting position.

I winked at Zoe. "It won't be long now."

"Jade, I'll get right to the point. We want you to teach the class."

I peered at her. "What?"

"You. We want you to teach the class."

"Wow. That's a nice gesture, but there are only three of you and…"

Alyssa shook her head and looked over her shoulder. "No. We all agreed. We want a woman, someone who understands us. You're our new instructor."

Two more of the attendees approached and a heavyset blonde asked, "Did you ask her?"

"She'll totally do it," Zoe said.

"Wait. I didn't say yes."

"And you didn't say no. We're all agreed."

Zoe glanced over her shoulder. All eyes were on us, and I suddenly realized when she said "we", she meant everyone. Well, except for Valerie, who was busy helping Jason to his feet.

Once he heard about this revolt, he'd go ballistic. I shook my head. "But you've all already paid Jason. He's not going to refund your money because you don't like him."

"He will once my husband gets done with him," Gail said. "He's an attorney, and he can be very intimidating."

Jason walked toward us, Valerie clinging to his arm. I had at most thirty seconds to decide.

"But I don't have a place or a curriculum or…"

"I'll help you get it organized," Zoe said. "My job hours are flexible, so I can totally help you out. Say you'll do it."

One-by-one, the others in the room joined our little group, which was now more than half the class. "Okay…sure. I guess if I can co-teach, I can teach."

"That's it, Jade, you went too far," Jason snapped.

I raised my hand to my chest and gave him an innocent smile. "But Jason, I just did what you trained me to do."

Snickers coursed through the group, which had grown to everyone in the class.

"We've decided we want a different instructor," Zoe said. She turned and pointed at me. "Her."

The veins on Jason's forehead bulged. Vesuvius time coming up. This was not going to be a pretty sight. Valerie was rubbing Jason's shoulder as though she expected that to calm him. Sorry, Val. I know him. You don't.

"Tell you what, Jason. Why don't you let me finish teaching the class? We'll still keep our same arrangement."

"No way. I'm in charge here."

"I don't think so," I said. "I do believe you've lost control."

Jason snorted. "And what do you know about control, Jade?"

"Apparently, I have more than you. I'm not the one who cheated."

Valerie blinked and did a fast double take. "Wait…were you two together?" She pulled away from Jason, but still kept her hands on his bicep.

"Five years…"

"Jade, shut your trap."

I crossed my arms over my chest and glared at him. "What are you going to do, Jason? Smack me around?"

"I've never hit a woman!"

"Not in the physical sense, but you gut punched me when you screwed that bimbo in our bed."

Valerie took another step back and stared at Jason. Her jaw hung slack. "Is that true? You did it in your own bedroom?"

"Well, yeah. Where else was I going to go?"

Grumblings ran through the group. Obviously, even Valerie was starting to see Jason the way I did.

"I'm not a hundred percent certain about this, Jason, but I think that might have been the wrong thing to say in front of your new girlfriend."

Valerie fell back in with the rest of her classmates, all the while glaring at him. "You are a…"

"Slime," I said. "I think that's the word you're looking for."

"Yeah," Val agreed. "You're a slime. And we're done."

She stepped forward and slapped Jason. Hard. "That's for using me in your little game."

The veins lining Jason's forehead flamed purple. "You want the class, Jade? Go ahead. You teach it." He glanced around the room quickly, then went and picked up his bag. "Just don't any of you come crying to me when she doesn't teach you good technique."

Zoe snickered. "Her technique looked pretty good to me."

11

TWO HOURS LATER, ZOE AND I were sharing a pitcher of margaritas at the Flying Pig. We'd been joined by Alyssa, Gail, and our new best friend, Valerie. So far, the night had been a total success. Not only had the class gone well, but Val had blown off Jason in public and sent him home alone. I still hadn't heard from Gina, but I was on a roll, so why worry about a little speed bump?

Another pitcher arrived, and we all shook our heads. Apparently, none of us had ordered it. The server pointed toward the bar. My eyes widened when I saw a familiar face smiling at me. Roger. I raised my glass, then excused myself from the group.

Roger and his two companions wore conservative dark suits. Talk about feeling intimidated. I was dressed in jeans and a tank top. Oh well. I waved as I approached. Did my best to sound casual.

"Thanks for the pitcher, but you really shouldn't have."

Roger dismissed my protest with a small headshake. "You looked like you were having a tough day at lunch. I saw you with your friends and thought maybe it would help brighten your evening." He raised a finger and added, "And just so you know, I'm not trying to pick you up. Go back to your friends and have fun. Maybe I'll see you at Charlie's sometime."

I held his gaze for several moments, then shook my head. "Charlie was right."

"About what?"

"You. She said you were a really nice guy. Thank you, again." I turned and walked back to the table. Before my butt hit the chair, the questions started.

"Who's the guy?"

"Are you hooking up afterwards?"

"How long have you been seeing him?"

"No, no, and never," I said as I poured the last of Roger's pitcher into our empty glasses. "He's just a friend of a friend. I met him today and…" I glanced over my shoulder at Roger. His gaze met mine and the room suddenly felt like a sauna. I turned back to the others. They each stared at me as though I were the biggest liar on the planet. Maybe I was.

"You're totally into him," Zoe said.

"I'm not. He's just being nice. That's all. Now, let's talk about something else. What do you guys do for a living?"

Zoe shook her head and exchanged a quick glance with the others. "Liar, liar," she laughed.

They all joined her, but at least they dropped the subject. Alyssa was a server in a high-end restaurant. Gail worked for the City, and Valerie was a legal assistant. When all eyes turned to Zoe, she shrugged.

"During the day, I wait tables, but at night, I'm a blogger."

"No way," Alyssa said.

"For real," Zoe countered. "I'm trying to build my readership and hope to eventually syndicate my content."

"Where can I find you?" Alyssa asked. "I totally want to follow you. What kind of stuff do you write?"

Zoe arched her eyebrows and smiled. "Well, right now, I'm working on the Amorous Assailant. That's why I attended the class." She stopped and peered at me. "Jade? Are you okay?"

Oh. My. God. This couldn't be a coincidence. What had Mom done? "You're Zoe Jessica Wright."

She did a fist pump and smiled. "Yes! You've heard of me?"

"My mom is following your blog. She was showing me your stuff. I was reading most of the afternoon."

"Awesome. I love it when word-of-mouth takes over. Tell your mom I said thanks for helping."

I nodded and smiled. "She says you're persistent." Mom was going to be surprised. Or maybe not.

"I totally think this guy needs to be found. I've researched all three of the victims. Their lives are so screwed up now because of him."

"What's with this guy, anyway?" Gail asked. "He doesn't hurt his victims."

Zoe shook her head and leaned forward. "That is so not true. He traumatizes these women. They feel totally helpless and don't know if he's going to kill them or what. And once they're attacked, they keep reliving the experience."

"That's why these classes are so important." Alyssa peered at her glass, then looked up and said, "We need another round."

We agreed to split the cost and flagged down our server. When she arrived table-side a few minutes later, she asked, "Another pitcher, ladies?"

Gail held up the money we'd collected.

"Awesome." She grabbed our little wad of cash, told us it would only take a couple of minutes, and left.

The buzz from the tequila was strong by the time she returned with our pitcher, and our discussion of the Amorous

Assailant had grown more heated. The bottom line was we all agreed he was instilling fear in women, even those who hadn't been victimized.

"What if we set up a watch group?" Gail asked.

Val, who was sitting next to her, nodded emphatically. "We should totally do that. We can all be on the lookout for suspicious behavior. "

"I don't know. It sounds pretty vigilante to me," I said.

"Jade, if you take down this guy, you'll be the biggest thing in town," Gail said. "Think of what it will do for your agency. You'll be turning away clients."

Boy, had I heard that one before. When I was growing up, all my friends' parents thought it would be cool to hire a PI, until they realized how much it cost—then they only thought it was expensive.

"There's no question I'd love to be the one to stop the Amorous Assailant, but I need to be working for paying clients."

"I'd hire you…if I had any money." Alyssa giggled as she drained the last of her glass. She turned to Zoe. "You two totally should work together."

Zoe grinned as she glanced at Alyssa. "You mean like partners?"

I didn't want to hurt Zoe's feelings, but she waited tables for a living. She had no experience. No training. I did not need a blogging server as a partner.

Alyssa piped up, her voice chirpy and positive. "For sure. You're working the case, anyway. Right, Zoe? And Jade needs to find new clients."

I'd had too much tequila. Why had I spilled my guts about the business? I had to get out of this. "My contract might be a little iffy, but I'm sure it's going to be renewed. I'll be too busy."

"You can work two cases at once, right?" Val said.

"Well, yeah. My dad always juggled multiple clients. But I can't call the Amorous Assailant a real case without a paying client."

Gail grabbed my arm and shook it. "It would totally boost your reputation."

"I suppose. And it would be awesome to find this guy." Oh, gawd, I had tequila mouth. "No—forget I said that. I need clients with money, not pro bono work. Besides, we have no idea where to look for him."

"Down by the boardwalk," Zoe said. "He always strikes in the early morning near there. I talked to the cops, and they said they don't have the resources to stake out the whole area indefinitely. And since nobody knows when this guy will strike again, they're being reactive."

"We need to be proactive," Gail said.

"For sure." Alyssa looked at me and gave me a thumbs up. "Just like you were with Jason. That was super proactive."

"We could totally work together. Right, Jade?" Zoe asked.

"What?"

"You and me. We could collaborate on finding and locking up the Amorous Assailant."

"I…I…"

"Awesome," Gail said.

Alyssa nudged Zoe. "Yeah, you get your story and Jade gets her agency supercharged."

Gail raised her glass. "To an awesome partnership and the capture of the Amorous Assailant."

Now they all had their glasses raised and mine was right there with them. We clinked glasses. I felt a flush of satisfaction. I had partners. My own watch group. We were totally going to do what the cops couldn't—take down the Amorous Assailant.

The moment I set my glass on the table, the euphoria faded.

Tequila. Once again, it had turned my brain to mush.

12

A FREIGHT TRAIN RUMBLED THROUGH my head. Its sole purpose, apparently, was to drag me from the dead of sleep. Squinting through one opened eyelid, I was nearly blinded by a narrow beam of sunshine streaming through a crack in the blinds. I peered at the clock, brought it into focus, and groaned at the time. I'd overslept. And my mouth tasted like a swamp.

The train rumbled louder when I lifted my head. No amount of effort was going to make this hangover go away. This was going to take painkillers, a shower, and coffee…lots and lots of coffee. Maybe I should add mouthwash to that list. I groaned and buried my face in the pillow as the memory of last night came rushing back…along with that stupid train.

When I'd recovered enough to face Mom and Dad, I headed downstairs. They both sat at the kitchen counter talking in hushed tones. When I walked in, they glanced my way and gave me smiles of disappointment.

"Morning, honey," Mom said. "Guess you overslept."

Dad gave the clock on the stove a purposeful look. "It's nine o'clock, Sunshine."

Oh, gawd. Talk about feeling like a loser. "Has anyone seen my phone?"

Mom pointed at the countertop next to the sink.

I went and stood looking down at a gooey mess. "What's it doing here? And why's it got all that…stuff on it?"

Mom shrugged. "Because it was in the trash. And that's where we put the garbage…unless it goes down the garbage disposal…"

I closed my eyes and took a deep breath. "I know where the garbage goes, Mom. What I'm trying to figure out is…" I moved my finger over the screen in small circles. "I want to know what all this slimy mess is."

Mom pointed at a dark brown blob. "Those are coffee grounds. And that…I think that's part of the peach I had this morning. It was bad, and I had to throw it away. And the pinkish purple…"

"Got it, Mom," I snapped, then took another deep breath. This was going to be a long morning. "I'm sorry. I didn't mean to bark at you. I was trying to figure out how my phone got in the trash in the first place."

"Oh. That." Mom shrugged. "I have no idea. I found it when the trash started ringing." Mom reached out and laid a hand on my shoulder. "Bad night?"

I rubbed my temples with my fingertips, then nudged the phone and wrinkled my nose. "I think I had too many margaritas."

"There was this one time your mother and I…"

"Don't, Thomas."

Mom in cranky mode. Got it. I'd really tested her patience this time. "I'm sorry, Mom."

The phone rang and a million firecrackers exploded in my head. In big, bold letters, which were smeared with all the food slime, Zoe's name appeared on the display. Oh no. I remembered something about…oh, gawd no.

"You're not going to answer it?" Mom went to the coffeepot, poured a mug, and shoved it into my hands. "What's going on, Jade?"

"It's kind of a long story, but I ended up teaching Jason's self-defense class last night."

"Good for you." Dad flipped me a thumbs-up and winked. "Was that before the tequila or after?"

Mom shot Dad a nasty look. He made a face and raised his mug to his lips. Mom sighed. "I meant, why was your phone in the trash?"

"Some of us went to the Flying Pig for margaritas afterwards. I guess you'd call it a celebration."

Mom let out a heavy sigh. "Was Jason with you?"

I frowned and stared at her. "No. Why?"

"He left you a few messages."

My shoulders sagged and the cotton in my head did nothing to stop the throbbing in my temples. "Oh gawd. That's right. He did show up. Later. He called me when we were on our…third pitcher."

"No wonder you have a hangover." Mom pointed at the mug in my hands. "Drink. Three pitchers. Wow."

"Um, actually…it was four, maybe five. Jason bought one. He said it was an apology pitcher."

Dad shook his head and held my gaze. "An apology pitcher? What a load of crap. You didn't fall for it, did you?"

"No. We sent him home. Alone." I took a sip from my mug and relished the slightly bitter taste. "He called me a few times while we were at the bar. The last time he called, I was here. I told him I wanted nothing to do with him." I massaged my temples again, then took another sip from my mug. "I'm not totally sure, but that might be when I got fed up and threw the phone in the trash. Anyway, I have a bigger problem than Jason Taylor. The girls I was with want to form a watch group to find the Amorous Assailant."

Mom and Dad both did the parental, "I see."

Then Dad shielded his face with his mug. No doubt he'd gone from parental disappointment to professional disapproval. I must be going for an all-time personal best.

"That's why Zoe keeps calling me," I said. "Oh, by the way, Mom, she's the blogger you've been following."

"Zoe Jessica Wright took your class? What a coincidence."

I pulled back and inspected her face. I'd been right. "What did you do, Mom?"

"Yeah, Jo. What did you do?"

Mom flushed exactly like I would, then looked at the mug she cradled in her hands. "Nothing, really. I just might have sent her a message after her last blog post. She was critical of women who see themselves as weak, so I wrote to her and said she should set the example."

Dad put down his mug and huffed. "This attacker is a police matter, Jo. You shouldn't be recommending people take the law into their own hands."

"Thomas, I merely suggested she learn how to defend herself. And that she encourage others to do the same. I didn't say she should form a watch group or anything of the sort."

My phone lit up again. Gina. Could this morning get any worse? "Please, can we put this discussion on hold?" I asked, then without waiting, brushed the slime off the phone and answered the call.

"Hi, Gina."

"Jade, where have you been? I called you three times last night."

"I was teaching a self-defense class."

"At ten o'clock at night?"

Oh, right, I'd had way too much tequila by then. Rather than lie outright, I just ignored the question. "You said there was something else you wanted to talk about?"

"Didn't you listen to my message?"

"It was a late night."

"Fine. Whatever. You need to get back on the job."

"Oh, okay. The retainer ran out yesterday and I didn't hear from you, so I wasn't sure what you wanted to do."

There was a long pause, followed by an exasperated sigh. "Jade, just bill me for your hours. I'll send you an open-ended contract this morning. I saw the report you sent me yesterday, and I'm impressed. Based on what you've turned up, I might not only be able to sue Bert for divorce, but fraud, too. I'd be happy to put the screws to him."

"Are you going to send me the detail for the payments you made to Bert?"

Gina huffed. "I'm working on it. Just get me all the dirt you can. I want to do more than get even. I want to bury him. You're on the payroll, Jade. I don't care how much this costs. I want to get Bert out of my life. And the sooner that happens, the better."

I started to thank Gina for trusting in me, but she'd already hung up. With a sigh, I looked at Mom and Dad. "Well, that was Gina Rose."

Mom snickered. "She sounds nice."

Dad shook his head. "Be careful, Jade. She sounds unstable to me, and just because she's rich doesn't mean she won't do something crazy. In fact, in my opinion, the richer they are, the loonier they are."

"Your dad's right, honey. You don't know what she'll do with the information you provide."

"Watch your back—and do what you think is right," Dad said. "It's all you can do."

"I think my head just exploded. I got my first client. She's got money, and now you're telling me I can't trust her." But I already suspected that.

"That's not exactly what I mean," Dad said. "When you're dealing with a client like Gina Rose, you can trust, but you have to verify everything. So drink your coffee, clean up your phone, and get to work."

Perfect. Just the kind of fatherly advice every girl wants to hear when she's got a hangover. Or maybe that was my mentor speaking. I plopped myself onto a stool and began sucking down caffeine. I had a lot of digging to do, and based on Dad's advice, the first order of business was to verify everything Gina had told me.

13

IT WAS NEARLY TEN BY the time I made it out of the house. It didn't take an ace detective to know Bert should have already left his morning haunts, so instead of pointing my car in the direction of his home or Joe's, I went directly to his work. Falling back on Mom and Dad's lessons to always look on the bright side, I told myself there was a huge advantage to starting the day late—traffic was light.

As expected, Bert's car was in its assigned space. I hung out for twenty minutes, then drove to the office to follow-up on something Gina had said in one of her three messages last night. Okay, her message had been more of a total rant, but she'd made a snide remark about Eric's past that left me wondering where I could find the unvarnished truth about him. I needed a source that wasn't tainted by personal opinion.

I found what I was looking for in the news in the form of a story about the departure of Eric Andrews from the law firm of Watson, Watson, and Oberdorf. The law firm hadn't discussed his departure, but a man named Israel Castillo said plenty to the press when his claims fell on deaf ears.

According to the story, Andrews had demonstrated a pattern of aggression at work. His temper had gotten him into more than one argument, and the final nail in his coffin was planted when he made verbal threats against Castillo. Based on the rendition of the facts given by Mr. Castillo—that Andrews had bullied him on multiple occasions—it sounded like Andrews had sweetened the story about his divorce substantially.

I checked the family court records and found the dissolution order, which included the mention of there being a minor child. If I wanted to see the actual record, I needed to go into the courthouse. For now, that seemed like overkill. After all, I was looking for information on Bert Darlington, not Andrews. And I knew what I needed to know—Andrews had not been on his way to becoming a partner when he'd joined forces with Bert; he'd been unemployed. He'd also told me Gina and Bert were soulmates. Another lie. At least now I knew how to handle him.

I dialed his number, waited, and left a suggestive message— call me for dinner, and maybe a little dessert. What the heck? He'd spilled his guts once, so he'd probably do it again, especially if I plied him with alcohol and plenty of flirtation. I just needed to make sure I got the truth instead of lies.

My phone rang with another call from Zoe while I was finishing my message to Eric. I let the call go to voicemail, waited a minute, then listened to her perky voice.

"Hey, Jade, this is Zoe. Me and the girls have been talking about the watch group. We agreed we totally need a name. Gail and Alyssa kinda thought we should have something descriptive like the 'Amorous Assailant Watch Group.' I told them we needed something with some bling. How about 'The Justice Seekers' or something like that?"

I rested my forehead on my palm and listened as Zoe prattled on.

"We got the scheduling worked out for the next few days. All of us are super-excited to be working with you, and we might have another couple members. I posted to my mailing list this morning and had a half-dozen responses in the first half hour. This is gonna be epic. Call me when you get a chance because we need someone to cover Saturday morning."

She'd sent a message to her mailing list? No way. This had to stop before things got out of hand. I tapped the option to call back. She answered on the first ring, her voice perkier than a high-school cheerleader riding the high of a date with the football captain.

"Hey Jade. You got my message, right?"

"That's why I'm calling. I wish you hadn't asked your mailing list for volunteers."

"Why not? I'm building an awesome list."

"Because if the Amorous Assailant is following his own press, he might have subscribed to your blog."

"That would be totally awesome."

"No, Zoe, it would be totally screwed up. He could be reading your every word. If you sent out an open invitation for watch group participants, he could even volunteer, and would always know where not to be."

There was a long pause, but Zoe did not sound deterred. "I never thought of that. At least none of the offers to help came from a man."

"These guys sometimes have an accomplice. I'm not so sure this watch group is going to work."

Zoe harrumphed, but her upbeat tone continued. "We're doing this for you, Jade. Don't be such a downer. It's totally going to work. We've got everything covered. This is so going to put you on the map."

I desperately wanted to tell her there should be a law about promises made while under the spell of tequila. Said promises should not be legally, ethically, or morally binding. The problem was Zoe. She was so upbeat and happy to be helping I did the only thing I could do—I chickened out.

"Zoe, you're awesome," I chirped. "I'm stuck on this other case, but I'll let you know when I can take a shift."

The call ended with Zoe's spirits soaring while mine went into a death spiral. How could I not have told her to disband the group? "Because I'm not Gina Rose," I muttered. "I like having friends, and people are important to me."

I stood, grabbed my bag, and sighed. Time for food therapy. If I couldn't be strong like Gina, I might as well load up on calories. I could work them off later at X Factor. I went to Joe's, grabbed a muffin and a medium coffee, then found an open table.

The boardwalk was again buzzing with activity. A couple sat on the pony wall posing for a selfie with the ocean in the background while skateboarders weaved through the maze of people. Surfers bobbed out on the ocean in anticipation of their next wave.

After finishing my muffin, I breathed in the smell of salt-laced air and walked back toward the office. On the way, I stopped at Sandy's Wiches.

Charlie was behind the counter doing her usual three things at once. The truth was, when I grew up, I wanted to be just like her—a confident, caring, multitasker who knew exactly where she wanted to go in life. When she saw me, I told her I just needed to talk. She pointed at an empty booth, where I plopped down as directed and waited.

I pulled my phone from my bag when it rang. "Ohhh…" I groaned, laid it on the table, and watched it ring. It was Eric. Why had I left that message? Maybe a little dessert? How cliché. Lame. And juvenile. He'd be expecting a booty call and the minute I didn't agree to hop into bed with him, my brilliant plan to extract the truth from him would go down in flames. Thank God my voicemail only gave my number. I let it ring and buried my face in my hands as I waited for Charlie, again beating myself up for not living up to everyone else's expectations.

"Hey, Jade. What's wrong?" Charlie said as she slid a cookie in front of me.

"Jason's self-defense class went haywire."

She slid into the booth on the opposite side of the table. "Did that jerk stiff you?"

"No, I taught the class."

"That's great!"

I unwrapped my cookie and sighed. "No, it's not. You know what? I don't want to talk about me right now. I want to hear about you. What's going on?"

"I have a big exam tonight. This is my final, and if I do well, I'll only have one class left."

"That's awesome. I'm happy for you." The words came out of my mouth, but they sounded hollow. I took a small bite of the cookie. Chocolate chip. My favorite. I sniffled. Charlie reached across the table and laid a hand on my arm.

"Oh, no. You didn't crash-and-burn, did you?"

"It was a huge success."

"Most people are happy when they succeed, Jade." Charlie's eyes widened, and she stared at me open-mouthed. "Oh, God. You didn't, not with Jason."

The memory of Jason lying on the floor, then of Valerie blowing him off, made me chuckle. "Nothing like that," I said, then filled her in with the details about the class. When I got to the part about the watch group, Charlie frowned. She shrugged and asked why I wasn't ecstatic about having my very own watch group.

"Because being the vigilante queen isn't why I took over the agency. What if something happens to one of the girls? How could I live with myself if they did something stupid and the Amorous Assailant turned violent?"

"Hey there, girlfriend. Back up the bus. First off, watch groups are commonplace. How many violent episodes do you hear about because someone saw a crime and dialed 9-1-1? Hello? It doesn't happen."

I scrunched up my face and nibbled on my cookie as I gave Charlie a begrudging shrug. "Okay, but…"

"No way. I'm not done. Second, all these women want to help others. You're helping them with what you're doing. And third, the chances of any of you actually catching the Amorous Assailant in the act are like zero."

I shrugged again. "Are you done?"

"Maybe. Depends on how much more I need to beat you over the head."

What she'd said made sense, but I'd already seen how Zoe's enthusiasm came with its own risks. "I understand all that, Charlie, but I feel like there are so many ways this could go wrong. I should call this whole watch group thing off."

"Jade, do you remember our Halloween party in first grade?"

"Um…yes, but what's that got to do with anything?" I took a larger bite, savoring the mix of chocolate and sugar.

"Most of the girls came as princesses and ballerinas…but you came as Sherlock Holmes. You had that stupid wool cap and the big magnifying glass."

I laughed and looked at her. "And I made you dress up as Watson."

"My mom was furious with you. She spent a week sewing my ballerina costume, but I told her my best friend was more important."

I ran my hand down my throat and sniffled at the memory. "You've always been there for me."

"Hey, what are friends for?"

My cheeks tightened as I watched Charlie's face. She knew me better than I knew myself. It was enough to make me cry. "So you're saying I have some friends who want to help me, and I should let them."

"I'm saying running the Beachtown Detective Agency is what you were meant to do. And face it. This watch group might be just what you need right now."

Charlie was right about one thing. Deep down, I really was enjoying my role as owner of the agency. I squared my shoulders and nodded. "What would I do without you? You're right, as usual. If I lay down some ground rules, this could work. That way, I can keep on Gina's case and not have to hurt anybody's feelings. Besides, what are the odds one of us will actually see the Amorous Assailant's next attack?"

14

WITH MY DRAMA-QUEEN ACT over, I finished my cookie while Charlie filled me in on the latest neighborhood gossip. She also kept a watchful eye on the staff as the line grew longer and, when one of them signaled her for help, she patted my hand and stood.

"I have to go, Jade. They're starting to get backed up."

I thanked Charlie for putting up with my momentary life crisis. We exchanged hugs, and I dumped my trash on the way out the door. Back at the office, I attacked Gina's case with a new fervor and a new perspective—I had to do this my way. Not Dad's way. Not Gina's. Not Zoe's. I wasn't going to pull the plug on the watch group, but I did intend to mother-hen them and keep them out of trouble.

With a decision about the group under my belt, I called Zoe, got voicemail, and left a message. *Sorry I went all Queen Bee on you. What's up? Need a status update.* At the end, I added a quick thank you for organizing the group. My second priority was dealing with Eric. Dad would call him a skirt-chasing dirtbag; I saw him as having a different perspective on Bert. As distasteful as I found flirting with Eric, I needed to suck it up and work the source. I listened to the message he'd left during my talk with Charlie.

"Hey, Mandy. I'm glad you called. I knew you and I had a thing. Sure, I'd love to have dinner and then a little…dessert." He chuckled, then continued. "Why don't I pick you up at seven? Text me your address."

Good. Eric wanted to play the game. It had been a while since I'd dressed for the game of love; that didn't matter. I had the perfect weapons of war—bright red lipstick, new false eyelashes, and a killer black dress that was sure to have Eric plenty willing to answer my questions. The next question was where to conduct my interrogation. I wanted a location that met three criteria: great atmosphere for teasing the idea of romance, busy enough to keep Eric from getting too out of line, and far from home. I knew just the place.

I dialed Eric's number. He answered almost immediately. We did the little hey-how-are-you thing and then I preempted him before he could ask for my address.

"Are you familiar with Carlucci's?" I asked. "It's on the beach, has a dynamite view, and isn't that far from my place. If everything goes the way I think it will, this will be a night you'll remember for a long time."

"Awesome," he said a little too quickly. "Seven? Do you want to handle the reservations since you know the place?"

"My pleasure." I paused and licked my lips for dramatic effect. I knew he couldn't see the action, but maybe he could—on some deep primal level—sense it. "Eric, I'm really looking forward to this."

"So am I," he breathed. "You sure you don't want to have that dessert first? I could stop by your place. Maybe leave here early…"

That would mean I'd have to give him my real address. Introduce him to Mom and Dad. No freaking way. "I wish I could," I lied, "but my boss has given me a deadline for some critical tasks this afternoon." I held back for a few seconds, then continued, "You were married so you know how women bosses can be."

"Tell me about it," he grumbled. "Okay, see you at seven."

He ended the phone call without another word. Eric was definitely living down to my expectations, which brought with it another problem. The little black dress was so short and tight it wouldn't let me conceal any kind of weapon. I was sure when Eric saw me, he'd be convinced I was ready to hop into the sack. Of course, his impressions and my intentions were two entirely different things, so while I was confident in my self-defense techniques, I knew my strategy was fraught with trouble.

My phone rang. Dad. He was probably going through work withdrawal. Either that or Mom was chasing him with a list of honey-dos.

"Hey, Dad, what's up?"

"Just wanted to see how it's going. That's all."

"Gina's case is going well—which reminds me, I have a date tonight. I'll be interviewing Bert's business partner."

"Great. Do you need any help? Backup maybe?"

Backup? Sure, someone to back me up would give me peace of mind with Eric. And it would create a monster Dad problem. Once I brought him in on this, I'd be setting a precedent. Did I really want to open that door? I bit my lip. It was the moment of truth. Time to prove I could be on my own.

"No, I'm good. I've lined up someone else to help me."

"Probably for the best. Your mother wants to go out to dinner tonight. You'll have to tell me all about it."

Oh no. I bit my lip, harder this time. Dinner? Dear God, you wouldn't do this to me. Would you? "Where are you going?"

"I don't know. Your mother wants to go someplace fancy. I tried to convince her we should keep it casual, but she said she's tired of casual."

The tightness in my shoulders ratcheted itself up a few notches. No. It couldn't be. "You're not going to Carlucci's, are you?"

"I don't know, Jade. Your mom's handling everything. You want me to ask?"

"No," I shot back, then winced. "You two have a great time. Okay? Right now, I have to go. I'll tell you all about tonight the next time I see you."

I hung up the phone, leaned back in my chair, and shook off my worry. There were plenty of other fancy restaurants for them to go to. Besides, my life was turning around. Things were going my way. I was contemplating calling Charlie and asking her if she'd be interested in going to Carlucci's, but then I remembered she had an exam tonight. Now what?

My phone rang again. It was Zoe. Providence, perhaps?

"Hey, I'm glad you called me back," I said. "How's everything with the watch group?"

"Oh, man, we are so pumped. We still need someone for Saturday, but other than that, we've got all the days covered. We've got backups for each day, so if one of us sees something happen, we can call out super fast. I knew you'd come around, Jade."

"I was just so worried about someone getting hurt, but if we can make sure everyone who's on watch is aware of the rules, there should be no problems. The really big one is to make sure all the girls know that if they do see something, the first thing they should do is call 9-1-1. I don't want any of them getting involved in a confrontation."

"But Jade…"

"No buts, Zoe. I'm serious. If anybody sees anything, they're to call the police first. I couldn't live with myself if one of them got hurt because they inserted themselves into the situation. We're a watch group, not vigilantes. Got it?"

"That's going to make Alyssa and Gail happy. They were both super concerned about security when I talked to them this morning. I'll let them know."

"And what happened to the new recruits?"

"I told them it wasn't going to work out. You were right. Even though it would be great to have more eyes watching, if we start bringing in people we don't know, we could lose control—or worse."

"Awesome. This is going to work out just fine."

"I agree. Hey, if you ever need any help on any other cases, let me know. I think we make an awesome team."

Zoe wasn't exactly an experienced surveillance expert, but my options were almost nonexistent. Charlie had her big exam. I sure wasn't going to call Jason. Or my dad. And the chances of me reaching out to someone like Dodger were positively remote.

"Actually, I could use some help on something else. Are you free tonight?"

"Totally. What do you need?"

"I've set up a dinner date with this guy who's peripheral to my other case. The thing is, he's a real sleaze, and I've had to let him think I'm attracted to him."

"You totally have him thinking he's getting a booty call. That's awesome!"

Dad would probably not approve of my methods, but I was doing this on my terms and, as a woman, I had assets he didn't. "I know. Right? But I need a backup just in case this guy doesn't want to take no for an answer. So I was thinking if you could show up at Carlucci's around seven…"

"Whoa. That's an expensive place."

"It's got everything I need. Mood lighting. Ocean view. Would you do it?"

"Totally. This is so awesome. So why's this guy so important to your case?"

Uh oh. I should have thought this through. I hadn't realized Zoe would ask why I needed help. I'd just assumed she'd jump at the chance to do some surveillance. How did I not tell her about Gina Rose? "This is not something you can talk about. Not to anyone, Zoe."

"My lips are sealed."

"And what about your fingers? You cannot blog about this. I'll get sued for breach of contract if anyone finds out I've said anything."

"I'm totally on board. But can I use it as deep background? If I think there's a story, I'll do my own investigation and never bring you into it."

I winced. Was I really going to do this? Trust Zoe? I took a deep breath and sat up straight.

"Okay. You're in."

15

IT SEEMED SO INCONGRUOUS TO me that to find a good beachfront restaurant I had to leave Carlsbad. There were plenty of multi-million-dollar homes with killer views, but beachfront restaurants were as rare as hen's teeth in my hometown.

To make sure everything went according to plan, I'd left early. My diligence helped me score one of the best tables. It had a perfect view of the beach and a gorgeous sunset. This was exactly the atmosphere I wanted. The place was already getting busy, so I congratulated myself on good planning.

Dad always said preparation was ninety percent of the solution to a problem, so I'd put a lot into tonight's dinner meeting. From hair and makeup to the little black dress, I'd covered all my bases. I felt naked without my crossbody bag and the protection I could jam inside, but to make the illusion work, I had to go with the plan.

The server, a tall man with a pencil-thin mustache and impeccable manners, was named Scott. He'd watched over me since I'd been seated, but when I told him my date wasn't arriving until seven, he reassured me there was no problem and said he'd check back with me periodically to see if I needed anything.

Zoe sat at the bar, which was to my right and about twenty feet away. She was working on her second glass of wine when a tall man dressed in a white guayabera shirt, baggy shorts, and sandals sat next to her. It hadn't occurred to me when I'd opened the bar tab that I might have been better off making her handle her own alcohol costs. Let's face it, when you're paying for your own drinks, you tend to be more frugal than when someone else tells you drinks are on them.

At five after seven, Eric arrived. From the way he carried himself, he looked like a confident businessman. He'd left his dark gray suit jacket unbuttoned. His monogrammed white shirt looked just like the one he'd worn at our last meeting. The power tie was, of course, loosened, probably to show me that he was not only successful, but busy.

Judging by how his eyes widened when I stood to greet him, he was already counting the number of bases he planned to round later tonight. He moved in for some sort of pre-dinner lip lock, but I dodged left. The end result was a poor excuse for an air-kiss.

Looking only slightly miffed, Eric motioned for our server, then sat and looked out the window. "What a great view, Mandy."

When he turned his leer back on me, I wasn't sure if he was referring to the sunset or my neckline. I wanted to be offended, but the Chardonnay had gone to my head. Oh man, did I regret not having ordered sparkling water. "It's beautiful," I muttered.

He winked at me. "The sunset is, but so are you. What are you drinking?"

"Chardonnay, but…"

He abruptly turned to Scott and ordered another glass of wine, along with a scotch for himself. I glanced to my right and spotted Zoe. She was chatting with the guayabera-shirt guy. The bar had filled up with diners waiting for tables. I wondered how many were singles hanging out with friends or looking for a new one. When Zoe glanced in my direction, I widened my eyes at her as if to say, 'What do you think you're doing, girl?'

Instead of getting rid of the guy, she laughed, flipped her hair, and put her hand on his arm. She was flirting while she was on the job? When I might need saving…from myself? Seriously?

"Mandy? Are you okay?"

"What? Oh sure, Eric. I just thought I saw someone I knew." I waved my hand nonchalantly and smiled. "I was wrong. This place is really busy tonight. So how'd work go?"

"You know, the usual. Make a deal here, another there. The life of a real estate tycoon."

"In other words, you sat around drinking coffee all afternoon."

Eric faked a laugh and sat back as Scott approached with our drinks. When Scott left, he said, "You're a funny girl. Actually, I spent my afternoon anticipating dinner with you." He leaned forward and planted one elbow on the table, rested his chin on his palm, and stared at me. "I just can't believe we hooked up."

Not in his wildest dreams would that happen, but I took my lead from Zoe and played with my hair the same way she had. "I know. Hey, did you talk to your business partner today?"

Eric rolled his eyes and downed another sip of his scotch. "I don't want to talk about him. Tonight's all about us." He flagged Scott with a raised hand and said, "You had a big project your boss gave you?"

News flash, Eric—we weren't here to talk about me. I flipped my hand dismissively and said, "A client we're doing work for had an emergency. It happens. Hey, I have a question. You're good with marketing, right?"

"Of course, that's part of my job. You need some advice?"

Scott arrived and asked if we were interested in appetizers.

"What do you want, Mandy?" Eric asked.

"How about the Fried Macaroni and Cheese? If you like comfort food, it's to die for. You can't get much closer to heaven."

While Eric ordered the appetizer along with another scotch, I glanced over at Zoe. She was still acting enthralled by the guayabera-shirt guy—and the bartender had just delivered another round. Had she forgotten why she was here?

I grabbed my cell and sent her a text. *Hey - remember me?*

She pulled her phone from her back pocket, glanced at it, and laid it face down on the bar.

I jumped when Eric grabbed my hand. "Earth to Mandy…"

"Sorry," I gushed. "I just…never mind, it's a work thing. Just kind of distracted, I guess." A movement in the lobby caught my attention. Oh no. This was not happening.

"What's going on, Mandy? You look like you've seen a ghost. You sure you're okay?"

"What? Oh, no, I'm fine." But I wasn't. Was that Dad's face I'd just seen waiting for a table? Oh gawd, please no.

Eric moved his hand up my arm. "Maybe you need a little consoling back at your place."

I smiled and eased his hand away. "So, you were saying you like marketing?" I took a sip from my glass, raised my eyebrows, and leaned forward.

Eric let his eyes roam downward as his tongue made slithering motions. If ever I'd felt like I was being sized up on the how-easy-is-she? scale, it was now.

"Okay, sure," he said. "I get it. You're going to play hard-to-get. Marketing's always interested me. It's always fascinated me how large corporations use it to make people forget how they've taken shortcuts with some of their products." He droned on about big manufacturing while I pretended to be oh-so-fascinated by his depth of knowledge. When he finished a story about the Ford Pinto, I caught Scott's eye and, even though Eric was only halfway through his second drink, ordered him a third.

He blinked, gave me a roguish smile, and chuckled. "Good idea. You need another, too."

"No, I'm good." I'd polished off the first glass of wine, but had only taken a sip of the second. I raised it to show him it was nearly full.

A high-pitched woman's laugh erupted at the bar. Even Eric turned to see who it was.

I touched his hand and winked. "So tell me more about yourself. You're such a fascinating man."

He sat a bit straighter in his seat, then leaned toward me and launched into another story, this one about his college days. Eric's third scotch appeared at the table. His eyes were glazing over and he now slurred his words with abandon. Our appetizers arrived—four perfectly round, evenly sized balls of macaroni and cheese that had been fried to a deep golden brown. Crispy on the outside and gooey inside, these were perfection on a plate —so good I wanted to tell Eric he should savor every morsel because this was as close to sex as he was getting tonight.

Midway through my second little ball of goodness, I said, "That's how you and Bert met, right? In college? You said you were on the soccer team?"

"Oh, I told you about that? I guess I did, didn't I?"

"You also said earlier that Bert and Gina were soulmates."

He grinned, made a show of looking around the room, then lowered his voice. "That's the public story. Bert's got this little problem. He's an adrenaline junkie."

"Meaning?"

Eric snorted, hit the scotch again, then whispered, "Bert likes two things in life—money and thrills. Gina has plenty of the first, which lets Bert satisfy the second. The bottom line is she has him by the short ones." He made a face like he'd said something naughty, then added, "Oh, sorry, didn't mean to offend."

"I'm not bothered by a little off-color remark. But I am curious. The papers keep painting him as this guy who cares so much about others. Is he a playboy? Does he chase women?"

Eric shook his head and grumbled, "You know, we're talking a lot about Bert. I want to talk about us."

"We'll have plenty of time for that. Later. I have to confess, I am doing a little work here because, well, I told you we might be able to put together a deal. But to do that, I need to know more about your partner—and whether we should cut him out." I winked at him. "We might only need you."

Eric sat back in his chair and swallowed the last of his third scotch. His upper lip curled into a sneer. "Okay, you want to talk about Bert Darlington? I'll tell you all about him. He's a double-crossing, two-bit hustler. He never worked a day in his life." He continued on, his words coming faster and louder, his face growing redder and redder by the moment. Soon, most of the restaurant was watching us.

I reached out in a desperate attempt to stop him. "Eric, you need to calm down. Let's take this down a notch, okay?"

The veins on Eric's forehead bulged purple. He slapped away my hand and then slammed his palms on the table. "You women are all alike," he bellowed. "You all have your agendas."

My jaw dropped. Was this what got him fired? I looked around. Everyone sitting near us was watching. And across the room, so were Mom and Dad. The blush started low and hard and came up fast.

"I'm sorry," I stammered to the nearest couple.

"Hey, I'm the one you owe the apology," Eric shot back. "You got me here pretending to be interested, and all you want to do is talk about Bert Darlington. I'm sick of talk."

"Stop this, Eric!" I hissed.

His stare, intense as it was, intimidated me less than the looks we were getting from the surrounding tables. I needed to find the manager and get this jerk subdued before the entire restaurant heard us.

"Why?" Eric bellowed. "Am I embarrassing you, Mandy?"

"Yes!"

But it was too late. Zoe and the dude in the guayabera shirt who'd picked her up had joined us. Zoe's new guy walked straight up to Eric and stood over him. He planted a hand on Eric's shoulder and spoke in his own boisterous tone.

"Hey, buddy, tone it down. The lady was only asking you some questions."

Oh, please, no. Now I was going to have two drunks fighting because of me—with my parents watching?

"Who are you?" Eric snapped.

"I'm with her." The dude cocked his head in Zoe's direction.

The answer seemed to confuse Eric. At least when he was confused, he was silent. Across the room, Scott gestured frantically to someone in the back. How perfect. We were probably about to get thrown out by the manager—or the cops.

"And I'm with Jade." Zoe pointed at me, then she winced and muttered, "Oops."

Eric shook his head again. He did an admirable job of trying to focus through the scotch haze. "Jade? I thought your name was Mandy."

"I can explain…"

"Jade? What's going on here? Is this man bothering you?"

I buried my face in my hands. So this was what it felt like to live in your most embarrassing nightmare? "Hi, Dad," I mumbled, then took a deep breath and looked up at him. "I have everything under control."

"Doesn't look much like it's under control to me," he growled.

Zoe stepped forward, her hand extended and a perky smile on her face.

I slumped back in my chair. "Okay, had."

"You're Jade's parents? I'm Zoe," she chirped. "I write the blog you've been following."

I groaned. My life was over.

Eric jumped out of his seat. The manager signaled to one of his staff. The staff member put a cell phone to her ear. Eric took a wild swing at Zoe's date.

Eric's blow went wild. Dad stepped in, grabbed Eric's arm, and twisted it behind his back. A collection of oohs, ah's, and cheers erupted as Dad escorted Eric away. Despite the noise, Eric's threats came through loud and clear.

"You're going to pay for this! Whatever your name is!"

I shot a glance at Zoe, expecting her to be embarrassed for her part in this debacle. Instead, she was videoing my dad march Eric out of the restaurant.

16

AFTER A BIG ARGUMENT WITH Mom and Dad about me running my own life, I'd taken the easy route and snuck out of the house in the wee hours of the morning. I was outside Gina's home when the sun peeked over the horizon. Actually, it was much less of a sunrise than it was a gradual brightening of the sky. It seemed like the perfect complement to last night, which had gone from one gray shade of disaster to another.

Bert started his day right on schedule. Now that I knew his routine, I was tempted to take a shortcut to Java Joe's and order myself a large coffee to go. Despite the temptation, I followed Bert to within a block of Joe's, then turned off on a side street where I could watch him through binoculars. I gritted my teeth as he ordered. Man, could I use some coffee. He found an empty table, slathered cream cheese all over the top of a perfectly browned bagel while he sipped his coffee and watched the ocean.

The guy sure had the life. He started each day the same way. From his habits to his dress, it was all perfectly casual. The only thing he'd changed today was his jacket. Instead of his brown leather bomber jacket, he wore what looked like a black nylon or cotton windbreaker.

My stomach growled. "Shut up," I muttered. "You need to lose two pounds, anyway."

I hoisted my binoculars back into place. If I couldn't eat, I might as well watch. I blinked twice and lowered the binoculars.

"Crap! Where'd you go?" I hissed.

I searched around the restaurant patio desperately, but Bert was not there. Had he gone to the restroom? Left? Putting down the binoculars, I scanned the boardwalk. When I spotted a black windbreaker, I went back to the glasses. Sure enough, it was Bert. What the heck? Why had he changed his pattern? What did that mean? I tossed the binoculars in the car, locked it, and followed the black windbreaker.

I had a big problem, though. Bert was on the ocean side of Carlsbad Blvd. I was on the opposite side. Did I cross over? Duh. No. Jaywalking on a four-lane road was a great way to draw attention to myself. The last thing I wanted was to have to listen to my dad and Gina explode when I told them I'd blown my cover right when I was getting my break.

Slowing my pace, I watched as Bert quickly turned toward the ocean and rested his hands on the railing. He'd been carrying a small paper sack. Had he taken that bag into Joe's? I couldn't say for sure. At Walnut Street, just one block ahead of me, a woman stopped to check for oncoming cars. That's when I realized Bert's sudden interest in the ocean view had been a reaction to the woman stopping to check traffic. The moment she'd stopped, Bert had decided to gaze out to sea. What was he up to?

The woman wore bright green-and-blue yoga pants and a cropped tee. She jogged across the road. Bert immediately speed walked to the same spot where she'd crossed and darted across the road between cars. My heart pounded in my chest. I fell to one knee and pretended to tie my shoelace, but all the while, kept a watchful eye on my subject. I was witnessing something. A crime? A rendezvous? A little game of cat and mouse?

When they'd both disappeared up Walnut, I jumped up and ran to the corner. Bert couldn't possibly be more than a half block ahead of me, so I slowed at the corner and peered cautiously down the street. My spirits plummeted. There was no sign of the black windbreaker. And no sign of the woman.

"This can't be happening," I muttered.

The gray in the skies was beginning to feel like the story of my life. I was so dead. I'd finally caught Bert. But I'd immediately lost him? Seriously? I followed in the same direction Bert had gone. As soon as I was off the main street, everything grew quieter. Ahead of me, there wasn't a soul in sight. Not a sound...except...scuffling? Someone moaning? A prickly sensation crawled the length of my spine. I crouched and crept forward until I was standing in the middle of a long driveway for a small apartment complex.

About fifty feet down the driveway, a man wearing a black sash mask that trailed down his back had the woman I'd seen earlier on the ground. A red rose lay next to her. Her hands were tied behind her back with red material. Oh. My. God. It was the Amorous Assailant.

"Stop fighting me. I won't hurt you," the man snapped.

"Hey! Get away from her!" I yelled.

The masked man darted a glance at me and stood. He was trapped between a cinderblock wall and the apartment building. He shot a look down the driveway. My thoughts cleared with one single exception—take this guy down.

The woman lashed out with one foot. She connected with the masked man and he stumbled sideways, but when he caught himself on the cinderblock wall, his mask came loose. I got a clear look at his face as the mask floated to the ground. The realization that Bert Darlington was the Amorous Assailant stopped me for a split second, but then my instincts kicked in.

I started after him, but stopped when I got to the woman. I could go after Bert, or I could help this poor woman. I knew who he was, but I didn't know what kind of injuries she had. I knelt beside her and loosened the sash from around her mouth. She leaned into me, her voice trembling as she alternately thanked me and cursed her attacker.

While I cradled her head on my lap, I called 9-1-1. After assuring her the police were on their way, I untied the red silk securing her wrists. We sat there on the ground, her sobbing uncontrollably and holding onto me with a vice-like grip while I tried to decide what I was going to tell Gina.

"What's your name?" I asked.

"Belinda. Belinda James," she muttered. "That…that was him, wasn't it?"

"The man who's been attacking women around here? I think so. Did he hurt you, Belinda?"

"My side hurts from where he tackled me." She shook her head, but continued to hold on. "He tried to kiss me on the cheek, but I kicked him. The cops are on their way?"

I assured her again that they were, then said, "I hear sirens. They should be here anytime now."

Sure enough, a patrol car arrived less than a minute later. They secured the scene and separated us to take our statements. I told the officer what and who I'd seen. He told me they would follow-up immediately.

By the time I got back to the office, the gray skies had lifted. Even though my world seemed filled with uncertainty, my spirits had lifted, too. Just because Bert had committed this morning's attack didn't mean he was the Amorous Assailant. It could be he was just a copycat. Why hadn't I thought to take a photo?

Because, I told myself, I'd been trying to stop him, not film a documentary.

The good news was the cops had the mask, so there should be DNA all over that as well as the sash he'd used. Add to that the fact that when Gina found out what her husband had done, she would probably castrate him first, then divorce him. Unless she was secretly attracted to prison inmates. No, not Gina. I doubted if she would take Bert back. Which left me wondering how Bert would afford the army of lawyers he'd need to fight the charges.

I stared at the plant in the corner I'd been trying to resurrect and sighed. With my elbows on the desk, I buried my face in my hands. The universe was so screwing with me. It was time to swallow my pride and get help. I pulled out my cell and called my dad.

"Hey, Dad."

There was a short pause, then he said, "Jade…about last night at the restaurant."

"No, it's all on me. I picked the wrong person to back me up and let the situation get out of hand. I take full responsibility."

"And I shouldn't have interfered unless you asked me to. I shouldn't be butting in before things play out."

"And you're still my hero. You taught me everything I know about the business." My stomach tightened at the thought of disappointing him. "Are you going to be home for a while?"

"Sure, why?" He paused, then asked, "Do you need to talk?"

I squeezed my eyes shut tight, took a deep breath, and blurted, "I might have discovered the identity of the Amorous Assailant."

"That's great. Wait…how come you sound so down?"

"It's Gina's husband. Bert."

There was a long pause, then Dad said, "You remember what I taught you about clients and their expectations? Right?"

"Yes. They're happy to get the bad news they expect, but they hate getting told about the unexpected. I think I might need some guidance."

"Come to the house. It's better if we talk here."

"I'm on my way."

I disconnected the call, picked up my go bag, and started for the door. My phone rang. I checked the display. Oh crap. Gina. Not who I wanted to talk to right now, but avoiding her call would make things worse. I punched the green button to answer, but never got a word out. She started yelling so loud I had to pull the phone away from my ear.

"Jade? Are you insane? I asked you to find out what he was doing with my money, not implicate him in a…a felony!"

Uh oh. How did she find out? The cops? Bert? Both?

I set my bag back on the desk. "This should be good news, Gina. It will give you plenty to divorce him…"

"I'll never see that money again now! He'll use it for his legal fees. And I'll probably get stuck with the rest of his legal defense, too."

"Why would you say that? Cut him loose. This is the perfect opportunity to stand up and say you won't tolerate any man terrorizing women."

"I can't do that," she said coldly. "You've ruined everything!"

The line went dead, leaving me staring at my phone. My fingers trembled as I replayed the confrontation in my head. "What just happened?" I asked.

Obviously, something wasn't right with Gina. What made me nervous was not knowing why she was so unhappy. I collected my bag and made myself a promise on the way out the door. I would not answer the phone again until after I spoke to my dad.

17

WHEN I ARRIVED AT THE house, Mom was on the front porch pacing—total bad news. Dad must have already spilled the beans. Fact of Life: Mom was going to dote. Period. End of discussion. The moment she saw me, she started in my direction. There was determination in every step she took. Driving away was not an option unless I wanted to live out of my car and eat junk food for a decade or two.

Resigning myself to the inevitable, I got out of the car and looked at her over the roof. "Before you say anything…"

She shook her head and rushed toward me with her arms outstretched. "My poor baby. You must be devastated."

My independent-big-girl-streak told me to be strong. Show her I could handle this. But the minute I felt her arms wrap around me, I melted into her embrace. Sympathy was good. I could work with that, so I extricated myself from Mom's spiderweb embrace and went with Surviving Mom Tactic #1. Fake it. "I know. Right?"

"In all the years your father ran the agency, he never had a client get arrested."

My client? As in Gina? My hand went to my heart, and I stared at her. "Are you saying Gina Rose was arrested?"

"No, honey. Her husband was. It's all over the news."

I glanced toward the house, hoping to see my dad. He wasn't there. I looked back at Mom and said, "Mom, Bert's not my… what happened?"

"He turned himself in during a traffic stop. He's claiming to be the Amorous Assailant."

I said a silent thank you that the cops hadn't blamed Bert's arrest on me, but why had he turned himself in? This was getting weirder and weirder. "A traffic stop? What did he do?"

"He ran a red light. When the officer asked for his license and registration, he broke down and confessed to what he'd done. He said he needed counseling and the only way he was going to get it was to confess."

What was Bert doing? Setting himself up for an insanity plea? Or maybe he—and Gina—both had different plans. There had been three previous attacks, and all of a sudden Bert had developed a conscience? It did beg the question—why now?

"Did Dad talk to you, Mom?"

"The news broke while you were talking to him. He said we'd discuss whatever it was when you got here. So you didn't know about your client?"

"Her husband, Mom. My client is Gina, not Bert."

"Yes, but you've been following the man every day. And you never had any inkling he might be a criminal?"

"Not until today."

Mom peered at me with a narrowed gaze. "What are you not telling me?"

"Nothing, Mom."

"Juliet Delores Cavendish, do not lie to me."

Oh, gawd, she was using my full name? What was I? Five? I knew where this would wind up, so I closed my eyes and, once again, reconciled myself to the inevitable. "I broke up the attack and chased him away."

"Oh." Mom pursed her lips and gazed out toward the street. She took a long breath. "The news didn't report that. At least your client doesn't know yet—wait… Is Gina aware of what you've done?"

Surviving Mom Tactic #2—Reverse Guilt Trip. "Wow, you make it sound like I'm the one who committed the attack. I'm the one who broke it up. Remember?"

"Sorry, honey. I don't mean to be critical, but your client will probably not take this well."

The tactic might have worked, but I felt terrible. Now I was lying to my mother? For what? So I could avoid having her comfort me? I let out a deep sigh that was filled with regret and the weight of what I'd done. I had to face facts. I could not lie to my mother. "You're right. Gina's not happy."

Dad opened the front door and came out onto the porch. He ran a hand through his gray hair as he watched us, then started down the stairs. His steps were slow and deliberate, and his attention flicked back-and-forth between me and Mom.

When he was a few feet away, I broke loose and threw my arms around his neck. I whispered, "Help me!"

He eased me to one side and looked at Mom. "Jo, let's take this inside. There's probably more to this story than we know."

I followed Mom and Dad up the steps to the porch, and with each one, I felt a stronger connection with a man taking his final steps to the gallows. In the kitchen, we sat at the center island. My mood teetered on the tipping point between a complete loss of appetite and wanting food therapy to cheer me up. Food therapy won. Junk food therapy, to be exact. I snatched one of the peanut butter cookies Mom had baked earlier along with a napkin and some water.

"Good idea," Dad said with a wink. He picked up the rack containing a batch of cookies and laid it on the table. "We might need these."

Mom immediately looked at me with raised eyebrows. "Jade, you said your client is not happy and you're resorting to sugar support? Is it that bad, honey?"

Oh, how well she knew me. I plucked a second cookie off the tray and placed it next to the first. "Could be. The bad news is she's ticked off because her husband is the Amorous Assailant…at least, that's what she says." I went on to tell the rest of the story. When I was done, even Mom grabbed one of those little support pills.

"So what do I do, Dad?"

He glanced sideways at Mom. "These are really good, Jo. What's in them?"

I sat with my mouth hanging open while Mom glared at him.

"Thomas, you know perfectly well what's in them."

"Right. Sugar and spice and everything nice."

"No, Thomas, there's peanut butter, sugar, and…"

"You're not listening. These cookies contain everything Jade needs to appease Gina." He looked at me and smiled. "This is where you find out if you can manage your client, Jade. You've proven you have good instincts. Now the question is if you can make your client listen to reason. If you can't, you won't last long in the business. I'm sorry, honey, but that's just the way it is."

Mom shook her head and made grumbling noises, then said, "Thomas, I don't see how that's helping her."

Instead of answering, Dad broke off a piece of the cookie over his napkin, popped it in his mouth, and rolled his eyes as he chewed.

A warm glow filled my chest. Dad was letting me—no, encouraging me—to be an adult and fight my own battles.

"Mom, do you remember when I was seven and Eddie Gould pushed me down on the playground?"

"Distinctly," Mom said with a huff. "I wanted to go to your school and have that boy suspended." She grimaced and gave Dad a sideways glance. "Your father told you to deal with him yourself."

"I think Dad was right, Mom. I stood up to Eddie the next day at recess."

"And that only made things worse, Jade. You came home with another skinned knee and cried for days."

"I remember it all too well. But when Eddie knocked me down, I got up and punched him. He got a black eye, and I got suspended for fighting. The thing is, Eddie never bothered me again. And then you both got me into karate lessons."

"I've never condoned fighting," Mom declared.

"But you do condone people standing up for themselves and believing in themselves. I think Dad's right. I'm going to go back to work, calculate the bill for Gina, and hand deliver it. I'll talk to her and hopefully she'll see the upside here. Whether Bert is the Amorous Assailant or not, her days as Mrs. Bert Darlington are numbered. She'll soon be able to get on with her life. She wants the money she gave him back, but that just may be something she can't have."

Mom scrunched up her cheeks as she held my gaze. "Honey, all I want is for you to succeed in life."

"And the only way I'll do that is to fight my own battles. Gina Rose is my problem. Bert is hers. There are no good solutions here. Maybe Gina just needs time to process this. You know what? I think I'll go to Bert's bail hearing tomorrow."

It was Dad's turn to sigh. "Are you sure that's a good idea?"

I nibbled on my cookie, nodded, and looked at him. "I don't know, but at the very least, I can try to offer Gina some moral support."

"What if she doesn't want it?" Mom asked.

"Well…I may get worse than a couple of skinned knees. But what's the worst she can do? The courtroom's a public place, and I don't see Gina as the type to go postal on me. Not there, anyway."

18

SITTING IN MY CAR WATCHING a cheap motel room for hours on
end while Gina and Bert did God knows what inside Room #11
was not how I'd pictured finishing up my day. It had started out
well enough—I'd finally caught up to Gina at the bail hearing
and given her my bill, which she'd accepted without incident.
Actually, she'd been quite civil about the whole thing.

After sitting through an hour of mind-numbing hearings and
not-guilty pleas, Bert's turn came. Bail was set at $500,000. In
some weird way, I could even understand it when Gina made the
arrangements to put up the money for the bond. What I couldn't
believe was when she gave him a couple of heartfelt I've-been-
missing-you hugs and kisses upon his release. On the other hand,
this was the power-couple universe, and the paparazzi were
always watching. Maybe they felt obligated; maybe Gina was
having second thoughts. Who was I to criticize? But just because
I wasn't going to judge didn't mean I couldn't follow.

I expected them to go home, but instead, Gina brought Bert
here to the Sunny Days Inn, a low-budget motel of questionable
repute. She stayed with him until four, then left. She returned an

hour later with a small suitcase and a grocery bag. Okay, I got the suitcase—Bert was out on his ear, which meant the public display of affection in the courtroom must have been for the press. I got that, too—a tearful reunion would play well in the tabloids. It was a perfect opportunity for Gina to cultivate the attention she loved. But the paparazzi were nowhere to be found now, and she was still playing nice with him? For real?

At five-thirty, a pizza-delivery guy showed up. Through my binoculars, I watched Gina pay the bill. She must have tipped well because he was grinning from ear-to-ear when he returned to his car. I still couldn't believe she was spending so much time with the man she claimed she wanted to divorce, so I followed the delivery guy's car. I parked behind him at his next stop and waited until he'd made his delivery. I was leaning against the side of his car when he returned.

He was young, probably eighteen or nineteen, with curly hair and a moderate case of acne. The poor guy stopped dead in his tracks when I waved to him.

"Hi, my name's Jade." I paused to let the introduction sink in. "I was wondering if you might answer a question for me about your delivery at the Sunny Days Inn."

He blinked a couple of times and peered at me. "Was there something wrong with the pizza?"

"No, nothing like that."

He pressed his lips together and rubbed the back of his neck. "The lady doesn't want her tip back, does she?"

"Not that either. The money's yours."

"Awesome. I totally need the cash." Apparently satisfied that he had no downside in this conversation, he craned his neck forward and peered at me closely. "What do you want to know?"

Good question. What did I want to know? "How did she seem?"

"What? Who?"

"The lady back at the motel."

Suddenly, he stood a little straighter. He fingered his chin and his worried look was replaced by good old-fashioned greed. "What's it worth to you?"

I hesitated. There were two ways to play this: the easy way —pay the kid money to tell me what he'd seen—or the hard way, which was to intimidate the crap out of him. Sorry, kid, I didn't have a Gina Rose sized bank account to draw on. I pulled out my credentials and shoved them in his face. "I'm a private investigator and you're interfering in an official investigation. The couple you delivered to are currently under observation. Do you know what obstruction of justice means?"

His confidence evaporated, and I thought the poor kid might pee all over himself. Obviously, he wasn't as worldly as he thought he was.

"Look, lady, I just deliver pizza," he stammered. "That's all. I don't want trouble."

"Then answer my question. How did she seem?"

"Happy to get her pizza? Can I go? I got another delivery to make."

"Was she in a good mood? I saw her smile at you."

He glanced past me at his car and winced. "I guess so. She was kinda…distracted. We see it all the time. People are…doing stuff…and they want to get back to it. We can be kinda like an interruption."

"Did you see the man she was with?"

He nodded quickly. "He was right there on the bed with his shirt open. There were a couple of beers on the nightstand. It looked kinda like they were…busy, you know?"

Holy crap. Gina was doing the nasty with Bert? And they had beer? Unbelievable. What was she really up to?

"Thanks. You've been a big help." I turned and walked back to my car. By the time I'd checked traffic, the pizza guy was already gone. I made a very illegal U-turn and drove back to the Sunny Days Inn. Gina's car was gone when I arrived. The sun had dropped into a bank of clouds out on the ocean, so our glorious day was ending in typical fashion for spring on the coast—gray. Bert's room light was on, so I decided to stroll by. Who knows? Maybe I could sneak a peek inside or something. I didn't get the peek, but I did hear a TV blaring with the sounds of the evening news from inside.

I resolved to sit tight for a while longer, mostly because Bert didn't strike me as the type to sit around in a sleazy motel room watching prime time TV—plus, I really didn't want to have to deal with Mom and Dad or their questions. There was a taco stand on the other side of the street just down the block. It took only a few minutes to walk there. All the while, I kept glancing back at Bert's door. The last thing I needed was him making an escape for a wild night on the town. Or to stage another attack.

19

Paco's Tacos had the appearance of a real dive. From outward appearances, it was the kind of place where cockroaches hung out for table scraps. I know. Don't judge a book…blah, blah, blah. That's why I was waiting in line to order. Along with five others. We all stood at an old-timey sliding window that kept the help in and us out.

There were a couple of well-worn—and fully occupied—picnic tables, but that was the extent of the amenities. The crowd ahead of me included a couple jabbering in Spanish, a grungy teen with a skateboard under her arm, and two guys dressed in suits. Obviously, Paco's drew an eclectic crowd, and from the sounds of the conversation between the guys in suits, Paco's tacos were killer.

I was second in line when Bert exited his motel room. I swore under my breath. One of the guys turned around. He gave me a smile and a wink. Across the street, Bert paced in front of his door like he was waiting for someone to give him a ride. I ignored the guy in front of me and rushed back to my car. A compact, blue sedan I didn't recognize pulled into the parking lot and stopped. Bert climbed into the back seat, and the car pulled away.

Now what was he up to? One thing was becoming clear—well, maybe two. First, the laws of normalcy did not apply to Gina and Bert. And second, I couldn't maintain a good surveillance on Bert all by myself, especially if he was meeting somebody. It had been one thing to watch him go back and forth from work, but if he was ubering around town tonight, I was so screwed. I needed help.

Dad was out. No way. Charlie? I dialed her number.

"Hey, Jade, what's up?"

Bert's driver hung a sudden left, leaving me to fend with oncoming traffic. I jammed on the brakes, ignored the blaring of horns, and squealed around the corner just ahead of an oncoming pickup. The maneuver earned me the ever-classic one-finger salute and what appeared to be a string of expletives I was glad I couldn't hear.

When I caught my breath, I said, "I've got a little situation. My client's husband is…well, he's acting kind of weird."

"You mean Bert Darlington? What's he doing?"

I told her about Gina's visit and then the car pickup. Charlie agreed that Bert wasn't acting like most people would if they'd just been released on bail, but she drew the line at joining me.

"I'm sorry, Jade, but I've got to study."

The blue sedan pulled into the parking lot of Fat Cat's, a swanky Mexican restaurant with a large bar and nightly entertainment. I had to say one thing about keeping up with Bert Darlington—it could get super-expensive, fast. The sedan dropped off Bert and drove away before I was even in the parking lot. Call me paranoid, but as I cruised by the entrance, I watched to make sure Bert really did go inside. When he disappeared through the front door, I said my goodbyes to Charlie, then found a parking spot at the end of the lot. The parking spaces were all minuscule. This was one of those lots where subcompacts could park without too much difficulty, but larger cars had to be shoehorned in.

I pulled my hair back into a ponytail, then added a Padres baseball cap along with a shorty denim jacket. It wasn't much of a disguise, but it was the best I could do on the spur of the moment. When I stepped out of the car, I froze at the sight of a black Mercedes pulling into a parking space near the front door. The driver was none other than Eric Andrews. I waited, watching over my roof.

Eric exited his car and did a cursory check for traffic as he crossed the lot and entered the front door. There was no way him being here was a coincidence. Especially since he'd shown up within two minutes of Bert's arrival. I definitely needed help. It was time to worry more about enthusiasm than credentials. I dialed Zoe's number, certain I'd get a positive response.

When she answered, I said, "Hey, this is Jade. How would you like to help me with a little surveillance?"

"Awesome!"

I could almost hear the fist pump on the other end of the line. "Great. How long will it take you to get to Fat Cat's?"

Zoe said she could join me in twenty minutes and agreed to text me when she arrived. I spent the next ten minutes watching the parking lot fill up and customers file into Fat Cat's. At this rate, there would be a waiting line when Zoe arrived. I went to the door and did a walkabout, more of a skulk-about, to find Bert and Eric. All I needed was a trench coat and sunglasses to qualify as the perfect movie cliché.

Bert and Eric had taken a small table in one corner of the bar. They were crowded around it with the one person I'd never expected to see here, Gina.

I kept walking, then stopped where I could step out of the line of traffic and think. Gina was having drinks with Bert and

Eric? What the heck was going on? I peeked around the corner. There were two empty stools at the far end of the bar. It was the ideal location for my purposes. I could see Bert's table, but would remain inconspicuous in the growing crowd. I grabbed one of the stools and ordered a club soda and some chips and salsa.

Even from my perch across the bar, it was obvious Bert, Gina, and Eric were engaged in a heated discussion. Gina had a glass of white wine, Bert and Eric both had a beer. Their glasses were nearly empty. Gina flagged the server, who gave her a nod and came directly to the bar.

Zoe's text came through just as the bartender finished Gina's order. I texted Zoe to let her know where I was. She came in, sat next to me, and said, "This place has killer nachos."

I pointed out Bert's table. Her eyes nearly popped out when she saw who was with Bert. She turned to me and leaned closer. "For real? He's meeting with his wife and his business partner?"

"It's getting to the point where nothing Gina does surprises me." I plucked a chip from the basket, dipped it in salsa, and munched. "I'm starving." I grabbed another chip and watched as the server delivered drinks to Bert's table.

"How about we split an order of nachos?" Zoe winked at me.

"Sure. The way this night's going, that's probably the closest thing to dinner I'm going to get. This could be a long one."

Zoe's eyebrows went up, and she peered at me. "You're going to watch him—like, til dawn?"

I nodded. "This whole Gina-Bert-Eric triangle has me wondering what little game they're playing. One minute Gina wants to divorce Bert, the next she's ordering pizza and drinking beer with him in his motel room."

"No way!"

"Oh, yes."

"Wow. We totally need those nachos." Zoe raised one hand, and the bartender acknowledged her. When he showed up a minute later, she ordered nachos and a glass of wine.

"I'm not sure wine is a good idea, Zoe. You need to stay sharp."

"No worries, partner. I can hold my liquor with the best of them."

Over at Bert's table, the conversation remained heated. Eventually, Gina ordered another round. While that was going on, Zoe flagged the bartender for a second, and we demolished most of the nachos. I was convinced the decision to go with enthusiasm had been the wrong one. Zoe's eyes were glazed, and she was flirting with the guy next to her. At one point, she turned to me and giggled.

"You have like the best job in the world, Jade. This PI stuff is awesome."

I closed my eyes, shook my head, and scooped up the last of the nachos. "You were supposed to stay sober, Zoe. You said you could hold your liquor."

She peered at her glass and shrugged. "Oh, well, guess I was wrong." Her eyes got wide and her face lit up with a huge smile. "I have an idea." She stood, pulled her phone from her back pocket, and tapped the display.

"What are you doing?"

"Getting you some answers." She winked at me, hopped off the stool, and giggled. "Oops," she said as she steadied herself, then marched across the floor to Bert's table.

I sucked in a breath, put my arms on the bar, and laid my head down. No. This couldn't be happening. But it was. I looked up just in time to see Zoe standing at Bert's table with her phone at the ready. The flash went off, along with Gina's temper.

"Who are you? What are you doing?"

"My name is Zoe Jessica Wright. I'm private press reporting on the Amorous Assailant case," she said in a loud voice.

The dull roar in the bar died down and soon the only background noise was what drifted in from the main dining room. I groaned and kept my forehead resting on my forearms. So much for inconspicuous. If Gina saw me now, I was dead. But I couldn't help myself. I had to peek.

Zoe held her phone in front of her, and I could see the screen. She was now recording video.

"People want to know why you're having drinks with your husband, a man you want to divorce," she demanded.

"Good God! Leave me alone!" Gina jumped up and darted left.

Zoe cut her off by slipping between two tables. "No. The people want to know the truth."

While they stood stock still locked in a staring contest, Bert and Eric rose. The server, who was carrying a fully loaded tray, stopped at a nearby table, effectively cutting off their escape.

All eyes in the bar were trained on Gina and Zoe. The color in Gina's cheeks darkened to scarlet, and then she must have reached her breaking point. She yelled an obscenity and raised her right hand, her middle finger extended. At least it hadn't been directed at me this time. Gina stormed away from the camera and Zoe, taking the only available escape route—right by me.

I reached up to lower the bill of my cap, but was too late.

No question. Gina had seen me.

20

GINA'S BROW FURROWED AS SHE stared at me, obviously trying to comprehend where she'd seen my face. Then, her jaw went slack, and she did a quick one-eighty to look back at Zoe. It didn't take a genius to guess what was coming next.

Gina spun back to face me, an intense look of hatred on her face. "You traitor! I give you a job, and this is how you repay me? By following me? Setting me up with the…the paparazzi?"

My gaze darted across the bar to where Zoe was now confronting Bert and Eric. I raised both hands and shook my head. "It's not what you think. I can explain."

But Gina was having none of my lame excuses. She stormed past me and out the door.

"Zoe, what have you done?" I muttered, then groaned as Eric, followed by Bert, marched toward me.

"You again?" Eric stood before me, his face red with anger. "You are the coldest, meanest…"

"Don't say it." I pointed at Zoe, who was standing to the side with her phone raised. "You're on the record."

He gritted his teeth, then turned to Bert.

"Let's get out of here," Bert said and jerked his head toward the exit.

I sat, watching them leave with Zoe on their tail. Both of the men waved Zoe off, but she was relentless. The buzz in the room returned, this time, louder than before—and I was now the object of pointing fingers and surreptitious glances. Thanks to Zoe—and now me—everybody had something juicy to talk about. The bartender appeared before me, a white towel in his hand, and began drying moisture off the bar.

"You want something stronger?" he said with a smug smile.

Staring morosely at the exit, I asked, "How about a bottle of Jack Daniels to go?"

"Can't sell it that way."

I huffed and handed over my credit card, then looked straight at him and wished I could've been nasty enough to tell him he'd missed the joke altogether. "Receipt, please."

While the bartender was finishing my transaction, I picked up Zoe's glass and downed the last of her wine. I sat glumly and watched as she returned, grinning from ear-to-ear. She sat next to me, reached for her glass, and did a double take.

"What happened to my wine? I had almost half a glass."

The bartender returned, handed me the credit card slip, and I signed. When I was done, I snapped, "The wine cops put you on suspension."

"What's wrong, Jade? I thought you wanted to break this open?"

"I said I wanted to know what was going on, not cause a public spectacle."

Zoe scrunched up her face and nodded. "Well, okay. It was a little over-the-top. But you have to admit, it got their attention."

"I didn't want their attention, Zoe. You know what? I'm done with you. This is a disaster." I hopped off my stool and left her standing at the bar.

What did I do now? Go home with my tail between my legs? No freaking way. I was returning to Bert's room and watching him. All night, if necessary. Somehow, I was going to figure out what little conspiracy he, Gina, and Eric were engaged in. Fifteen minutes later, I was once again across the street from the Sunny Days Inn, my binoculars in hand. Eric's Mercedes was parked directly in front of Room #11.

About five minutes later, a dark Honda pulled into the far end of the motel parking lot. Oddly enough, I didn't see anyone get out of the car, so I dismissed it as one of those weird cheap-motel things. Eric left about ten minutes later, which left me wondering whether I should follow him or stick with Bert. I chose Bert.

I spent the next half hour watching Room #11. Bert had no visitors, didn't leave, and the light remained on. At eight-thirty, the driver of the Honda got out of the car. Though the driver wore a dark hoodie and jeans, I could easily tell that it was a woman. She passed three doors before I recognized her. It was Zoe. Again. And I'd bet anything she was going straight to #11.

"No!" I yelled and jerked on the door handle.

Zoe crept along the walkway. Did she really think moving slowly made her invisible? I made it out of the car just as she snuck past the door.

My relief was short-lived, however, because she was headed straight to the office.

Enough was enough. If Zoe started asking questions, the motel staff might tell Bert, then he'd tell Gina, and I'd be in even deeper trouble than I was right now. I ran to the street corner. Pressed the pedestrian crossing button. The light remained red. I jabbed it again. And again.

There were no cars coming from either direction. Zoe was almost to the office. Forget the light. I darted across the street.

Just as my foot hit the opposite sidewalk, the little green man lit up.

"Screw you," I muttered and rushed toward the office.

Zoe stood at the desk, leaning forward and craning her neck like a swan. A young man with long stringy hair and a bad goatee drifted out of the back room, said something, and approached her. They both jumped about a foot when I burst through the door a split second later.

"There you are!" I exclaimed.

The guy behind the counter peered at me. I gave him an apologetic look as I grabbed Zoe's arm. She blinked and tried to pull away, but I applied pressure until she yelped. "She got away again." I cocked my head and screwed up my face. "I'm so sorry. Was she bothering you? I hope not."

I lifted Zoe's arm slightly and pushed her toward the exit.

"Jade, what are you doing? Let me go!"

"Once she's off her meds..." I called over my shoulder as I pushed her through the front door.

Outside, I cast another glance at the desk clerk. He was watching us from behind the counter like we were a pair of loonies. To be honest, I couldn't blame him.

"Let me go!" Zoe cried.

"When I get you back to my car." I pushed the crossing button again. "What did you think you were doing?"

"I was trying to get information."

"You're trying to blow my investigation."

The light changed, so I pushed Zoe forward. She resisted, but my grip was too strong for her to fight me off.

"This is kidnapping. I'm going to call the police!"

"Zip it, Zoe."

She stopped in her tracks, then her shoulders slumped, and she began to sob. I rolled my eyes and kept my grip, but by the time we were approaching my car, Zoe was in a full-on meltdown, barely able to walk because she was crying so hard.

"What is wrong with you?" I demanded.

"No." She pouted, then started blubbering again.

"Oh, for God's sake, Zoe. What is it?"

"My…father." She sniffled a couple of times while I unlocked the passenger's door.

"Your father what?" I snapped, then realized how awful I sounded and sucked in a quick breath. "Did he die or something?"

"No, back when he was drinking, he always said that same thing when he got tired of listening to me. He'd get drunk and if I talked at all, he'd tell me to zip it." She burst into tears again.

I opened the door, eased her into the seat, then went around to the driver's side and got in. We sat in silence for a minute, then I handed her a tissue and reached out to console her. She pulled away and sniffled a few more times.

"I'm sorry I blew your cover." She dabbed at her eyes with the tissue. Even in the dim light, it looked like it had been used for target practice in a game of paintball. "My dad always pushed me to be more assertive, so I put on this big front and act all impetuous, you know? For real. Something just came over me and I thought, my friend Jade needs help and if I do what I did to make my dad happy and get these guys to panic, it's going to make her like me more."

Wow. Talk about rambling. I leaned over and hugged her. She leaned in and now we were both blubbering.

"I do like you, Zoe. But what you did was exactly the opposite of what I needed at the time."

She sat back in her seat and dabbed at her eyes again. "I know. It was stupid."

The polite thing would have been to tell her it wasn't. It would have been the kind response, too. But I chose honesty.

"Yes, it was. You got me in big trouble with Gina, and now Bert probably suspects he's being watched."

"Oh man, I'm sorry, Jade."

"So am I, Zoe."

I leaned back in my seat and stared across the street at Room #11. The light was still on, and I wondered how long it would be before he would turn it off and go to sleep. Zoe and I sat in silence for several minutes before I finally broke the quiet.

"You might as well go home, Zoe."

"No way. I'm making this up to you. I'm staying as long as you are."

The light was still on. The Sunny Days Inn parking lot was almost filled to capacity, and it was getting cold. "I'm here all night," I said.

"Me, too, then."

"I've got a blanket in the trunk." I stepped out of the car, retrieved the blanket, and gave Zoe half. She snuggled up under it. "I'll take the first shift," I said. "Get some sleep."

Zoe leaned to one side with her head cradled between the headrest and the window. A few minutes later, her sniffles subsided and her breathing settled into a soft and low rhythm.

At around ten, Gina's car pulled into the parking spot two doors down from Bert's room. She went straight to the door of #11, knocked, and waited until Bert opened the door. Judging by what I could see through the binoculars, neither of them was happy.

I didn't dare say a word. If I woke Zoe, she'd probably go charging across the street. Though the idea of confronting Gina while she was with Bert was tempting, it was my job to watch, not influence. It was one of those times I'd love to go with my gut, not the rules. As a precaution, I fished out my phone and placed it on the dashboard. Gina exited the room at ten-forty-five, went to her car, and left. This time, I got her on video. This was starting to look like the strangest breakup I'd ever seen, so I logged the contact and settled back in.

At eleven-fifteen, all was quiet, and I was wondering if Bert might stay up all night. I resolved to wake Zoe at midnight. It was only forty-five minutes, but it would give her some sleep before I grabbed a short nap.

Not only was it getting colder, but all of Zoe's drama had drained my energy. The half glass of wine I'd drunk at Fat Cat's was making my eyelids heavy. I pulled the blanket up to my chin and enjoyed the cozy warmth. Sitting in the car for hours on end wasn't so bad. Especially when you had a friend…or memories…to comfort you.

While most kids heard fairytales before bed, Dad had often talked me to sleep with stories about long stakeouts. The more he had talked about being tired, the heavier my eyelids had gotten. I blinked a few times, rubbed my eyelids, and sat up straight.

Thirty minutes. I only had thirty minutes to go. Then I'd wake Zoe. Next to me, her breathing was still slow and regular. Almost like a lullaby…or one of Dad's stories.

I snuggled under the blanket and stared without blinking at the light coming from the window of Room #11, smiling as I relived a memory of Dad telling me stakeout stories at bedtime.

21

THE CRASH OF METAL ON metal jolted me awake. Zoe sat next to me, rubbing the back of her neck and blinking away the dregs of sleep. I jerked sideways, bumped my head on the window, and saw the source of the noise. A garbage truck was emptying a large green dumpster.

"What happened?" Zoe asked. "My neck is killing me."

I rubbed my eyes and gazed across the street to Bert's room. "I fell asleep," I confessed.

Zoe nodded, blinked, and grimaced. "Me, too."

"I know. I was going to wake you at midnight, but I must have dropped off right before then." My back felt like a stale, malformed pretzel. "I have to move."

I opened my door and watched the garbage truck retreat from the lot. The driver seemed oblivious to our presence. For all I knew, the sight of people sleeping in cars was a regular thing for him.

"I need a bathroom," Zoe said as she came around the car. "And coffee."

"No kidding." I gazed across the street. "Bert never did turn the lights off. The guy must have an alcohol tolerance that's off the charts. And he must never sleep. Or he fell asleep with the light on."

Zoe groaned. "Or he left."

I leaned against the roof of the car and stretched my legs. "The blanket was a bad idea. I was okay until I got all cozy and warm. I don't know how my dad ever did those all-night stakeouts."

"What happened last night?"

"Gina showed up. She was here for about forty-five minutes. It's possible Bert left after her."

"My mom always left a light on in a motel room when she went out. She said she never wanted to be surprised when she came back."

I glanced over at Zoe. She was staring at the motel, presumably Room #11. "It would really suck if he's not there," I groaned, then grabbed my phone and dialed the number for the Sunny Days Inn.

"What are you doing?"

I signaled Zoe to be patient with a raised index finger, then said sweetly, "I'd like to speak with Bert Darlington in Room #11."

"Ma'am, it's very early," the desk clerk replied. She sounded older and not the least bit interested in being helpful.

Seriously? I'd never stayed in a motel where the staff or the guests had any sense of day or night. It was time to call on my inner Gina. What would she do? Get all snippy, of course. "This is his wife," I snapped. "He's an early riser and there's been a change to his schedule today. I need to contact him immediately. Put me through right now."

The woman's reply came almost immediately. "Yes, ma'am."

There was silence when the clerk put me on hold, which was followed by ringing. After ten rings, I hung up.

"He didn't answer," I said.

"Totally weird. Maybe he's in the shower."

Rather than play twenty questions about where Bert Darlington might be, we agreed to wait thirty minutes and try again. During the wait, Zoe went down the street to a twenty-four-hour fast-food burger joint. She returned fifteen minutes later, a cup of coffee in one hand, an anemic-looking egg sandwich in the other. I left her in charge, ran down the street, used the facilities, and spent two bucks on a cup of coffee that was way too strong and tasted burnt.

When I told the clerk, she peered at me like I was insane. "Are you sure?"

"Am I…of course I'm sure."

"Well, you don't need to get nasty about it."

Nasty? She didn't have a clue. "Haven't you been taught that the customer's always right?"

Again, the look. Then a shrug. "I guess I could make a fresh batch."

"You guess you could?" I rolled my eyes, shook my head, and left, tossing the cup of mud in the trash on the way out.

When I got back to the car, Zoe was sitting in the passenger seat watching the motel. I climbed behind the wheel and looked over at her. "Any change?"

She shook her head. "I thought you wanted coffee."

"It tasted like day-old sludge."

Zoe nodded and eyed the cup sitting in the holder next to her. "It's so gross. And my egg sandwich was, like, cold. I said something about it and she just blew me off."

"Blonde girl with a ponytail and bad attitude?"

"That's the one."

"She said she guessed she could make a fresh batch. I walked out and threw the cup in the trash. I probably should have forced her to make more."

"Yeah. You totally should have."

I pointed at her untouched cup. "What about you? Why didn't you make her fix the problem?"

Zoe looked away, then pointed at the motel lot. "So, you gonna call the office again?"

Got it. Zoe was also a chicken. "Sure." I dialed the motel. This time, the clerk must have recognized my voice, or maybe we were now beyond the too-early hour, because she put me right through. The phone rang about seven times before I hung up.

Zoe pursed her lips. "This totally sucks," she grumbled.

Her jaw tightened, and she jumped out of the car, then strode toward the crosswalk. Now what? I hurried after her, this time happy the signal light was slow to respond.

"What are you doing, Zoe?"

She jabbed the button for about the third time. "We're totally gonna find out if he's in there."

"No, we're not. Surveillance means to watch, not participate."

She huffed. A car zoomed by. And Zoe made a dash for the other side of the street amidst a flurry of honking horns and speeding vehicles. I stood staring after her.

"Wait!" I yelled.

By the time the light changed, Zoe was passing the office and well on her way to Bert's room. I sprinted across the street just as she planted her feet and knocked.

"Zoe," I hissed. What was she trying to do? Ruin my life forever?

I ran the rest of the way. She was pounding her fist on the door for the third time when I got there.

"He's not here," she announced.

"You're not sane," I snapped. "Come with me."

I grabbed Zoe's arm and started to guide her away, but stopped when a maid pushed her cart out of the office and into the walkway directly in front of us. With a huff, I pulled Zoe into the opening between a pair of parked cars, but she shook loose of my grip and rushed back to the maid.

"Hi," Zoe chirped. "I was in a hurry to get to a meeting in San Diego and totally locked myself out of my room." She held up her car keys and pointed at a white four-by-four. "See? I'm parked right there. Can you let me in so I can grab my room key?"

The maid, a woman with graying hair who must have weighed more than Zoe and me put together, shook her head. "No. You need to talk to the office," she said in halting English.

Thank goodness somebody had some sense. If I had any sense, I'd drag Zoe back across the street and handcuff her to my car. But trying to stop her now would call even more attention to what we were doing. I went and stood next to one of the cars. When the maid wasn't looking, I jerked my thumb and glared at Zoe. "Get over here," I hissed.

She ignored me and instead wrinkled her nose. "I totally don't have time to deal with them. Also, the traffic's awful this morning. And I don't want to go into the office tonight when I get back. I've got a super busy day today and that dude on nights like creeps me out."

The maid looked over her shoulder at the office. She wore a name tag with the name Esme engraved on it.

"Look, if you want, you can just grab the key for me," Zoe said. "It's like right on the…the dresser. And I really don't want to have to deal with the office. Please? I'm totally late."

This time, Esme sighed and fished a keyring out of her pocket. "You stay outside when I open the door."

"Awesome," Zoe said with a nod.

She was still gushing her thanks as Esme went to the room, knocked on the door, and announced herself. When there was no answer, she slipped her key into the lock, opened the door, and announced herself again. Once again, there was no answer.

She stepped inside and let out a bloodcurdling scream.

22

ZOE AND I EXCHANGED A wide-eyed look, then started toward the room. We didn't make it through the door because Esme charged out like a linebacker rushing full speed ahead. We both backed away just in time to avoid the impact. Esme slammed the door behind her, then stood between us screeching like a wounded cat.

I checked the door, but it was locked. Esme shook her head violently and shoved the keys in her pocket. "No! No!" Her screeching and sobs subsided and were replaced by ragged breaths, which were soon followed by hiccups. The next thing I knew, she was the one in meltdown mode, babbling in Spanish as she gestured wildly toward the office.

"You want to call the police?" I asked.

She nodded vigorously, hiccuped once, then nodded again.

I hadn't realized it, but Zoe was off to the side with her phone pointed at the maid. "Is he dead?" she asked.

Another nod.

"Zoe, put down the phone."

"No freaking way, Jade."

I looked at Esme. "How do you know he's dead?"

The maid shook her head vigorously. She was obviously in shock and wasn't going to answer questions, and Zoe wasn't going to stop the video. Enough was enough. I dialed 9-1-1, reported what Esme had told us, and was assured help would arrive in a few minutes.

"The police will be here soon," I said. "I know CPR and first aid. Do you want me to check on…" I glanced at the door. "The man inside?"

The maid shook her head again, this time more vehemently. Okay, I was very confused now. Was there blood? How did she know Bert was actually dead? She'd been in the room for a total of maybe ten seconds.

During the next few agonizing minutes, Zoe peppered Esme with questions she either didn't understand or didn't know the answers to. My Spanish wasn't the best, but I got the gist when she held her hand in front of her face and snapped at Zoe. I wished the cops would arrive. That would force Zoe to play nice and stop badgering this poor woman.

I inserted myself between the two of them and made a cutting motion across my neck with my fingers. Zoe must have understood—she was getting nothing more from this witness. She put away the phone with an exaggerated huff.

A hulking paramedic truck, bright red with lights flashing and siren wailing, lumbered into the parking lot. Two guys with crew cuts, big chests, and tiny butts were out of the vehicle within seconds. Esme let them into the room, then stood guard at the open door. Zoe whipped out her phone again and tried to enter, but Esme pulled the door shut in her face.

Standing only inches from the closed door, her lower lip sticking out in a pout, Zoe grumbled, "Not cool." A moment later, she added a weak, "I'm with the press."

The response, delivered in Spanish, sounded much like a mother scolding a recalcitrant child. I didn't need the words to understand that she'd had enough of Zoe. A police cruiser rolled to a stop in the parking lot directly behind the ambulance. The cop, who was so clean-cut he looked like he was fresh out of junior high, got out of his vehicle and approached.

He introduced himself as Officer Caputo and was soon talking to Esme in Spanish. She shot Zoe a nasty look before she responded to one of the officer's question. His expression darkened, but he gestured for her to open the door.

Officer Caputo fixed Zoe with a stern gaze. "Ma'am, you'll need to stay out. No pictures. No video."

"Haven't you ever heard of freedom of the press?" Zoe shot back.

"Ma'am, please."

"Fine," Zoe huffed.

She started to put the phone in her back pocket, but I snatched it from her hands.

"I'll hang onto this. We don't want her to be tempted."

Zoe flashed me a black look, but didn't complain. Officer Caputo went inside and left the door open behind him. Before he went deeper into the room, he looked at all three of us, but let his gaze linger on Zoe.

"Do not enter," he said.

I grabbed Zoe's arm, smiled at Caputo, and nodded. "Got it. Yes, Officer."

It didn't take long to figure out that Bert really was dead. Officially, none of the responders would say a word, but when the paramedics left, I overheard one of them mutter something about hanging being a crappy way to die. I swallowed hard and thought back to last night's surveillance.

Officer Caputo called for homicide and the cops soon had the room cordoned off. The desk clerk showed up to whine about the complaints she was receiving from guests, but Caputo chased her off with a brusque comment, then returned to Esme and told her she needed to give a full statement.

I returned Zoe's phone to her right before the detectives arrived at ten. They began interviewing all of us. While Zoe stood off to the side talking in animated tones to her inquisitor, I was in the midst of being grilled by Detective Des Martini. The detective was one of those women I'd classify as fire-and-ice. Hot enough to ignite the passions of any man while simultaneously exuding a cold if-you-mess-with-me-I'll-rip-your-face-off-and-throw-you-in-jail aura. Even Zoe had been cowed into submission with a single raised eyebrow when Martini told her to give her statement to a different officer.

At first, I thought things might go well for me with Martini. We were both professional women; we both wanted to see justice done—and then she started in with the questions. Things like, why was I here?

"I'm a private investigator and was on surveillance last night."

"Who were you conducting surveillance on?"

"Mr. Darlington."

Martini gave me the raised eyebrow and pursed her lips. "Interesting. So, did you see who went into the room last night?"

"Up until almost midnight." There was no sense in belaboring this, I might as well just confess. "That's when I fell asleep."

Her reaction was almost undetectable, but Martini did stop writing and her chin puckered. "Do you have a record of who went in and out prior to midnight?"

I bit my lower lip and wrinkled my brow. "Uh, that's a difficult question."

"Really?" The detective stopped writing again and looked me in the eye. "It seems like a very straightforward question to me. So tell me, Ms. Cavendish, why is it so difficult?"

Talk about ice in her tone. This lady could freeze steel with a single voice command. This was not going well. How did I tell Detective Martini that I was protecting my client when I didn't have a client?

"I'm waiting, Ms. Cavendish."

Ewww. The raised eyebrow again. That couldn't be good. I'd been fired. Right? I had no current obligation to Gina. Right? I said, "Detective, this is sort of a problem for me. I saw two people enter the room last night. One of them might have been a client."

"Might have been?" Martini stared at me, raised the eyebrow again, and waited.

How many of those raised eyebrows did I get before the ice queen sent me to jail?

"You have an obligation under the law to tell me what you saw, Ms. Cavendish. I can subpoena your records if necessary. What do you mean by 'might have been' a client?"

Okay, I had my answer—three. I could just hear the conversation with my dad—something like, *Oh gee, Dad, I'm super sorry I destroyed your life's work in less than a week.*

Zoe was talking to the other detective—I'll bet she wasn't having the same moral dilemma. I had to tell the truth.

"Mr. Darlington had two visitors I know of last night."

The detective sighed. "Are you stalling, Ms. Cavendish? I want names and times." She fixed me with a steely gaze that clearly conveyed her annoyance at having to repeat her question and deal with a lowly PI—a newbie at that.

I swallowed the lump in my throat and took a deep breath. "Detective, mind if I refer to my notes from last night?"

"Not in the least, Ms. Cavendish. You'll be signing your statement under penalty of perjury, so let's make this as accurate as possible."

Sure, I thought. Let's.

23

I HADN'T FELT LIKE SUCH a rat since ninth grade when I gave up my best friend Amelia for smoking in the girl's restroom. Amelia's parents grounded her for a month. Amelia didn't talk to me for two. And I became *persona non grata* until I started going out with Jason. I guess that's one reason I stayed with him —even though on some deep level I'd always known he was a philanderer, he'd been good for my cool factor.

The big problem was Gina had done all the things I related to Detective Martini. Even though I was selling out my client, Martini didn't seem terribly appreciative. Then again, if I were in her size eights, I'd probably be spouting a bunch of civic-duty rigmarole too. When I got to Gina's last visit, the detective raised both eyebrows and gave me a sly smile.

"Do you think it was a booty call?" she asked.

Holy crap. I did not see that question coming. Wow, maybe Detective Des and I could be friends after all. I shrugged, then pursed my lips and peered at her. "I don't know. Maybe. What do you think?"

The smile disappeared, and the detective made a note. "I'll take that as a yes, Ms. Cavendish."

"Wait! That's not what I said."

"You've been very helpful. I'll be in touch if I have further questions for you." Detective Des Martini slapped her notepad shut and walked away.

Talk about feeling used. She'd tricked me into implying my client had slept with her husband the night he'd been charged as the Amorous Assailant. What was I? Intent on destroying the last of Gina's reputation? Man, Dad had told me stories about some heartless women over the years, but Detective Des had them all beat, hands down.

So, that's the way my morning went. I was back in ninth grade with no friends, lots of questions, and a bad case of the woe-is-me's. The big difference was, this was not ninth grade and my actions carried some serious consequences for Gina. To make matters worse, I was now sure Martini wouldn't answer any questions. At least Zoe would talk, which made me regret not even attempting to say goodbye when I left the motel.

I had a bad case of guilt building, so I texted Zoe. She ignored my first message…and the second…but sent me an emoji on the third. Oh man, I had no idea that gesture could be done with an emoji. I shrugged it off and replied, asking if she'd meet me for lunch. Once again, she didn't reply. Undeterred, I was confident that I knew Zoe well enough and upped the ante with another text offering to make lunch my treat.

Thirty seconds later, we were making arrangements to meet at Sandy's Wiches. At quarter to twelve, I staked out my table. Charlie plopped down opposite me. She wanted to know what was wrong; I filled her in. As I was wrapping up, Zoe appeared in the doorway, looked around, and waved.

"My lunch date's here," I said.

"Good luck." Charlie winked and gave my hand a squeeze as she stood and turned sideways to face Zoe. "Hi, I'm Charlie. I'm the owner and a friend of Jade's."

"I'm Zoe." She shot me an uncertain glance, then smiled at Charlie. "Nice to meet you."

"I'll let you two talk." Charlie gestured for Zoe to sit, then hurried away.

Zoe sat in the seat opposite mine. "So what's good here?"

"I'm addicted to the California Sub and the jalapeño potato chips."

She studied the menu board for a minute, then nodded. "Sounds good. Should we get in line?"

"No worries." I caught Charlie's eye and held up two fingers. She gave me a thumbs-up. "Order in," I said.

"Awesome."

"So you want to talk about this morning?"

"Not really." Zoe stuck out her lower lip and sighed. After a moment, she said, "I think I just keep trying too hard, you know?"

"Like what you were telling me last night?"

"Yeah. It's super hard to come across a story on your own, so I got desperate and started acting stupid again. I'm sorry, Jade. I did it to you again after I promised that I wouldn't."

"No worries, Zoe. It happens." I reached across the table and took her hand.

She responded by returning the pressure and looking at me. "At least I'm not as screwed up as Gina. Right?"

"Well, now that you mention it…it was all pretty weird last night. I'm trying to figure it out myself. Gina told me she wanted to divorce Bert, so I don't get why she spent so much time with him."

"And that Eric dude…he's like, super aggressive, you know?"

"Totally," I said. "You saw how he was at Carlucci's, so him being at the bar shocked me."

"Maybe Gina's got some weird mental disorder. Like her mother."

"Could be…wait…her mother is mentally ill?" My pulse kicked up, and I so wanted to tell her she couldn't drop a bomb like that and not explain, but Charlie was coming our way, and I didn't want to drag her into this.

Zoe glanced sideways and her face lit up. "Food's here."

"Hey," Charlie said as she laid a tray in front of us. "Two California Subs, jalapeño chips, and a couple of cups for drinks. Jade, you look like you're in shock. What's up?"

Zoe grabbed one of the sandwiches and began unwrapping it. "I'm famished."

I waved my hand nonchalantly and shook my head. "Oh, nothing. Zoe just told me something that surprised me."

"Really?" Zoe leaned back and peered at me. "You didn't know?"

"I had no idea," I grumbled.

"Gina's mother is like demented. She's in this super expensive mental hospital down in San Diego."

"Wow." Charlie looked at me. "You had no clue?"

I shook my head and peered at Zoe. "You checked out my client?"

She bit into a chip and rolled her eyes. "Oh, God, these are so good."

"Zoe? Answer my question."

She sighed. "Technically, she's not your client. Right? I mean, didn't she, like, fire you?"

"Well…"

"And besides, she totally can't afford to be spending money. She won't even be able to pay for her mother's care pretty soon."

"Of course she will. She's rich," I blurted.

"No way. She's almost broke. She like squandered the family fortune."

Charlie looked at me, made a face, and took a step back. "Sounds like you two have some catching up to do."

"This sandwich is to die for," Zoe said. "I totally have to start coming here."

"Thanks," Charlie said, then shot me one of her we-need-to-talk glances before she slipped away.

"What do you want to drink?" Zoe asked.

"Iced tea." I nodded numbly and watched as she went to fill our cups. Today was definitely my day for being caught off guard. In that moment, I could have been standing down at the shore listening to monster waves. The surrounding sounds slipped away and the only thing I heard was a rushing in my head. Zoe returned, slid a drink across the table, and took another bite of her sandwich.

"Why did you check out Gina?" I croaked.

"I'm doing a series on her and need to find all the dirt."

"What do you mean you're doing a series? You said you wouldn't write about Gina."

"No. I said I would only use what I got from you as deep background. Mostly, it's just like a lot of questions right now. But I think my readers are going to totally love the theme—rich girl turns bad girl. It's going to be awesome. The first piece was published an hour ago. Here, you can read it."

She pulled out her phone, tapped the screen a couple of times, and handed it to me.

I read the headline and the opening paragraph and muttered, "This is your blog?"

"Totally. Isn't it awesome?"

Not exactly the word I had in mind. More like, disastrous. I kept reading. The gist was that Zoe had put into words everything about last night. It began with the dinner and went right up to this morning's discovery of Bert's body. She'd even included her photo of Esme looking distraught.

When I was finished reading, I gaped at her with my mouth hanging open. My sandwich lay in front of me, untouched. "Zoe, you can't publish this. It's…libel."

She blew off my comment with a flip of her hand. "First Amendment, Jade. Freedom of the Press. Besides, it's already live."

I was not going to win an argument with Zoe about journalistic standards and liability, but maybe I could get her to make some changes. "Let's go over a few of these things. You said the dinner was a meeting of conspirators. You can't call it that."

"Why not? I didn't say it *was* a meeting of conspirators. I only said it looked like one. And the photo I got of that Eric dude talking with Bert confirms it. If I don't raise the question, my readers will. I'd be derelict if I didn't connect the dots."

I groaned, then hung my head and asked, "Why did you call Gina's visit to the motel a booty call?"

Zoe smiled. "Pretty awesome, right? I can't take credit for it. I heard that detective ask you the question, and I totally knew I had to include it."

"But there's no proof it was anything other than…a social call."

"Seriously? You're going with a social call?"

"Zoe, you can't say these things without proof."

"And I intend to get it. I'm going to find the proof that Gina Rose is a black widow. She totally did it with her husband in a sleazy motel and then killed him."

My phone vibrated, and I jumped about a foot in the air. I didn't even want to know who was calling. The way this day was going, it could only be one person, Gina.

I checked the display. It was Mom. Maybe I'd caught a break —unless she'd seen Zoe's blog already.

24

ZOE SNATCHED UP ANOTHER JALAPEÑO potato chip and peered at me from across the table. "Aren't you going to answer that?"

"Yes," I grumbled, then took a deep breath. Two things I knew for sure. First, Mom didn't call unless it was serious. Second, not answering wasn't an option, unless I wanted her to go into worry mode, in which case she'd be calling every five minutes. And if she found out I'd been avoiding her in the middle of the day? Total disaster.

I put on a smile and tapped the green button on the screen. "Hey, Mom. What's up?"

"Have you read this?"

Okay, no 'hi, how are you?' or anything. Not a good sign. Technically, I wasn't clairvoyant and didn't know what she was referring to, but based on Zoe's revelation, I had a pretty good idea. "Have I read what, Mom?" I said innocently.

"This blog post from your friend Zoe Jessica Wright."

I groaned and glared across the table at Zoe's empty spot. She'd finished her drink and was getting a refill. "I just saw it a few minutes ago. In fact, she showed it to me. I'm in shock."

"So's your father—what do you mean, she showed it to you?"

Zoe was still at the drink machine. She'd filled her cup, but was putting the lid back on. "We're having lunch. I was trying to follow Dad's advice to always keep your enemies closer."

There was a momentary pause, then Mom said, "Tell me she's not sitting with you right now."

"No, she's chatting up some guy who's getting a refill at Charlie's drink station. She's flipping her hair, so I might have a few minutes."

"Then I'll make this quick. This post is very inflammatory. You cannot ignore it. When your client hears about this…who knows what she'll do? Your father and I agree you need to get ahead of this."

"Sounds great, Mom, but what do I do about Zoe? She's so determined to build her readership that she's just making wild accusations."

"I know, Jade. Figure it out. You'll find a way."

I shot another glance over at Zoe, who was laughing at some supposedly funny remark made by the new Mr. Wonderful. She reached out and touched his arm and laughed again. "Oh, man, she's going all out."

"Excuse me?"

My phone buzzed again; I took a quick look at the display. So much for catching a break. It was Gina. "I have to go, Mom. Gina's calling me. See you tonight." I clicked off the one call and accepted the other. "Hi, Gina."

"Where are you?" she hissed. "I need to see you right away." Her voice held a note of desperation I hadn't heard before.

I listened closely to the background noises—voices, the rush of wind, the distant rhythm of the surf. It all sounded very familiar. Kind of like she was down on the boardwalk. "I'm having lunch right now. What's up?"

"I was at your office, but you weren't there. I got away from them, but there are reporters everywhere looking for me. I'm hiding out in some coffee place on the beach called Joe's Java or something like that."

"Got away from who, Gina?"

"All the reporters!"

My gaze darted back to Zoe, who was nodding agreeably, smiling, and drifting this way slowly. Behind the counter, Charlie was alternately checking out Zoe, then me, as she worked.

"I'm kind of busy right now. In fact, I'm trying to deal with something that affects…"

Before I could finish, she snapped, "This all started because of that stupid blogger. She printed lies about me and now all the real reporters think I killed Bert. You have to do something about her!"

Zoe slid into the booth opposite me, raised her eyebrows a couple of times, then bit back a self-satisfied smile and glanced at Mr. Wonderful. My insides tightened. Now what? My untouched sandwich still lay on the table. The frontrunner for the Most Unreliable Reporter award was watching me, obviously eager to tell me all about the new guy.

"I'll be there in a few minutes. Just stay where you are." I ended the call, told Zoe I had to leave, and stood. "I can't stay. I have to go see someone. You can tell me all about that guy later. Okay?"

"But…"

"No buts, Zoe. I have to go."

I turned to leave, but Charlie was standing in my way. She handed me a paper bag, hugged me, then returned to her spot behind the counter. Zoe didn't say another word as I packed up my sandwich and chips. On my way to the exit, I looked back at her and saw her watching me. She gave me a weak, little-girl wave as I darted out the door. I speed walked to Java Joe's, all the time wondering why I didn't just cut Zoe out of my life.

I double-timed it to the boardwalk. When I arrived, Gina was nowhere in sight. I swore under my breath for letting her disrupt my attempt to deal with Zoe, then jumped when someone tapped me on the shoulder. It was a woman in baggy jeans, an Army sweatshirt, and oversized sunglasses. She had tucked her hair under a baseball cap.

"Jade," she whispered. "It's me, Gina."

"Why are you dressed like that? And why are we whispering?"

"Because I don't want to be recognized. I had to buy a disguise in some…second-hand store." She waved her hand in the general direction of the downtown.

I tried, I really did, but I couldn't help myself. With a smile, I said, "It's a good disguise."

For a moment, I expected Gina to tell me what a rotten person I was for making fun of her. Instead, the corners of her mouth curled up ever so slightly. "It is. Isn't it?"

We both laughed as though we'd been friends for years, and as we stood there, I realized Gina's disguise gave her the ability to do something she couldn't normally do—relax. "Come on. Let's walk back to my office. You might as well enjoy your freedom."

We took our time heading back to the office. Unless I was mistaken, Gina was actually enjoying not being recognized for once. When we arrived, I pulled out my keys to open the door. There was nobody in sight, so I told Gina we were in the clear. She pulled off the cap and sunglasses and plopped into the chair she'd used on her last visit.

"My life is a disaster because of that blogger person. I can't believe someone printed all those lies. The worst part is they'll probably get away with it."

I pushed the bag off to the side.

Gina nodded at it. "Is that your lunch?"

"There's a shop down the street I go to a lot. Sandy's Wiches. A friend of mine runs it."

"I'm starved."

Oh, what the heck? I wasn't hungry, anyway. "I'll split it with you."

I cut the sandwich with a plastic knife, gave Gina the larger half, and split the chips.

Gina took her first bite of the sandwich, rolled her eyes, and sighed. "This is so good."

I nodded, smiled, and gestured with my chin. "Wait till you try the chips."

Gina's reaction was much like Zoe's. She was soon professing her love of jalapeño potato chips. Maybe I'd missed my calling in life. I should've been a jalapeño potato chip pusher.

In between bites, I asked, "So, what happened with the reporters?"

"That post came out and right after that, I got a call at my office from a reporter. He asked if I killed Bert."

"You're missing the point of my question. What I mean is, you fired me at Fat Cat's. Now you want my help. Which is it? Am I fired, or not?"

"Did I do that? Of course you're not fired. Just because I got angry doesn't mean I don't want you to work for me."

"Then why haven't you gotten me that list of payments you made to Bert?"

Gina grimaced, then let out a little huff. "I'm working on it. My accountant is busy…you'll get it."

When? At the trial? Obviously, Gina was stonewalling me. For now, I could let that slide. "All right. Then you need to level with me. How much of what Zoe wrote is true?"

Gina stared at me, swallowed hard, then took a deep breath. "Zoe?"

Uh oh. Why had I mentioned her name? "What I meant was…"

"The woman from the bar? She's the blogger? And you're on a first-name basis with her? Were you working with her from the beginning?"

"Gina…"

"Oh my God, you were! Jade, how could you? After I gave you a chance? After I trusted you?"

Should I lie? It was tempting, but my karma was already in the toilet. Why make things worse? "That's not how it was supposed to happen."

Gina shook her head and stared at me. "How what was supposed to happen?" she croaked. "My public embarrassment?" Her lower lip quivered. Her eyes filled with tears and she looked away, gazing off into space.

Mom's words echoed in my head. I needed to fix this. Now. I reached across the desk and laid my hand on Gina's. "I never meant to hurt you. That whole thing at Fat Cat's went sideways. I went there because I was following Bert. When I saw you visiting him at the motel, and then having drinks with him and Eric, I got suspicious. I knew I couldn't do a decent surveillance without help, so I called a woman I met during a self-defense class that I taught. She wasn't my first choice."

The excuse sounded lame. Even to me. Sad as it was, the excuse might have placated Gina had the door not burst open.

There, standing with her phone pointing at Gina and me, stood Zoe. "Gina Rose. I'm Zoe Jessica Wright with the press. Would you like to comment on the allegations that you conspired to kill your husband?"

25

I WANTED TO STAND UP, march over to Zoe, and yell at her, *Are you out of your freaking mind?* My other option was to grab my surfboard, walk to the beach, and paddle away—forever. While I wrestled with that idea, Gina and Zoe launched into a mean-girl staring contest.

My life as a private investigator was most likely over. I'd become convinced Zoe was an alien sent to Earth for the sole purpose of ruining my life. With the power of the universe behind her, my best option felt like throwing in the towel right now.

"I did not kill my husband!" Gina practically spat the words at Zoe.

"I never said you did," Zoe shot back. "What I asked was, how you'd like to respond to the allegations you killed your husband?"

Oh, dear God. Someone just shoot me. More staring. More drama. Finally, my brain kicked into gear. Maybe Zoe wasn't trying to ruin my life after all. It was a long shot, but what the heck? I asked, "Who's making those allegations, Zoe?"

"People."

"What people?"

"I'm sorry, Jade, but you ought to know I can't reveal my sources."

"Sources?" Gina scoffed. She pointed an accusing finger at Zoe. "You paparazzi are vicious. All you want to do is get your story and you don't care how many lives you ruin to do it."

Zoe stood straighter and held Gina's gaze. "I'm not the one who started the rumors. In fact, I'd like nothing better than to prove them wrong."

Maybe for the next thirty seconds, but from what I'd seen, Zoe could flip-flop on a coin toss. On the other hand, she was also relentless. The relentless part could make her a good ally— assuming I could keep her under control by keeping her out of touch with her home planet.

"Zoe, why don't you tell us what the rumors are so Gina can respond to them?"

"What?" Scarlet lines mapped the anger on Gina's face. Her jaw worked furiously for a moment, then she snapped, "You're enabling her? That's it, Jade. I've had it with you."

I held up my hands, and to my surprise, Gina stopped talking. Her angry stare did nothing to warm the cold silence, but at least I felt like she might be having something vaguely resembling a rational moment. I swallowed hard, knowing my next comment might be the last I ever made to her directly.

"Both of you, listen to me. Zoe, you need to get the facts before you go making accusations—or even sound like you're making them. And if you want to keep working with me, you have to accept my terms. It comes down to one simple principle —Gina is innocent until proven guilty. If you'd rather make unsubstantiated claims on your blog, go ahead—just don't expect me to stand by and let you get away with it."

Gina raised her chin, smiled at me, then gave Zoe a self-satisfied smirk. "Take that."

Oh, gawd. Really? "No. I'm not saying you're innocent in all this, Gina. Or that I totally believe in you. Right now, I'm on the fence. I'd like to help prove your innocence, but you need to think about the predicament you're in. You could potentially be facing a murder charge. Your typical rich-girl persona won't get you out of this."

"But…"

"No buts, Gina. Level with me now or I'm walking away. I won't work for a client who keeps secrets from me."

It was Zoe's turn to smirk at Gina. I rolled my eyes, threw my head back, and huffed. "That's it. I'm done with both of you."

They both gave me an open-mouthed stare. "What?" they asked in unison.

"Seriously? You two don't get it? I'm out of here." I stood to walk out, but stopped when Zoe grabbed my arm.

"I'm sorry, Jade. I told you, I'm an overachiever. I wish I could turn it off." She faced Gina. "I was wrong. I totally came across as way too accusatory. For what it's worth, I don't believe the rumors, but I have an obligation to print what I know."

"You have an obligation to print the truth, which is that I didn't kill my husband." A moment later, Gina grimaced and shoved out her lower lip. She shot a melodramatic sideways glance at Zoe, then fixed me with a hurt-puppy-dog gaze. "What I want to know is why you didn't tell me you were working with her."

Did it really matter why I was working with Zoe? Probably not, but Gina did like drama. I took a deep breath, nodded, and said, "We've all made mistakes. I should have told you about Zoe. I'm sorry."

The apology seemed to appease Gina, and the conversation gradually became less confrontational. Soon, we were talking like real adults and then the unthinkable happened—we agreed to a truce—of sorts. The three of us would work together. A good sales guy would call it a win-win-win. I called it a triumph of desperation. Whatever it was, Zoe was going to get her exclusive inside story. I was getting a helper. And Gina? Well, she would tell all. Finally.

She began by denying any involvement in Bert's death. At that point Zoe brought up the Gina-is-broke rumor. I thought for sure our pact would go down in flames, but Gina surprised me again—instead of going into another rant, she sighed and buried her face in her hands.

"Why not?" she wailed. "It's all going to come out. If it's not you people, it will be the police or someone else. Yes, most of my money's gone."

"What?" I gasped, unable to erase a vision of nasty notices from my bank informing me I'd overdrawn my account. "How gone is gone?"

"I still have enough to pay you. If that's what you're asking. I just have so many…obligations." Her voice faltered and the little worry lines at the corners of her eyes crinkled.

Something in the way she stumbled on that last word made it impossible for me to not ask. "What kind of obligations?"

"Daddy always liked it when I did charity work. He said it was good for the family name…for the business."

"Gina, you're not answering my question."

She sucked in a breath and shook her head. "Like I said, it's all going to come out. I have this problem with saying no. I…I can't."

The Gina Rose image flashed before me. Gina helping to save the whales. Gina at the children's hospital. Feeding the homeless. My breath caught, and I asked softly, "Have you given away all your money?"

"I have some monthly income from the properties the business owns, but I committed so much that I had to tap the trust my father set up to pay for my mother's care. It only has about a hundred thousand left."

I exchanged a glance with Zoe. If I had a hundred grand sitting around, I wouldn't be calling myself broke. "A hundred thousand is a lot of money."

Gina grimaced and shook her head. "My mom's in dementia care. That will barely cover another year. Before his death, my father made some terrible decisions. He never told me and I made all these commitments and…and then Bert bled me dry."

She leaned her elbows on the desk and buried her face in her hands. Her sigh—a combination of a heavy breath and a groan— reminded me of a dying animal. When she spoke, her voice cracked.

"The reason I went to see Bert that night was to talk him into selling off the business assets. I figured if he put the land in Carlsbad up for sale, I could replenish my mother's trust and nobody would even know."

I had to consciously warn myself to not be a gawker. Gina Rose—*the Gina Rose*—was broke? And she'd borrowed from her mother's trust? It wasn't exactly the same thing, but I'd stolen from the cookie jar a few times. Maybe it was the same— for me it was a few cookies, for Gina it was…

"How much?" I asked. "How much money did you borrow from your mother's trust?"

"Oh, I don't know…a million—give or take."

A million? Thank God I kept my mouth shut, but from the look on Zoe's face, she was equally shocked. I swallowed and took a deep breath. "Well, that's…um…interesting."

"Interesting?" Zoe gaped at me with her mouth hanging open. "She embezzled a million bucks from her mother's trust and you call it interesting? Are you nuts? It's illegal…it's…it's…bigger than grand theft auto."

Gina sniffled. I pulled a tissue from the box in my desk drawer and handed it to her. "Here." I gave Zoe a disapproving glance as Gina dabbed at her cheeks. "Zoe, we're all on the same side. Right?"

She nodded, then mumbled a weak apology followed by a justification. "It's just that a million bucks is more money than we'll make in our lives."

I narrowed my gaze until Zoe glanced away. "Are we on the same side? Or not?"

"Yes."

Gina blew her nose, sniffled a few more times, then wadded the tissue into a tight ball and held it out. Ewww. I picked up the trash can so she could throw her own little germ bomb away. "What did Bert say when you said you wanted him to sell the property?"

"Bert was being Bert."

"Meaning?"

Gina closed her eyes and sighed. "Really? Do I have to spell it out for you? He wanted to get back together. He said we were so good together and had lots of fun, and he'd consider selling the land if I dropped the idea of a divorce."

"Do these guys all work from the same playbook?" I blurted.

Both Gina and Zoe frowned as they looked at me. It was Gina who caught on first. "That guy you were with did the same thing?"

"Not exactly, but close enough," I muttered.

Zoe crossed her arms over her chest and scrutinized Gina. "So you totally walked out on him. Right?"

Gina and I looked at each other, and I knew exactly how she felt. The signs were there. How had I missed them? I'd been in her shoes. Made the same mistake with Jason—multiple times. Which put Gina's role in a whole new light.

"You didn't walk out on him, did you?" I asked.

Gina fixed a bleary-eyed gaze on me for a few seconds, then burst into tears again. I knew it. There was something else she wasn't telling me.

26

ZOE AND I WATCHED GINA have another meltdown in an awkward silence. I kept expecting Gina or Zoe to say something, but neither seemed ready to make the first move. I desperately wanted Gina to tell me she hadn't slept with Bert, but deep down, I knew she had. The only question was, why? And I didn't think it was because of the money.

To break the silence, I pretended to shiver, then said, "Getting chilly in here again."

Zoe rolled her eyes; Gina sniffled a couple of times and whimpered something I interpreted to be a yes.

"Gina, I understand you didn't actually kill Bert, but did you help him along?" I asked.

The color in her cheeks slowly drained. She croaked, "No."

Gone was the rich-girl persona. Gone was the aura of confidence. Those pretend images had been replaced by the real emotions of fear and worry. I might have only been a PI for a week, but I was sure my client finally got it—she was in trouble.

"Then you're innocent," I said, doing my best to sound reassuring.

Zoe was still silent and biting her lower lip as she watched Gina. She caught me looking at her and glanced away.

I frowned and peered at her. "Zoe?"

"I'm like thinking."

"It's more than that. What's up?"

She chomped down on her lower lip again and winced. "I totally want to believe this is for real, Jade, but how do we know she's telling the truth?"

"Hello? I'm right here," Gina snapped. She glared at Zoe and let out a loud huff, but a moment later, she added, "I get it. You hate me because I went to private schools and wore thousand-dollar prom dresses."

Zoe gaped at Gina for several seconds before she responded. "You spent a thousand bucks on a prom dress? My mom got mine second-hand, and I totally hated it."

A wry smile formed at the corner of Gina's mouth, and she bit her lower lip. "For real? My mom picked mine out, too. It was so beyond ugly."

They both laughed, and I was happy they'd finally found common ground. But Gina still hadn't answered Zoe's question —how did we know if she was telling the truth? "So what did you do, Gina? I mean, when you found out what Bert wanted, did you walk out on him or did you give in?"

"Bert got all handsy," she blurted. "I guess he thought he could turn me on by…I told him to stop."

"And?"

The single word hung in the air like a dark cloud on the horizon and the color in Gina's cheeks reversed direction by deepening to a bright scarlet.

"Tell me you didn't," I groaned.

Gina sat straighter and glared at me, her eyes growing redder by the second until they brimmed with tears. "It's not like we'd never done it before!"

"Oh, gawd." I sighed and handed Gina another tissue. Slowly, very slowly, the puzzle pieces fell into place—the woman I'd once seen as the strongest of role models—was human. Just like me and Zoe. And like us, she was in need of constant reassurance.

In between sobs, Gina croaked, "I'm getting a massive headache. Can I go?"

Wow. Gina Rose asking for my permission to leave? I still had so many unanswered questions. Questions that could mean the difference between her standing trial or not. As long as she didn't start avoiding me, most of the questions could be answered later. "I think we have what we need for now. Zoe and I will get to work, but I'll need to follow up with you. Maybe tomorrow?"

Gina nodded, sniffled, and held her head as she rushed out. Zoe sat across from me, staring at the front door and muttering to herself. "This sucks so bad."

"Tell me about it."

She took a deep breath and gazed at me. "You get it, right? If she felt forced into doing it with that guy, the cops will for sure use that against her."

"I know. The cops will claim she asked Bert to sell the assets and that he refused, so she killed him." Oh, no. What if she had an even stronger motive? A deeper secret only Bert knew? Something that might have died with him?

"You said she was the last one in the motel room with him. Right?"

"I fell asleep. I have no idea who else might have gone into that room. Maybe we should go talk to the night clerk. It's possible he saw something. I doubt if there are any other witnesses. It was almost eleven when Gina left. The DA will have a field day with this."

Zoe nodded enthusiastically. "We should totally go to the motel and talk to the dude."

After contemplating the foot traffic visible through my front window for a few seconds, I called the Sunny Days Inn. When I was done, I said, "The night clerk's name is Harvey Longo. He comes in at seven, and the woman I talked to said it usually quiets down around eight. The problem is he won't be in until tomorrow night. I guess the good news is, that's Sunday and the motel should be slow. Let's meet then and hope this guy has time to talk."

"Awesome," Zoe said as she packed up her stuff.

When she was gone, I headed for home. Mom and Dad were in the kitchen assembling the ingredients for shredded chicken tacos. To be more precise, they were searching the pantry for a couple of the ingredients that had missed the grocery list.

After hugs and greetings all around, Mom took a long look at me and frowned. "Is your problem fixed, Jade?"

"Sort of," I lied.

Mom shook her head; Dad pretended to read the label on a can from the pantry.

"More problems at the agency?" he asked absently.

I wanted to talk to him alone, but Mom was like Sherlock Holmes on speed—she zeroed in on clues with lightning efficiency and wouldn't stop asking questions until she had the answer. I shrugged, cast around for a prop to delay the inevitable, and gave up. "Fine. It's Gina."

Dad's smile reminded me of when I was eight and he'd let me sit on his lap. In those days, life had seemed so difficult. In retrospect, I realized how easy it had been and how it was all part of some cosmic game plan to prepare me for adulthood. It was time to suck it up and cop to reality.

"What's going on, Jade?" Dad asked.

I plopped down on one of the stools and confessed. "I need help."

Dad came and sat next to me, listening patiently as I explained my concerns about Gina and how she might be keeping secrets from me.

"Sometimes the best defense is a good offense," he said.

"Meaning?"

"Find the real killer."

"Thomas!" Mom sputtered. "Jade isn't ready to take on a murder case. She has no experience, no training, no…"

"Hush, Jo," Dad said. He folded his arms in front of him and leaned on the counter, then continued in a clear, strong voice. "I wasn't ready for my first murder, either, but that didn't stop me. I took the case because it's what my client needed."

Mom took a deep breath and the muscles in her jaw tightened. "I don't like it."

"You didn't like it when I was in the same situation, Jo." Dad looked at me. "Jade, the reality is you may never have another murder case in your entire career. It just doesn't happen very often. But what you have to do right now is believe fully in your client's innocence. You know why, right?"

I sighed and held Dad's gaze. "Because if she's innocent, someone else isn't."

"For now, you have to assume the police want to prove your client is guilty. Which means it's up to you to create the counterargument."

Good intentions were all well and good, but without my own game plan, I was toast. "How do I create the counterargument? Where do I begin?"

"That's the easy part, honey." Mom smiled at me. "Bert Darlington was the Amorous Assailant."

I sucked in a breath and stared at her. I'd been so busy thinking about Gina that I'd lost sight of Bert's role. "So I begin with the victims. Find out if any of them have a motive."

Dad cleared his throat. "Or someone related to them. How many times have you wanted to kill Jason Taylor?" Before I could answer, he added, "How many times did I?"

I gaped at him. "You?"

"And me," Mom said. "Jade, you're our little girl. When Jason hurt you, we felt your pain. There were plenty of times I would have gladly shot Jason myself if it would have made you feel better."

"Holy crap. I never considered how my breakup with him might have affected you guys. I'm sorry."

Mom shook her head. "It's life, honey. Love and anguish are all part of the game. Some people deal with it better than others. Besides, murder only makes things worse, and worse was the last thing you needed."

"You made a good call when you started digging into Bert's past," Dad said. "The trail led you to finding out he was the Amorous Assailant. Don't let your client's reluctance to be truthful throw you off course. What you want to know is, who in Bert's life would have suffered so much they'd actually commit murder?"

The good news was Zoe knew who all those victims were. I let out a mental groan. Given her record of unpredictability, that might also be the bad news.

27

I SPENT THE REMAINDER OF Saturday working on the backgrounds
of the victims. After weighing my options, I decided to start with
Belinda James, the last victim. We had met, sort of. It hadn't
been under good circumstances, but at least we had something in
common. Second, I felt a need to check in on her to see how she
was recovering from her ordeal. She might not want to talk
about it, but it was worth a try. Last, she worked at a florist just a
few blocks from the agency.

On Sunday morning, I parked in my usual space, an
unmetered spot on a sidestreet several blocks from the office.
Though it was only ten, there were already strollers about. No
big surprise. The sun had issued its call—if you're cool, be here.
As a result, the village was a hive of activity buzzing with
tourists and locals. They stood, strolled, and swayed elbow-to-
elbow. With food, without, it didn't matter. They all did their
thing.

Like a bird caught in the flock, I meandered along, allowing
the momentum of those around me to pull me as I
simultaneously tried to avoid—and answer—the dilemma at

hand. Should I drop Zoe as a partner, or not? The entire question hinged on whether I believed I could keep her from doing something impulsive and possibly dangerous. While I wanted desperately to believe in her, I didn't know if I could control her.

Midway down the block, I came across Beachtown Florist. In some ways, I found it odd that they were open on Sunday. But then, Sundays were huge family gathering days. Maybe the florist did a big walk-in business.

Even when the open doorway loomed in front of me, I still wasn't sure what to say. Rather than standing out front and drawing attention to myself, I ducked into the shop. A refrigerated case stood to one side. The section nearest me was filled with red, yellow, and white roses. There were also bouquets from the simple to the elaborate. I could tell these guys had every occasion covered—from a simple apology to a funeral—flowers covered them all.

Belinda stood behind the counter, her blonde hair pulled back and up into a loose chignon. She carried a few extra pounds on her hips, but I could envision her still turning the head of almost any man. She appeared calm and serene as she arranged white daisies in a glass vase already containing button poms and lush greens. When she glanced up, she gave me one of those I-know-you-but-can't-place-you smiles.

"Welcome to Beachtown Florist. Are you looking for something in particular?"

"Hi, I'm Jade Cavendish."

She frowned, then looked at the business card I held out. She took it, read the card, then said, "You're the one who saved me from that awful man. Sorry I didn't recognize you. Everything from that day is just a big blur."

I nodded. "No worries. It's totally understandable. What's strange is that we've never met before. My business is around the corner and down the block. Are you doing okay?"

A quick nod, a sideways glance, then a shrug. She didn't seem very 'okay' to me.

"My boyfriend tells me I've changed since the attack."

"Tell him to be patient. You'll need a little time."

She nodded absently, then grabbed a daisy from the countertop. "Why would anyone call that man the Amorous Assailant?" Her voice turned hard, and she snapped, "There was nothing amorous about him. He was so…vicious."

I leaned against the counter and nodded. "Sometimes emotional hurt can be worse than something physical."

She peered at me closely. "Why are you here? I want to put that whole thing behind me."

"I understand. Actually, I'm investigating the death of Bert Darlington. He is…was…the Amorous Assailant."

Belinda blinked a couple of times and stood straighter. "Was? What do you mean?"

"He died while he was out on bail."

I watched her face for some sort of reaction. There was none for several seconds. Then, with deliberate precision, she placed the daisy into the arrangement on the counter. "Good riddance," she muttered. "The man was a pervert."

"I understand how you feel. But he didn't die from natural causes. Would you mind answering a few questions for me?"

"About what?" Her eyes widened. "Wait! Are you thinking I had something to do with it?"

"I'm just interviewing all the victims. If I can find some commonality, there could be a clue as to who killed him."

"Are you saying it was murder?" Belinda stared at me.

What did I say to that question? *Well, duh, somebody strung him up. Did you put the noose around his neck?* I shrugged and chose to make my answer sound like what the cops might say. "A final determination still has to be made."

She eyed me for a few seconds, then said, "So you don't think I had anything to do with his death?"

"Scout's honor." Okay, another lie. But if I came out and asked her if and why she killed Bert Darlington, I was sure Belinda would throw me out immediately. "I wondered if you'd ever met him before."

She shook her head. "No. I didn't even know who he was until afterwards."

"What about Gina Rose? Have you ever met her?"

"Is that his wife?"

"Yes."

"Never heard of her. Should I have?"

"She's pretty well known. Lots of money. Big real estate developments. That sort of thing."

"Look, I run a small business. I don't hang out with the rich and famous. I've never met them. And I don't follow that kind of news." She paused and started to remove one of the greens from the arrangement, but then stopped and looked at me. "All I know is this random guy jumped me on the way to my apartment. He tied me up, then tried to kiss me. I freaked out. I didn't know what he was going to do. Then you showed up. That's it."

I breathed in the air's fragrance. It was fresh and clean and made me want to fill my office with plants and flowers. "This is a nice shop. I don't know why I've never been in before. Maybe I'm just not a flower sender."

Belinda grimaced. "The walk-in business is tough these days. Everybody wants to buy online. We still get people who need something at the last minute, but that's the exception." She smiled and held up the arrangement she'd been working on. "That's why we have these."

"It's pretty." I paused and a heartbeat later, added, "Do you get many orders for a single red rose?"

"You mean like the one he used during the attack?"

169

"Exactly. Could he have bought it here, seen you, and decided...how do I say this? To make you his next victim?"

"I haven't made any sales like that. I suppose my business partner might have. I'd have to ask."

I scrunched up my face and shrugged. "That would be great. Like I said, I'm trying to figure out how he found you. I know he was at Java Joe's that morning. Were you there that morning?"

"I was. Come to think of it. A guy was watching me and it kind of creeped me out." She cocked her head to the side and her brow furrowed. "You know, he might have been there before, too."

"Do you go there every day?"

"Only when I work mornings. That was the week Tommy and I traded off. He's divorced and had his son for the week. Tommy wanted to spend time with him. You know, do a lot of the tourist things."

"How long have you been business partners?"

"We've known each other forever. He's like a brother. When he said he wanted to buy this business, I asked him if we could go in together. It's worked out better than other parts of my life." She rolled her eyes, grimaced, and muttered, "My ex."

"They're wonderful until they're not. Right?" I smiled at her.

She rolled her eyes again. "Isn't that the truth? I got a wonderful daughter out of the deal, so I guess it was worth it."

"How old is she?"

Belinda snickered. "Five going on fifteen. Smart as a whip. We're trying to get her into an accelerated program at school."

"We?" I raised my eyebrows and held her gaze. "You and your ex must be on decent terms."

"Oh, heavens no." She made a face as though someone had forced her to bite into a lemon. "My ex is long gone. My boyfriend Gareth says Ashley's too smart for regular classes. He wants her to be challenged."

Something felt off in her response. "It doesn't sound like you're completely onboard."

She bit her lip and glanced away. "I made a mistake in my marriage by being too independent. Gareth can be demanding, but he loves Ashley as much as I do. And let's face it, I'm not a supermodel, so I want to keep what I've got."

"Are you kidding?" I blurted. "You're beautiful."

I stopped myself before I made things worse by telling her she didn't have to give up control of her daughter to appease a boyfriend. Maybe it was just my bitterness over Jason's perpetual betrayals, but Belinda seemed to be capitulating, not living her life.

"When I was younger, I thought marriage was a game. Now I realize it's more of a business. You do what you've got to do to make it work. Besides, Gareth still wants to get married. Even after the attack. That's more than my ex would have done."

Suddenly, my outlook on the day felt tarnished. This talk about exes was too déjà vu. "I hope it works out for you."

Belinda turned back to the arrangement on the counter. She transferred one of the green poms from one side to the other. "Is there anything else? I need to get back to work."

"No worries. You've answered all my questions." With one exception.

The one thing I could say for Jason was that he always encouraged me and the women in his classes to be strong. Maybe Jason's "strength" was all an act to hide an inner fragility, but at least he'd gone through the motions. I said goodbye to Belinda and walked back toward the office.

In some ways, Belinda reminded me of Jason. They both seemed a lesson in duality. Strong and weak at the same time. And for that reason alone, I wasn't about to cross Belinda James off my list of suspects.

28

MY CONVERSATION WITH BELINDA HAD done little other than to whet my anxiety. I still didn't know what to do about Zoe. Or Gina, because…well, Gina was Gina. Dad would call her an enigma. I had to agree—the real Gina was nothing like her public persona.

With my uncertainty running in the red zone, I decided it was time for a little heavy-bag therapy at the gym. During the first month after my breakup with Jason, the owner of X Factor Self Defense had not only become one of my crying posts, but also my drill sergeant. Each time I wailed, Kimberley drove me to new heights in my strength training, channeling my negative energy into positive. X Factor became my refuge, the place where I could work out, beat the crap out of the bag, and lose my sorrows in something other than a bottle of tequila or junk food.

I warmed up slowly, then launched into full-on attack mode. I had sweat dripping down my chin when I landed a perfectly placed fist into the sweet spot on the bag. It swayed away from me. To the side, a woman chuckled.

"Nice form, Jade."

I bent over and sucked in air to catch my breath. "Thanks, Kimberley… didn't…see you there."

"No worries." She planted her hands on her hips and studied my face. "You're hitting harder than usual. Are you trying to kill my bag, or is Jason back?"

"Neither." I rubbed a trickle of sweat from my chin and gave her the sanitized version of my Gina-Zoe-Bert dilemma.

Kimberley let out a long sigh and looked around. "The Amorous Assailant was good for my business. Those attacks motivated a lot of women to come in and get started, but they also caused a lot of fear, and I hate to see someone get away with that. You do what you've got to do to focus, Jade. It will help you sort out who you can trust and who you can't. Now, get back to work."

She winked and walked away. The more punches I landed, the more the solution to my problem seemed clear. Gina was a client—I had to believe in her. Zoe was a resource—I had to manage her. And me? I was the one who had to find a killer. Which meant I needed to use my resources to save my client. Even if that meant uncovering her deepest, darkest secrets. I'd keep the meeting with Zoe, hold the reins tight to prevent her from doing something impulsive, and get what I could from the night clerk.

I drove home, took a shower, and grabbed a quick dinner. At 7:40, I parked in front of the Sunny Days Inn to wait for Zoe. It was a short wait. She pulled in next to me a few minutes later, slammed her car door, and huffed as she plopped into the seat next to mine.

"Hey, Zoe, what's up?"

"I'm being evicted," she grumbled.

"That sucks. How long do you have?"

"A couple weeks, I guess. I don't know."

"You mean your landlord didn't give you a deadline? He can't do that. Go to Legal Aid. Landlords have strict rules to follow. You should get advice on the process before this goes too far."

She shook her head, then stuck out her lower lip. "I need a job."

"The other night you said you were waiting tables. When did that change?"

"Yesterday," she grumbled. "I quit. It's just the blogging gig now." She paused, grumbled something under her breath, then looked at me with puppy-dog eyes. "Why's he doing this to me, Jade?"

"Your landlord? My guess is he wants the rent paid."

"I don't pay rent."

I shook my head. "What? How can you not… Wait! Are you living with your parents?"

"My dad. He says I need a real job. The whole thing's totally unfair."

I licked my lips, watched Zoe's face for a moment, and hoped she didn't ask if I had any openings. "You know what, Zoe? You'll work it out. I know you can. Let's go talk to the night clerk."

Without waiting for a response, I got out of the car and stood with my door still open. Zoe hadn't moved. I summoned my most chipper tone and poked my head back inside. "Coming?"

She still didn't move. Enough. I sighed, slammed the door, and started toward the motel lobby. About two seconds later, Zoe flung her door open and hurried to catch up.

"Not cool, Jade. Locking me in a car like that."

I stopped and studied her face. "What's really going on? You realize you can't be a blogger for the rest of your life. Don't you? Why don't you want to get a job?"

She avoided my gaze and muttered, "I want to be a journalist."

"And you were hoping your blog would be your ticket to the big time?"

Zoe's complexion, a pure peaches-and-cream most women I know would kill to have, took on a rosy hue as she glared at me. "Wow, that's like…"

"Don't go there. You quit a perfectly good job because you'd rather do something else. That's fine, but you need to take control of your life. Ask your dad if you can go to school. Now, would you rather be with me when we do what we came here to do? Or would you prefer to stand here and pout? That's another choice you get to make."

Turning away, I opened the lobby door and entered. Zoe tagged along behind me as I strode confidently toward the desk, a business card in my hand. The guy behind the counter had long, stringy hair and a bad goatee he stroked when he gave me a look reminiscent of Donny in the liquor store.

Ignoring his visual undressing, I handed him my card. "Jade Cavendish, Beachtown Detective Agency. We're investigating the death of Bert Darlington."

The clerk got a blank look on his face. "That the dude who offed himself in our room?"

Yes, doofus. That's the one. "Are you Harvey Longo?" I asked.

He hesitated, then glanced again at the business card. "Well, yeah."

"And you were the one who checked him in?"

"Nah. Never saw the dude. Didn't hear nothing, either."

"That's BS," Zoe blurted. "Somebody killed him in the room. There had to be some kind of noise."

Harvey peered at Zoe, then at me. "You two together?"

I shot a sideways look at Zoe. Apparently, she'd forgotten her depression and was now back in what she'd probably call journalist mode. I said, "She's working with me. So if you didn't check him in, who did?"

"Day shift."

"Who on the day shift?" Zoe asked.

Harvey shrugged. "How should I know?"

"You could totally find out if you wanted to. You work here and have access to the records."

I could almost hear Kimberley yelling at me, pushing me to channel my strength. Zoe stepped forward like she was going into attack mode. I gave her a sideways kick in the shin.

"Ow!" she wailed.

She glared at me with her mouth hanging open. I made a few clucking noises in response. "Is your knee acting up again?" I mimicked one of her pouts, then turned a smile on Harvey. "Mr. Longo, what my partner is saying is, would you mind looking at the record to see who checked in Mr. Darlington?"

The phone buzzed and Harvey gave it a cursory glance. "For real? That one again? I been here like one hour and had two calls from him already." He made a face at the phone, then stroked his goatee. "I guess I could find out who checked him in. Since you asked nice."

He muttered something about crazy chicks as he poked around the keyboard of his computer. While he did that, I took another look at the parking lot. There were two cars out there. This place was almost deserted. Zoe drifted out of striking distance, but she kept her mouth shut. At one point, the phone rang again. Harvey let out an exaggerated sigh and rolled his eyes. I'd had it with all the drama from both him and Zoe, but gave him another pleasant smile. He dropped his gaze back to the screen.

"It was Sharon," he said. "She checked him in. Dude paid in cash."

"What hours does Sharon work?" I asked.

"She comes in at three. Only works part time."

I knew what I was doing tomorrow afternoon—coming back here. The phone rang again, and Harvey huffed. "This dude ain't gonna stop until I answer." He didn't wait for a response, but picked up the handset and barked out a curt greeting. "Office."

I crooked my neck toward the front door. Zoe followed me out to my car where we stood listening to the rush of traffic while trying to avoid the obvious. Zoe needed to deal with her dad, and I needed to get back to the investigation.

"I'm sorry I kicked you," I said. Well, not really.

Zoe winced and nodded. "And I'm sorry I lost it in there. It just, like, happened."

"I understand. Been there, done that. Look, I want to talk to all the victims before I go any further, but you need to take some time and get this thing with your dad straightened out."

She choked back a sniffle, then peered at me. "What am I gonna say to him?"

Really? Now I was becoming the Life Coach? Granted, I'd heard a lifetime's worth of advice after the breakup. Why not put it to good use? I could BS my way through and hope for the best with something easy. "You'll figure it out. All you have to do is to be positive and speak from your heart."

Zoe nodded as though I'd just given her profound advice. I pulled in a deep breath, relieved my simple little suggestion had played so well. I wondered if the people who had helped me put my life back together had felt the same as I did now.

"I'll do it," Zoe said. "Text me if you need anything. I'm totally serious."

I could always go back to the police reports, but Resourceful Zoe might have found other ways to reach them. "How about your contact information for the victims? I've already talked to Belinda James, but you've chased down all the others. If I can get their information from you, I can save some time."

"Awesome. That makes me feel like I'm helping."

Zoe texted me the contact information for each of the victims. The first one worked the night shift at Don's Diner on the other side of town. Great. Just what I needed. A late-night snack.

29

MY CELL PHONE PINGED WHILE I was backing out of the parking space in front of the Sunny Days Inn. I glanced at the screen and did a double take. Roger Lowe had sent me a message to call him. What was up with that?

I let the engine idle while I considered my options. Roger was an attractive man. A slow glow filled my chest. Was I really thinking of him—that way? A shrink would say I wasn't ready. For what? A conversation? Maybe he needed a PI? Or wanted to know Charlie's favorite restaurant. Or…who was I kidding? Roger was hot, and I was lonely.

My finger hit the button to dial his number. I bit my lower lip and my heart thumped in my chest faster than the phone could vibrate.

"Hey, Jade. Thanks for calling me back."

"No problem. What's up?"

"We need to talk."

"Oh?" I asked with a slight lilt in my voice. I glanced at my image in the rearview mirror and blanched. Oh, gawd. I was twirling my hair. Just like Zoe had with that guy in the bar.

"Before you get the wrong idea, this is strictly professional. It's about your client."

My heart thudded in my chest, but for a whole different reason. "What client?"

"Gina Rose."

I hesitated and stared out the front windshield. Forget the pathetic, girly, I'm-flirting-with-you moves—my interest in romance had dropped to zero. I wanted to know who Roger Lowe really was and how he knew about Gina.

"Meet me in twenty minutes at the Flying Pig. I'll explain then."

The line went dead, and I was left staring at the display.

Traffic to the Flying Pig was light. I arrived with ten minutes to spare. Parking was easy, and it only took about another minute to find Roger, who sat at a table for two in the bar with a tall, half-finished schooner of beer. He'd exchanged his suit and tie for a dark hoodie and a gray T-shirt. His eyes seemed in constant surveillance mode as they bounced around the room. When they settled on me, he gestured at the chair opposite his.

Roger rose to greet me. We exchanged pleasantries, after which he offered to buy me a drink.

"Club soda. I'm working tonight," I said.

He nodded, then smiled. "You probably have a lot of questions."

No kidding. So why dance around the subject? "How did you know I was working for Gina Rose?"

"Before I can answer your question, I need your assurance that you will hold what we discuss in strictest confidence."

"I don't know if I can promise that, Roger," I shot back. "You haven't told me what 'we' are going to discuss."

He pursed his lips and motioned for the waitress, who was wearing a tight-fitting tee and shorts. The shirt bore the restaurant's logo—a pig with wings flying through the air. The server stood with one hip cocked and her trusty tray at the ready, her body language suggesting she was willing to flirt to increase her tip. Roger finished his beer, ordered another, and asked me if I wanted something other than club soda. I declined and ordered directly from the server. Roger did a much better job than Jason ever had of focusing his full attention on me as the server sauntered away.

"Let's say I'm here on behalf of a mutual friend," he said.

I leaned forward and looked him in the eye. "I'm not here to play twenty questions. Who's this friend?"

"Des Martini."

For the longest moment, I couldn't speak, but inside I could feel my anger building over being played. "Oh, I get it. This is a joke. Not funny, Roger. Not funny at all." I pushed back my chair and stood.

He held up one hand and shook his head. "Don't leave. Not until you've heard me out. Des said you'd be tough. She also said you were codependent and an overachiever."

Every fiber in my body screamed at me to walk away. I knew I should. It was the smart thing to do. There was no need to take these kinds of backhanded compliments. What gave Detective Des the right to call me codependent?

The server arrived with our drinks, placed them on the table, and gave us each a polite smile. Gone was her coy game from before. She slipped away as though she could sense the tension in the air.

"She said I was tough?" I found myself slowly lowering my butt back into my chair.

He snickered. "She did." After a short pause, he added, "Just listen for a minute. After you've heard me out, if you want to go, it's your choice."

"Okay," I muttered.

His eyes made another pass around the room, then returned to me.

"Looking for someone?" I asked.

"Sorry, but Des wants to keep this on the QT. She and I have a mutually beneficial arrangement. We do each other favors now and again."

I couldn't stop myself from smiling as I asked, "Are these favors personal in nature?"

His cheeks tightened, and he looked at me. "You said you were going to listen."

"And you can't drop a bomb like you and Detective Martini have an arrangement and expect me to not have questions."

"Let's just say I'm a good listener."

"You haven't given me an answer."

"We're friends," he said flatly.

I desperately wanted to ask if that was 'with benefits,' but suspected I'd already pushed back more than I should. "Go on," I said.

"Des told me she's got a problem with this case. She doesn't want to believe your client killed her husband, but that's where the evidence is pointing. Basically, on paper, your client is guilty. That, unfortunately, is how the DA has to look at it. You know what happens if the DA believes she can get a conviction."

Somewhere between Detective Des having a problem with this case and pointing evidence, my brain exploded. I stared at Roger. No way. No freaking way. But I had to know. "Are you saying Detective Des wants my help?"

Roger chuckled. "Detective Des—I like that." He did another scan of the room before returning his attention to me. "You're a quick learner—for someone who doesn't listen well."

Holy crap. The detective who had practically entrapped me was asking me to save her butt? Through an intermediary? This day had just taken a turn for the better. It might even qualify for a Best Day Ever nomination. Talk about awesome. "How do I know you're on the level?"

"Relationships are built on trust, Jade. I'm going to provide you with some information not available to the general public. Hopefully, it will help you avoid the inevitable."

"Which is?"

"Gina Rose standing trial for the murder of her husband."

All the noise in the Flying Pig—the clinking of silverware on plates, the loud voices, the laughter—suddenly seemed far away.

"Jade? Are you listening?"

"Yes," I murmured. "It just…hit me."

Roger paused and frowned at me. "Which part?"

"Gina's future," I said absently.

"When you step back and look at the big picture, your abilities as an investigator might determine what happens to her."

I took a deep breath. "I hadn't really thought about it that way." If I wanted to be successful with the agency or even just do everything I could to help Gina, I needed contacts like Des Martini, and quite possibly, Roger Lowe. "What's the evidence?" I asked.

"Your client had means, motive, and opportunity. She had access to his medications, including his antidepressant, Norpramin."

"Bert was on antidepressants?"

"The bottle was in the room, and the prescription checked out. The bottle also had your client's fingerprints on it."

"But she's his wife. Just because they found fingerprints doesn't mean she administered the drug."

"She booked the room and brought him alcohol, probably at the same time as his prescription. Norpramin has very serious side-effects when taken with alcohol and preliminary indications are that Bert Darlington died from a drug overdose."

"Wait a minute. How do you know Gina booked the room?"

"Your client admitted it. Confirm it for yourself."

"I will," I muttered. With Sharon on the day shift tomorrow. "So the hanging was…what? Staged?"

Roger nodded, his expression grim.

"And Detective Martini doesn't think Gina is strong enough to stage a hanging. Does she?"

"Bingo. Looks like Des was right. You are an overachiever."

"There's another problem. I don't see how Gina had a motive. She came to me wanting to divorce Bert, not kill him."

Roger held my gaze as he drank from his glass. He placed the schooner on the table and sighed. "There was no prenup with her husband. A divorce would have cost her a fortune."

A fortune she didn't have. I held my tongue. Roger had said he wanted me to listen, so why should I reveal something I hadn't confirmed? "I don't see how there's a motive, Roger. Gina admitted up front that neither of them signed a prenup."

"You should know the police have already searched your client's records. We know she's in financial trouble. The search also uncovered a letter from her attorney dated April 21. In the letter, he advised her about the financial risks involved in a divorce proceeding. It all points to her knowing her assets were in jeopardy if she divorced her husband."

I wanted to stick my head into a trash can and scream like Charlie and I had done when we were kids. How could Gina have been so stupid? Unless she hadn't been stupid at all. This could have been her attempt at the perfect murder.

We'd taken the fast slope all the way from Best Day Ever down to the Absolute Worst. The attorney's letter had been written on a Friday, and Gina had hired me the following Monday. The worst part was I already knew what was behind Door Number 3—the Big O.

"And she had opportunity," I said. "She was with Bert the night of his death and was the last one to see him alive."

Roger nodded. "It's the trifecta of guilt. I'm sorry."

I placed my fingertips on my forehead and stared at the table. "How long before the police charge Gina?" I asked quietly.

"Forty-eight hours."

Forty-eight hours? That was barely enough time to make a cursory contact with the former victims. I glanced up at Roger, hoping for some sort of miracle. "Is there any way to extend it? Maybe a week?"

Roger grimaced and shook his head. "I'm sorry. That's all Des can give you. She's under pressure to wrap this up and turn over what she has to the DA."

30

DON'S DINER WAS LOCATED IMMEDIATELY off Interstate 5 and only a few miles from the Flying Pig. By San Diego standards, the drive went well, clocking in at less than twenty minutes. But after the deadline Roger had given me, every mile, every traffic light, every slowdown, felt like an impediment to my investigation.

I'd been by Don's many times, but hadn't been inside since high school. With its low-profile roof and sedate colors, it wasn't a restaurant that screamed for attention. In sharp contrast to the Flying Pig's parking lot, this one was nearly empty. Nevertheless, this was where Bert's first victim worked.

A perky redhead with frizzy hair and more freckles than I could count greeted me. She was two shades beyond wholesome, and I was certain she'd blush at the mere suggestion of working in a place like the Flying Pig.

When I told her I was here to see Jacqueline, she gestured at one of the occupied booths. "She's on break. That's her, down there. She's talking to Armand. Her boyfriend. Can I get you something? Coffee, maybe?"

"No, thank you," I said. "I've had my limit of caffeine for the day."

"No problem." She sighed and glanced toward the other occupied booth. "I better check on my customer. It might be the only tip I see tonight. It's so dead."

I gave her a polite smile, then looked down the length of the restaurant to where Jacqueline sat. She had straight blonde hair parted just off center, blue eyes, and thin lips. Except for the dark green golf shirt she was wearing, she looked exactly like she did in the photo Zoe had sent me.

With his roguish good looks, including jet-black hair, a close-cropped beard, and a leather bomber jacket, I could picture her boyfriend working anywhere from a construction site to the boardroom.

They each had a cup of coffee in front of them and were holding hands. I introduced myself and explained the reason for my visit, at which point Jacqueline invited me to sit and asked if I wanted coffee or some pie.

I had a desperate urge to scream that I was on a deadline, but held my cool and gave her the same spiel as the girl up front. At the end, I added, "I'm trying to lose a few pounds."

Jacqueline laughed and blew out a breath. "Tell me about it. I'm tempted constantly. I need to lose five pounds before our wedding."

Armand squeezed Jacqueline's hand and winked at her. "You'll get there, babe. You'll get there."

I smiled at them. "Congratulations. When's the big day?"

"Two months," Armand said. "Can't wait."

He squeezed Jacqueline's hand again, and they goo-goo eyed each other. Obviously, love was in the air for these two.

"I wish you all the best." I hoped I didn't sound bitter, but the truth was, despite all the help my support group gave me, the memory of walking in on Jason and his bimbo was still an open wound on my psyche. "How long have you two been together?"

"Just over a year," Jacqueline said as she pulled her hand from Armand's and leaned back.

Talk about rubbing salt in the wound—I'd spent five years grooming Jason for marriage. Armand's smile revealed straight, white teeth, which caused me to change my earlier evaluation— this guy was definitely boardroom material.

"We met on Valentine's Day last year," Armand said. "She was wearing a super-hot, red cocktail dress, matching heels, and black fishnet stockings. She was the hottest girl in the room, and I knew I had to meet her."

Jacqueline shook her head. "You were just sitting at the bar drinking a beer. I sat down next to you."

Armand winked at Jacqueline, then smiled at me. "Anyway, I asked her to dance, and she said yes. We both hated the dating scene, so it worked out for the best."

"Sounds like it," I said.

"What did you want to know?" Jacqueline asked. "I need to get back to work soon."

"Had you ever met Bert Darlington before the day he attacked you?"

Jacqueline frowned and gave me a quizzical look. "No. Why would you think that?"

"I'm looking for links between Bert and his victims." I resisted the urge to say, *And big guys strong enough to stage a hanging. Your boyfriend will do.* Instead, I added, "If it's not too painful, could you describe the attack?"

Armand shifted in his seat and leaned forward on his elbows. "Is this really necessary? The police have all the details."

"It's okay, Armand. Really." Jacqueline sat up straight and grimaced, then described an attack much like the one experienced by Belinda James. At the end, she added, "I've reconciled myself to the facts—he didn't hurt me physically. In fact, I kind of feel sorry for the guy. I mean, how pathetic do you have to be to tie up a woman just so you can kiss her?"

Armand reached out and squeezed Jacqueline's hand. "Nobody will ever do that to you again, babe. I promise."

Jacqueline smiled weakly and glanced at her watch. "You're going to miss your flight if you don't get going."

He leaned toward her, and they exchanged a quick kiss. "You're right," he said, then eased himself around the booth.

I stood to the side so he could get out. "Where are you flying to?"

"San Francisco. I'm meeting clients tomorrow. I fly back tomorrow night. Long day. Gotta run."

"Sorry to hold you up," I said.

"Not a problem at all." He smiled, then winked at Jacqueline. "I'll call you when I land."

She nodded, waved goodbye, and let out a slow breath the moment he turned his back. "Thank God," she muttered.

I raised my eyebrows, slid into the booth, and cocked my head to one side. "What's the matter, Jacqueline?"

"Oh, nothing. Just Armand being Armand. Sometimes when I'm around him, I feel like I can't breathe."

"Maybe you're suffering from wedding jitters."

Jacqueline's mouth turned down, and she rolled her eyes. After a quick huff, she said, "I have no concerns about the wedding. It's the marriage I'm thinking about. Armand likes being together."

"And you don't?"

She sighed again and leaned forward on the table as though she were about to explain the facts of life to a child. "Are you married, Jade?"

I hesitated as an urge to defend myself rose within me. "I was with a guy for five years, but we broke up recently."

"And let me guess. You're devastated."

This conversation was definitely going off the rails. How had it become about my love life…again? "Why are you so negative about being engaged? You could've turned him down when he asked."

"I'm not saying Armand doesn't love me." She shrugged. "He does. Unconditionally. I could do whatever I wanted, and he'd be there for me."

Anything? Did that include murder? "Do you love him?"

"Yes, but lately, things have been different."

"Because of the attack?" I asked.

"I don't think so. It's him, not me."

I felt sorry for Armand. Did he know what he was in for? And I guess that was why I just couldn't let it go. "Why did you sit down next to him in the bar?"

"He was cute. My girlfriend had disappeared. Maybe all I wanted was a little positive reinforcement. You know, someone to tell me I was pretty."

"So you two hit it off?"

"We shared horror stories. I told him about my failed marriage. He told me about his most recent break-up. When the party got kind of crazy, he volunteered to give me a ride home. My girlfriend hadn't shown up, so I took him up on the offer. We left, and when he was dropping me off, I gave him my number."

"Did he call you right away?"

"Next morning. He asked me out. I figured, what the heck? The guy was on the rebound, so we could have some fun and I'd move on when it was time. Next thing I know, he's proposing and making plans."

My gaze flitted down to Jacqueline's arms. Like the rest of her, they were trim and fit. She wasn't skinny, nor was she fat. She was curvy in all the right places, but I wondered how much weight she could lift.

"He seems head-over-heels in love, Jacqueline. You're not?"

She rolled her eyes. "I guess. Armand dotes on me."

"Not a lot of the girls I know would complain about their guy paying attention to them."

"Whatever. I like my space."

"You said he was on the rebound when you met?"

"His ex broke up with him a few days before Valentine's Day." She stopped, shook her head, and cleared her throat. "You know what? You're right. Armand's a good guy, he loves me, and my love life is not your concern. Is there anything else you need to know? I really should be getting back to work."

"I understand." I paused, then added, "So you weren't bothered by the attack? Really?"

She folded her arms in front of her and glanced away. Her eyes teared up, but after a few moments, she blinked and smiled weakly.

"It's possible. Maybe I'm just resentful because Armand had a business meeting that morning. I guess it irritates me that while I was being attacked, he was schmoozing with clients. I feel like if he wants all this closeness, he should've been there. It's stupid, but I guess I'm mad at him because he was working the one time I needed him. Anyway, I have to get back. You sure you don't want something? Our chocolate cream pie is fabulous."

Actually, all this talk about couples and love and one-sided relationships was bringing me down. Add in Roger's deadline, and I needed something to pull me out of a growing funk. It was late enough that X Factor was closed, but early enough for Mom and Dad to still be up. I planted my elbows on the table and gazed at her.

"Chocolate cream? I haven't had that in years."

Her face lit up. It might have been the only smile I'd seen since we met. Why not indulge? I was making two people happy. And if I was going for junk food therapy, I might as well go big.

31

I AWOKE MONDAY MORNING WITH a bad case of the foggy-headed jitters. Long story short, I was working on about three hours of sleep thanks to one—no, two—bad decisions. The first was the chocolate cream pie. Don't get me wrong, Jacqueline was right —it was divine. But it had been way too much sugar, way too late at night.

The second mistake was the one that had totally done me in. I'd let Jacqueline convince me a cup of coffee would counterbalance the calories and sugar in the pie. I know. I'd been a fully willing participant in that little masquerade. Add sugar and caffeine to my Gina worries—enough said.

Mom and Dad seemed to sense my condition and let me muddle through the morning routine without interference, but at one point, Dad did tell me to maintain my focus for the next two days. Got it. No more chocolate cream pie. No more late-night caffeine.

I checked messages midway through breakfast. One caught my eye—it was from Hailey Robinson, Amorous Assailant

Victim #2. She'd replied to my text from last night asking if we could meet today.

—*Sure. I'm at Campus Coffee on Campanile from 9-12.*

Truly. The universe is one twisted place. I had to walk into a coffee shop now? I texted back to confirm.

—*Will be there at 10*

Campus Coffee was located near UCSD in San Diego amid a sea of earth-toned dormitories. From the looks of the pedestrians, most of whom carried backpacks while they traipsed along in tee shirts and shorts, they were students. Open parking spaces were an endangered species in this area. Fortunately, a little VW vacated a spot right in front of me on a side street. This parking spot was three blocks from the coffee shop. A total score. I grabbed the spot and joined the ranks of the walkers.

Campus Coffee's interior was typical of a modern cafe-hangout. It had an open ceiling with exposed ductwork and beams that had been painted a dark brown. Pendant lights hung from above, making the space feel larger and giving it a hip appearance. The lights cast a warm glow throughout. They received an assist from spot lighting on the walls, which were covered with photos of campus life ranging from sports-team shots to alumni of local fame.

Two-top tables predominated, but there were at least a half dozen tables for four and a long bar where stools lined each side. The place was packed with students bent over their laptops and paper cups.

Thanks to Zoe's thorough research, I had a photo of Hailey on my phone. She sat at one of the small tables, her papers, books, and laptop arranged in a delicate balance around a paper cup and a bottle of water. Nostalgia crept into my veins as I recalled many a study session in my favorite coffee shop near UCLA.

As if I needed more caffeine, I ordered a mocha and then hung out with a few of the others while we waited for our orders. Hailey was engrossed in something on her computer and hadn't yet noticed me. She had curly red hair and wore a grey scoop-neck tee I recognized immediately. Unless I was mistaken, she and I shopped the same sales.

When my order arrived, I made my way to her table. I was just a few feet away when she must have noticed me approaching and glanced up. Her dimpled smile fell immediately. I countered with a can-we-be-friends? expression —raised eyebrows, chipper tone, and a smile.

"Hailey?"

She narrowed her gaze and eyed me suspiciously. "Yes."

"I texted you. I'm Jade Cavendish."

She took the business card I offered, read it, then sighed. "Have a seat, I guess." She looked away and, a moment later, said, "I just want to forget that whole thing."

With blue eyes, enviable eyebrows, and a milky complexion, Hailey was drop-dead gorgeous. Judging from the textbook on the table, she was also incredibly smart—how many people read about the ecological effects of the industrial age for fun?

"I understand you don't want to think about it, and I don't mean to dredge up bad memories, but I'm investigating the death of Bert Darlington. He's the man who attacked you."

Her jaw tightened, and she clenched both fists. "I know who he is."

She closed her eyes for a moment, took a deep breath, then picked up her cup. Her fingers trembled, and she steadied the cup, using both hands as she sipped. When she set it back on the table, her lower lip quivered.

"Why?" she croaked.

Her voice, so filled with pain and fear, triggered a deep ache in my heart. I swallowed hard and tried to find an answer.

"I don't know," I whispered.

"I'm glad he's dead," she hissed. "How could he get away with that for so long?"

"He varied his pattern." It wasn't the answer she was looking for—she wanted someone to blame. Feeling like it was too little, too late, I added, "The police couldn't predict when or where he'd strike next. You were assaulted in January, but the first attack occurred in November. And the third wasn't until mid-April."

She stared at me for a few seconds, then blew out a little puff of air and shook her head. "You don't get it. I don't care what his pattern was. It doesn't matter that all he did was kiss me. For those few minutes in time, he took away my freedom. My life."

Hailey was wrong. I did get it. I also saw a new intensity in her blue eyes, which were now rimmed in red. It was as though all her energy was being focused into a laser beam of anger and hurt.

I nodded sympathetically and hoped my next question wasn't going to distress her further. "Have you talked to someone?"

"You mean like a therapist?" She huffed and fingered the neckline of her gray tee. "Of course. Two, in fact. Plus my parents—and a few of my girlfriends."

I scooted my chair forward and took her trembling fingers in my hands. She looked down, seemed to realize what I'd done, but didn't pull away.

"You can't get past it. Can you?" I said.

Her shoulders slumped inwards as she looked at me. "I can't eat. Can't sleep. Forget studying or doing my research. It's like my mind is stuck in constant replay mode. I try to work on my thesis, but my attention span is like zero."

"Can you get an extension?"

"I haven't asked." She sighed. "I guess I'll have to."

As we sat in silence, I wondered if Hailey was playing back the attack in her mind at this moment. "I hate to ask, but had you ever met Bert Darlington prior to the attack?"

"No. I'd seen him a few times hanging out at Beachtown Mocha, but he was always just sitting there minding his own business."

"You saw him there? Prior to the attack? Was he a regular?"

Hailey scrunched up her face. "I don't really know. The owner has been a family friend since forever, so I go there when I'm staying with my parents, but I don't get home that much."

"So you live near the campus?"

"I hate driving in rush hour traffic. It just drains me."

"I don't know anybody who likes that part of living here. How long were you in town?"

"I'd been up there for winter break and my classes weren't starting until mid-January, so I stayed for an extra couple of weeks."

Bert's first two attacks originated with victims who'd been at Beachtown Mocha. According to Zoe's notes, the third victim had been at Cool Beans and Belinda, the fourth victim, had been at Java Joe's. If Bert had stuck with the same venue for all of his attacks, there's a good chance he'd have been stopped sooner. My professors in school always told us criminals were caught because of their stupidity. Bert started out stupid, then got smart. How and why he changed his pattern was another mystery I found intriguing.

"Would your friend talk to me? Maybe confirm if Bert was a regular there? If I can sort out why he committed the attacks, it might…"

She jerked her hands away from mine and snapped, "What? You want to psychoanalyze this pervert to make me and the other victims feel better? Maybe help you or the cops find his killer? I hope you don't. Whoever killed him did the world a favor."

"Hailey, I understand your anger. You have every right to it. But revenge isn't the answer. Bert Darlington should have faced justice."

"He did," Hailey spat. She narrowed her gaze and looked straight at me. "The pervert got what he deserved."

"You don't really feel that way."

"Don't tell me how I feel. I'm glad he's dead." The fire in her tone made it clear she was deadly serious.

But were her words being driven by the pain of her attack? Or out of remorse because she'd played a role in Bert's death? I still had so many questions and needed to turn this around. It was time for a safe harbor.

"What's your major?" I asked.

She blinked as though the question surprised her, then her anger seemed to dissipate. "It involves the impact of coastal urban density on benthic invertebrates."

"What is a…"

She laughed. "Don't worry. It's the same reaction I get from everybody. The simple answer is I'm writing about how all the crap we put into the ocean affects the little guys living on the bottom."

"Oh. That's way harder than what I studied—criminal justice."

Hailey used both hands to take another sip from her cup, then said, "I don't think I could deal with something so dark."

"My dad was a PI. I was always tagging along when I was little. I was eight when he took me on my first stakeout. I didn't find out until high school that he just picked a random neighborhood and told me we were watching a house for dangerous criminals."

The corners of her mouth curled up. "Did you see anything suspicious?"

"Not really. I got bored after about an hour and fell asleep." Oh, great. Was that going to be the story of my life? Jade missed her chance because she nodded off? I cleared my throat. "You know, my clients are like your benthic invertebrates. I want to help them just like you want to help those little guys."

She nodded knowingly, then frowned. "I still don't get why you care who killed Bert Darlington."

"Because they could put my client on trial for his murder—and I'm convinced she's innocent."

"I see."

That was it? *I see*?

It wasn't just the caffeine ratcheting up my sense of angst. I felt like Hailey had more concern for little creatures living on the bottom of the ocean than she had for people and justice.

Unless she'd dispensed it herself.

But the truth was, to call Hailey Robinson erratic would be an understatement. She'd seesawed between fearful and angry almost on a minute-by-minute basis. The volatility worked to her advantage because eventually, all physical limitations aside, I wondered if she was even capable of planning and orchestrating the murder of Bert Darlington. I just couldn't see her pulling off a cold-blooded murder.

I'd hoped this trip wouldn't have been a complete waste, but so far all I had to show for my effort was an unfinished mocha that had cost me almost five bucks and a bad case of the jitters that would probably last me the rest of the day.

32

"I JUST NEED A LITTLE information before we finish," I said to Hailey. "All of the Amorous Assailant attacks took place after the woman was in a coffee shop. Do you think that's where he first saw you? Or could it be that he spotted you somewhere else and followed you there?"

She leaned back and stared off into space, her far-off look reminiscent of a lost child's. "I'd come from home. He must have found me there. The attack happened just a few blocks away."

"And you never realized a strange man was following you?"

"No." She shrugged, then winced. "I guess I wasn't paying attention. I grew up in Carlsbad. It was always a fun place, and it was safe. You know?"

"Yes. I grew up there, too."

"Then you understand. It was always like this small town surrounded by a gigantic metropolis."

"Go on," I said.

"There's not much else to tell. I'm not—wasn't—one of those people who spends all their time looking around because they're paranoid."

"And now?"

Even though she was wearing a long-sleeved tee, she rubbed her arms as though she were cold. Her gaze flitted around the room and she shuddered. "I'm different. I don't like it. You know what? I don't want to do this anymore. I didn't think you'd have so many questions. I can't handle it."

I felt another pang of sympathy for Hailey. I envisioned her before the attack—smart, confident, working towards an advanced degree. I swallowed my urge to carry this further. "Sure. I have what I need."

If only. What I needed was solid evidence that someone other than Gina killed Bert, and all I had so far were more questions without answers. I stood, watched her for a moment, and added, "I'm sorry. I didn't mean to upset you."

We said our goodbyes, and I left her sitting alone and staring at her computer. I never had found out what on her monitor was so fascinating, but as I neared the door, I looked back over my shoulder. Hailey was focused on the screen and smiling. For all I knew, she was watching cat videos.

I'd now spoken to three of Bert's victims and had discovered nothing I could remotely call a pattern—unless you considered the damaged lives he'd created. If anything, Bert seemed to know how to wreak havoc with the women surrounding him. From Gina to the victims I'd spoken with, he'd demonstrated a mastery of the sport.

It was time to talk to Esther Simpson. She'd been the third victim and, according to Zoe's notes, lived in Carlsbad, but worked three different retail jobs in different parts of the county. All were part-time, but between them she put in about seven hours a day, six or seven days a week. The routine struck me as one which would eventually put her on a collision path with burnout.

Craft World, the store where Esther worked her weekday-morning job, was only a few miles away. Given how close I was, it made perfect sense from my perspective to just show up. If I called, she could tell me to get lost. If I was standing in front of her, getting rid of me would be a lot harder to do.

Walking through the entrance, my reaction was, "color me gobsmacked, this place is massive." Craft World was a super-sized superstore, a giant upscale warehouse where a hundred people could walk around and have no clue how many others were there.

A seventies rock song played softly through the overhead speakers. It was an upbeat melody no doubt intended to keep crafters crafting and shoppers shopping. Between the white walls, ceiling, and overhead lighting, this was like walking around craft-store heaven. In addition to supplies for hobbies from drawing to painting to scrapbooking, there were rows of shelves for those of us craft-challenged heathens who wanted something cute, but had no talent.

I checked the time twice while walking the perimeter of the store in search of an employee—any employee. My forty-eight hour deadline had dwindled to thirty-six, so by the time I spotted an employee talking to a female customer I was weary of Craft World.

Thanks to the photo Zoe had given me and the name tag on her white cotton blouse, I knew the employee was Esther. She and the customer were discussing the differences between milk paint and chalk paint. After a few minutes of listening, I felt like an expert. I knew that milk paint chipped and chalk paint weathered, and that they gave different effects depending on your desired result. Now that I was an expert on distressing furniture, I felt empowered to hop over a couple of aisles and buy the supplies—especially if it would let me bang on wood with a hammer.

The moment Esther's conversation with the customer finished, I closed in. Esther had a wide mouth and large teeth, which gave her an oversized smile. Her eyebrows almost knitted themselves together when she peered at me. If it wasn't for the overzealous application of makeup—dark eyeliner, heavy mascara, and a lipstick color I didn't recognize—I'd definitely classify Esther as plain.

"May I help you?" she asked.

I held out a business card and introduced myself as Jade Cavendish with the Beachtown Detective Agency. By the time I got to the word agency, the smile was gone and Esther had closed down. It was becoming a familiar image—crossed arms, steely gaze, yada yada.

"I have nothing to say to you. Now, if you'll excuse me, I have customers to attend to."

So much for it being difficult to blow me off. I didn't see anyone else standing around waiting to talk to her. Then again, maybe I was just being snarky.

"This will only take a moment," I said. "Your attack happened after you were in Cool Beans. Is that correct?"

Esther stared at me, her gaze unflinching. "There's no point in beating the horse—it's dead. I'm done with the whole thing. I've put it out of my head, and I don't want to let it back in. Now, I have work to do."

"You're not bothered by the attack?"

She blinked and scrunched up her face. "What he did irks me. But it wasn't like he…well, you know. All he did was tie me up and kiss me."

Really? Being tied up and held against her will didn't bother her? Jacqueline had said something similar—and it turned out to be a lie. I spread my hands to my sides. "The other victims say they've been traumatized by the attack. You're not?"

Esther rolled her eyes, then huffed. "Seriously? Traumatized? Isn't that a bit overdramatic? He made me late for work. I was supposed to open that morning and my manager said corporate wanted a copy of the police report. Dealing with all the bureaucracy was scarier than anything he did." A moment later, she added, "I've said more than I wanted to. I told you. I'm over the whole thing. There's no point in belaboring it."

She turned and walked away. I stared after her, wondering whether she'd rehearsed her lines. In fact, the responses of each victim had, in some ways, sounded rehearsed. But even though Esther's responses seemed practiced, it didn't seem like she was hiding something. Or was she? I definitely wanted to know whether she was telling me how she really felt, or whether her responses were a defense mechanism, possibly even an outright lie.

A lie. It had to be. If she didn't care, she'd be willing to talk about the attack. And she wouldn't be trying so hard to avoid my questions.

Now what? Rush after her and force her to tell all? Like that would work. No, I needed one of those brilliant aha moments— some insight into what Dad would do. Given his Three Eggs story, there had to be a ready solution—some way to be persistent and get Esther to drop her guard.

I listened to the music and looked around. Of course. Everything I needed was right here. This was Craft World. I hurried after her. When I caught up to Esther and tapped her on the shoulder, she turned around and her smile fell again.

"Now what?" she snapped.

"I'm interested in distressing my desk. How do I go about doing that?"

"Oh, good Lord. Are you going to badger me all day?"

"Not if I get answers to a few questions. You could be rid of me faster than you can say milk paint chips and chalk paint doesn't."

She blinked, then stared at me, apparently realizing I'd eavesdropped on her earlier conversation. She swallowed hard and took a slow breath.

"What do you want to know?"

"Had you ever met Bert Darlington prior to the attack?"

"No."

"Had you ever seen him in Cool Beans prior to that day?"

"No."

"Do you have a boyfriend?"

She rolled her eyes and huffed, but her lower lip trembled. "No," she hissed.

Okay, I could see where this was going. "Esther, this isn't going to work if you shut down."

"Then we're done?" She peered at me with both eyebrows raised.

"The attack really got to you, didn't it?" I fixed her with a steady gaze, the one that Dad always used on me when he knew I was lying. Esther gripped her sides, and her eyes brimmed with moisture. She glanced away, down one of the endlessly long aisles. The background music became the only noticeable sound.

After a few sniffles, she muttered, "I can't talk about it." Her attempts to swipe away the tears tracking mascara down her cheeks only made things worse. After just a couple of attempts, she looked very much like a one-eyed raccoon.

"Can't talk about what?"

She looked up at the ceiling and choked back a sob. "My reaction. I hated it. The whole thing scared me to death."

I reached out and squeezed her shoulder. "That's perfectly natural. There's nothing wrong with being afraid. The other victims felt the same way."

Her hand went to her neck. When she pulled it away, her fingers left black smudges from her mascara. She sucked in a few short breaths. "You don't understand. I thought I was going to die."

"Of course. You didn't know what he planned to do."

"My heart was pounding so hard I thought it might burst."

I recognized the feeling. It was the same one I felt in a karate match—an adrenaline rush so strong it ought to be illegal. It was better than any drug-induced high. Its pull was addictive and— oh gawd, I got it.

"Esther? Did you want to see Bert again…afterwards?"

She shuddered and shook her head. "No! The man petrified me. But I can't stop thinking about it—that feeling." An unchecked tear dribbled down her cheek. "Boring," she muttered. "My life has always been so boring."

"Come on, Esther. You must have done something for excitement. Procrastinated in school so you'd get a last-minute study rush, made a snide comment in class to see if you could get away with it…"

She stared at me. "I never did anything like that. My parents would have killed me."

Okay. We were different. I'd pushed those same boundaries regularly. I even wound up in the principal's office once—okay, more than once. "What you felt is called an adrenaline rush. If you've never felt it before—I can see how it would confuse you."

"I keep wanting to feel that way again." She folded her arms over her chest. "What kind of pervert does that make me?"

I sighed. Gazed at her. And gave her arm a reassuring squeeze. "You're not a pervert. You just need some sort of outlet —something positive."

She nodded as though she understood, but I suspected I'd only confused her more. If Innocent Esther didn't understand adrenaline, there was no way she'd committed murder. Not that being an adrenaline junkie made you commit murder—otherwise, I'd be doing twenty-to-life.

The pattern was so clear to me now. All the victims had broken lives, thanks to Bert. And if I stopped grasping at straws and was really being truthful, I couldn't consider any of them serious suspects. I needed a break, something I wasn't going to find on the shelves of Craft World.

33

AFTER LEAVING CRAFT WORLD, I fully intended to drop in at X Factor Self Defense. Esther Simpson might not understand adrenaline and what it did to the human body, but I did—and I intended to use that rush to clear my head and lift my spirits. Until an overturned big rig on I-5 snarled traffic. And my plans.

I suppose the good news is all this driving at one mile per hour gave me plenty of time to hold my own little one-person brainstorming session. With the radio off, the air cranked up, and my mind racing through scenarios, I mentally ran through what I'd learned.

It initially appeared Bert Darlington had died by hanging, but according to Roger, the cops were now calling his death an overdose. Any of Bert's victims could have drugged him, but none were physically capable of lifting him high enough to slip a noose around his neck. Unless he had been looking for his own adrenaline rush. Maybe cooperated in the act? How had he done that if he'd overdosed?

The lane to my left surged forward, and I briefly considered jumping over. Moments later, the cars came to an abrupt halt. I sighed and surrendered to the reality. This was traffic hell—a fact of life on San Diego freeways.

My eyelids drooped. The monotony numbed my senses until my forehead and eyes felt like they were swathed in cotton. It was a side effect of mind-numbing gridlock—the driver's trance.

I suddenly jerked upright and blinked hard. What if there had been more than one killer? A Let's Kill Bert Club seemed farfetched, but wasn't impossible. That could put the victims back in play—assuming they found each other, agreed to a murder pact, created a plan—good grief, who was I kidding? I dialed Zoe's number, waited impatiently for her to answer, then launched straight into the question that had hit me in my semi-comatose state.

"When you researched the victims, did you check for relationships between them?"

"You mean like family?"

"More like, do they know each other?"

There was a long pause on the line. I was about to ask if Zoe was still there when she replied. "What are you getting at, Jade?"

I could see where this was going. So far, I hadn't gotten a single answer, and I had the feeling we could play this game of Q&A tit-for-tat the rest of the afternoon. "I've visited with all the victims and can't find any connections. There has to be something we're missing."

"I just assumed the only links between them were the attacks," Zoe said.

My other line rang. Roger Lowe. I contemplated letting his call go to voicemail for about a millisecond. "I'll get back to you, Zoe. I have to answer another call." I disconnected before she could complain and picked up the other line.

"What's up, Roger?"

"There have been a couple of developments you need to know about."

Roger's tone was somber, the kind I might expect to hear while he was laying out facts in a courtroom, not while I was stuck in bumper-to-bumper traffic. I bit my lower lip and glanced around, feeling much like a caged animal. There was nothing I could do. No way to even change lanes. Everyone around me was either zombie-driving or chatting on a cellphone. We were dead in the water.

"What kind of developments?"

"Des wanted me to tell you she's changed her mind. Your assistance is no longer needed. Mine, either."

"But I still have almost thirty-six hours left. And what do you mean, your services aren't needed either?"

"Apparently, I misunderstood what Des intended. That's not your concern. What Des did tell me before she told me to back off is your client and her husband took out life insurance policies on each other. A million dollars each."

A million bucks? That was a lot of motive. And I was feeling cornered. "Lots of couples take out insurance policies."

"True, but one of them doesn't usually end up dead shortly thereafter. Also, given your client's financial condition, she could use that money. Right now, she doesn't have enough cash to continue operating the empire her father built."

The police had obviously been doing a thorough investigation of Gina. This was happening a lot sooner than I'd expected. "I know," I said, then added, "Is that what made Des change her mind?"

"No. There's something else. Des brought your client in for questioning."

"What happened?"

"Des couldn't just let the case lie. She had to keep working it. After she discovered the insurance policies and your client's cash situation, she took another look at her. It was all part of the investigation."

This could not be good news. Roger Lowe was an attorney. He did not strike me as the kind of man who beat around the bush. He'd recruited me in less time than this. "You're stalling, Roger. What's going on?"

"Do you remember what I told you about your client having access to her husband's antidepressant?"

"What about it?"

"During the interrogation, your client admitted to bringing the bottle of Norpramin to her husband's motel room. While she claims she doesn't remember what happened, she admits he was very drunk. When Des asked her if she administered the pills, your client responded in the affirmative. And when Des told her that mixing Norpramin and alcohol could have deadly side effects, the meaning must have become clear to her. She stopped talking and demanded she have an attorney. The bottom line is Des now considers her the primary suspect."

34

ROGER'S CALL—AND THE IMPLICATIONS of Gina being charged with Bert's murder—haunted me for the remainder of the drive. My emotions ranged from wanting to berate Gina for talking to the police alone to wishing I could console her for this entire ordeal to doling out self-recriminations because I hadn't yet found the real killer.

Somehow, over the clash of emotions, the urge to call her finally won out. My call went unanswered. I didn't even get voicemail. And that ticked me off more. On the other hand, who was I to criticize Gina's phone etiquette? I'd cut Zoe off and never gotten back to her. In part, because I didn't know what to say.

Don't get me wrong, Zoe was growing on me, but she was high maintenance, and right now I was operating in low-power mode. Despite my misgivings, I did the deed, and of course, she answered. Obviously, my karma was in the crapper today.

"I have bad news," I said.

"It totally couldn't be worse than mine. My dad still wants me to get a job. He said school's not an option."

"You'll work something out, Zoe."

"I was thinking maybe you could hire me. Don't you like need an assistant or something? We could work cases and I could run the blog and…"

Blog? What blog? I didn't have a blog. I didn't have money. And I certainly had no more patience for her drama. "Zoe! I can't hire you. I have one client. That's Gina. And she's confessed to murdering her husband. Which probably means I'm fired—again."

"Oh, man. Talk about suck city. She confessed? To the cops?"

Okay. So maybe it hadn't exactly been a confession, but when you tell the cops you brought the murder weapon to the crime scene, what else could it be called? Tempting as it was to zing Zoe with something totally snarky, I said quietly, "Yes, to the cops."

"I guess that means you don't want to hear my plan?"

"If it involves me doing any hiring, the answer is no. Unless I get more clients, my first month as the new owner of the Beachtown Detective Agency will be my last."

Putting the thought into words suddenly made it so much more real. The Beachtown Detective Agency—the business my dad had run for most of my entire life—would be gone. And it would be my fault. With my vision blurring, I ran a mental debate session in my head over all the things I should be doing. It wasn't until someone honked their horn that I realized I hadn't been listening. At all.

"I'm sorry, Zoe. What did you say?"

"I said, I'm super bummed out now."

A pair of red-rimmed eyes looked back at me from the rearview mirror. Mine. "At least you're not the one who's going to destroy the business their father spent a lifetime building," I grumbled.

"Whoa. That's like intense, Jade. But just between you and me, I never did buy Gina's innocent-rich-girl routine. Right? I mean, those people don't think the rules apply to them, so why wouldn't she try to get away with murder?"

"I thought you were on board. You weren't?"

"At first I was. But afterwards, I was like, why wouldn't she try to kill her husband? She had nothing to lose. I'm gonna write one more post on it, then I'm done with Gina Rose and the whole Amorous Assailant story. It's old news and I need to find something hot. Rich girl kills deadbeat husband doesn't work. Where's the viral potential in that?"

"You need a job. And an open mind. Gina's innocent until proven guilty."

"Hello? You said she confessed. That's like game over, Jade."

I groaned. "You could be right. Maybe I'm just hanging on because I don't know what else to do. At this rate, I'll be living with my parents and working three part-time jobs like Esther Simpson."

"She's a piece of work."

"I admit she's kind of strange. Naïve, for sure."

"Her whole story was bizarre. Right down to the part where she says she was saved by a mystery man."

I glanced at the rearview mirror. Yup. I was frowning. "What are you talking about?"

"The dude who came running when he heard Esther screaming. He like showed up and the attacker ran away. The mystery man untied her and then split before the cops got there. I wrote up the whole story on my blog. You did read it, right?"

Crap. The question I hadn't wanted to answer. "I, um, scanned it. Things have been hectic since Gina hired me."

"Seriously? I'm, like, totally hurt that you didn't listen when I told you I'd done loads of research."

"Maybe I missed it," I muttered. "Or got interrupted while I was reading." Or spaced out because I hadn't taken her blog seriously.

"You don't like my blog? Have you read any of my posts? I totally put a ton of effort into each one."

"Let's leave my reading habits and my opinions about your blog out of this for the moment. Okay?"

I could almost hear her pout, and I certainly had a picture in my head of her glaring at the phone, lower lip pushed out. She might have even stuck her tongue out at me.

"I'm sorry," I said. "Look, I'll go back and read all the entries. Okay?"

"Whatever. This is so not fair."

I crossed my fingers. I needed to maneuver this conversation away from the looming cliff—the one where one of us said something we could never take back. That was the other lesson I learned during the breakup with Jason—I'd said things, terrible things. Even if he suddenly devoted himself to me like Armand did with Jacqueline, I would always remember what I'd done and said. I did not want to feel the same guilt with Zoe.

"Telling me about this mystery man was a big help," I said. "I just finished talking to Esther, and she didn't mention him once. In fact, now that I think about it, she never said anything about the actual attack. All she talked about was her reaction and how much of an adrenaline rush it gave her. When did she tell you about this guy?"

"Um…"

"Never mind. The exact date doesn't matter. Do you know who he was? How to contact him?"

"No."

"What did she tell you about him?"

"Um…?"

Seriously? She wasn't sure? I rolled my eyes, thankful this wasn't a video call. "Come on. You might want to give up on Gina, but I don't. This mystery man could be important."

"Whatever. I suppose."

How could Esther not even mention this mystery man in passing? Unless someone was lying—or coloring outside the lines. Esther seemed super straight, but Zoe was definitely a 'creative' problem solver. Esther worked three part-time jobs in different parts of the county; Zoe didn't even want one. And Zoe was impulsive. I had a hard time seeing her staying on task long enough to track down and drive all the way to Craft World. "Zoe, when did you interview her?"

"You mean like in person?"

"Or over the phone. When did you actually talk to her?"

"Uh…"

I was almost positive about the answer. "Zoe?" I demanded.

"Okay, fine," she huffed. "I got it from the police report."

I hung my head and massaged my temples. What an idiot I'd been. The wannabe reporter must have gone over the report from each attack of the Amorous Assailant in detail. I, the professional PI with a criminal justice degree, had barely skimmed them. There had to be other little gems in those reports I knew nothing about. My afternoon was now booked, but for the moment, I might as well see what else the amateur had discovered.

"I know," she said. "You're going to chew me out for journalistic incompetence because I took a shortcut." She continued almost without taking a breath. "It was a super-stressful time for me, Jade. I had a deadline and didn't have time to drive halfway across the state to spend five seconds getting brushed off."

"Actually, that's not what I was going to say. You're right, my talk with Esther wasn't very productive. I get it. Do I think you were wrong in not reaching out to her? Yes. But I made my own mistakes because I didn't read those police reports thoroughly. Or your blog. We're both learning and the fact is, you picked up things I should've known about before I started my interviews."

After a long pause, Zoe said, "So we're, like, okay?"

"Better than okay. We're good. I'd like to find this mystery man and have a conversation—in person, if possible."

"That could totally be a problem. The dude must be super cop-averse because Esther's statement said he broke up the attack and then split the second he heard sirens."

"Doesn't this whole story strike you as odd?"

"Um…no. I mean, like, why would she lie to the cops when she was the victim?"

"So some guy just happens to be in the same location as the attack at exactly the time when it occurs? Then he decides to play superhero and take on a masked man who's assaulting a woman he doesn't know? And then he leaves the minute he hears sirens? We are talking so bogus."

I waited, determined to give Zoe time to process what I'd said. In a dejected tone, she finally said, "When you put it that way, it does sound weird."

"Not weird, Zoe. Coincidental. And if there was one thing my dad taught me early on, it's that there's no such thing as coincidence. I need to find this guy."

"I guess."

"You might not be sure, but I am. This mystery man had to be there for a reason. He was either following Esther, or he was following Bert."

There was another long pause, then Zoe chirped, "Awesome. That means he could totally be the killer!"

Leave it to Zoe. Impulsive to the end.

35

FOR THE REST OF THE drive home, I alternately played back Zoe's last words and contemplated their truth. Maybe the mystery man from Esther's attack was the killer. More likely, not. Either way, my dad's philosophy about coincidence kept rearing its head. He always said coincidence was way overrated. Now that I was in charge of my own investigation, I understood what he meant. Coincidence was a crutch, a way to justify something you didn't yet understand.

It was time for a little mentoring session with the experienced private investigator in the family. When I arrived at Mom and Dad's, I found my parents in the kitchen. The three of us sat at the center island, a plate of warm oatmeal-raisin cookies in the middle. I grabbed one, took a bite, and let out a little moan of delight at the mix of flavors.

"Do you like them, honey?" Mom asked.

I took another nibble, rolled my eyes, and sighed. "They're wonderful. When did you become so interested in baking?"

Mom and Dad cast sideways glances at each other, then she said, "Your father and I get along much better when I'm in the kitchen and he's working on projects in the garage."

I gawped at my dad. I could count on one hand the number of times he'd done something around the house. And he'd never spent time in the garage—he'd always been on a case. "Projects? What are you working on?"

He rolled his neck as if he were trying to release tension and grumbled, "Twenty years of catch-up."

Oh. "Is that a note of irritation I detect?"

He shook his head and shrugged as he broke a cookie into quarters over his napkin. "Being around the house full time is a big adjustment. I guess I wasn't as prepared for all this freedom as I thought I was. I can tell you this. We're both glad to see you spending a little time at home." He winked and popped the bite-sized piece into his mouth.

"Yeah…about that. I'm actually working on Gina's case— and I need some advice."

Mom and Dad exchanged a glance. Mom smiled, Dad, not so much. Then Mom stuck out her hand, her palm up.

"You owe me five bucks, Thomas."

Dad reached for his wallet and scowled at me. "Your mother said if we saw you during the day, it would be to ask me for advice about a case. I told her you'd do fine on your own."

My jaw hung slack as I stared first at Mom, then at Dad. "You bet on me?"

"And a good bet it was," Mom snickered as she wiggled her fingers. "Pay up."

Dad playfully slapped the bill on her open palm and grunted.

Mom beamed as she stretched the bill taut and kissed it. "Hello, Mr. President. I promise to spend you well." A moment later, she stood. "I'll let you two talk. Right now, Mr. Lincoln and I have some gardening to do. Oh, and Jade, I packed a little something for you just in case you have to work late."

Once Mom was out of the room, Dad winked at me. "I never should have taken that bet."

I didn't know whether to feel worse because my parents were gambling on when they'd see me next or because Mom knew me so well. I winced. "I'm sorry, Dad."

"No worries, honey. I know what the job's like. What do you need?"

His tone, light and breezy, made me feel almost guilty about asking for help. He was right, though. He knew what the agency was like. "I have a huge problem with Gina. She's confessed. Sort of."

"Confessions aren't generally…" Dad paused and glanced upwards. "Shall I say, flexible? Did she admit to killing her husband?"

"Not exactly. You have to work with the cards you're dealt. That's what you always told me." I went on to detail what I'd learned. Dad and I each went through another cookie during the explanation, and when I finished, his face was somber.

"Do you remember what I told you about Locard's Principle?"

"How could I forget? You drummed it into me every time you had a case—there's no such thing as a perfect crime."

"Exactly. Which means that for your mystery man, and for Bert Darlington's murder, Locard's Principle says there is evidence. It just hasn't been found yet. The limiting factor here is time. You have a finite number of available hours. What it comes down to, honey, is you have to prioritize. The last thing you need is me telling you what to do, but I will ask you one question. What's most important to you at this very moment? Finding this mystery man, or what the police may have missed?"

I swallowed hard and listened to the beating of my heart. Dad waited patiently, his elbow crooked and resting on the countertop while he watched me as though I were ten and working through a math problem.

"It never occurred to me to question the police investigation," I said. Standing, I hugged him and gave him a kiss on the cheek. "Thank you."

"You feel like you've got a course of action?"

Not only that, but I also had a nice little sugar high going on. The rush might only last a short time, but hopefully, my renewed sense of confidence would last. I grabbed the lunch bag Mom had packed and stopped to say goodbye on the way out. She gave me a huge hug, which seemed a bit overdone. I wasn't sure what was going on with her, but resolved to ask when I got home tonight.

I returned to the office, intending to spend an hour or two poring over the police reports and making notes. It was way too soon for conclusions, but at least I might be able to break out the similarities and differences between each of the attacks. At three p.m., I packed up my go bag and pulled my keys from my pocket. A piece of paper fluttered to the floor. Without even bending down to pick it up, I recognized it. It was Mr. Lincoln.

I smiled as I picked up the five-dollar bill and put it in my bag. "Thanks, Mom,"

The drive to the Sunny Days Inn was uneventful. I just hoped I was really getting the clerk who had rented the room to Gina. The moment I walked into the motel office, I sensed a different vibe from my last visit. The woman behind the counter was middle-aged, had sandy blonde hair, and a friendly smile. Unlike the smarmy guy who worked nights, this woman made me feel welcome with her friendly smile and eye contact.

I introduced myself and handed her a card. She glanced at it and stuck it in her back pocket. "I'm Sharon West. How can I help you?"

"I understand you booked Room #11. That's the one Bert Darlington stayed in."

She shook her head and grimaced. "I did. To a woman. Blonde. Young. Expensive taste in clothing."

I gazed at her, wide-eyed. Her description fit Gina well enough, and I wondered what else she could tell me. "Wow. You have a good memory. How do you remember all that?"

"Honey, when you've been doing this as long as I have, you learn to forget the bad ones and play nice with the good ones. It was obvious the lady had money, so her renting a room in a dive like this was definitely an experience to remember. And you can drop the little Miss Innocent act. If you're a PI, you came here for information, not to compliment me on my memory."

Oh crap. The room felt warm. One of these days, I had to take a class on how to maintain a poker face. Sure that my cheeks were burning, I said, "Okay. No problem."

She winked at me. "I give you props for trying, though. That little act would work wonders on Harvey, but most of his thinking is done below the belt."

"We've met. He's the one who told me I should talk to you. Did you get the name of the woman who rented the room?"

"Smith. Jane Smith." Sharon planted her hands on the counter and laughed. "She was probably banking on us not asking questions because she paid in cash, but I recognized her. It was Gina Rose. She's in the legit news, as well as all the tabloids." Sharon shrugged one shoulder and cocked her head to the side. "I assumed she was setting up for an evening fling with someone's husband, so I let her off easy. It wasn't until the next day when I came in that I found out what happened." She shook her head and grimaced again.

"What else do you remember?" I asked.

"There's nothing else to remember. After she paid, I gave her the key, and then she got in her car and drove away."

"That seems odd. She never went into the room?"

"I distinctly remember her walking out the door and getting in her car."

"Did you get her license plate number?"

Sharon shook her head. "No. I had another couple checking in. I think she might have been driving a black Mercedes. One of those little convertibles. The lady wanted anonymity, so I let her believe she was getting away with something. Harvey wouldn't have been nearly so accommodating."

"Did you tell all this to the police?" I asked.

"Some junior detective. Young guy. Don't remember his name. You probably know him, though."

She looked at me as though she were expecting an answer. The description was vague, but it could have been the one who interviewed Zoe. I didn't know his name, but the way Zoe had been flirting with anything wearing pants it wouldn't surprise me if she did.

"Got it," I said. "Can I see the room?"

"Sure. For all the good it will do you. Esme did a deep cleaning after the police finished." She turned away, went to a rack of keys on the wall, and plucked one from its hook. "Here you go. Knock yourself out."

The overpowering scent of cleaners blasted me in the face the moment I opened the door. After catching my breath, I stepped into the room. Could there be such a thing as a Clorox high? The smell, combined with the heat that had been building in the enclosed space, made the room feel like a disinfected sweat lodge. "Wow," I muttered. "When Esme deep cleans, she doesn't fool around."

I walked through the living area, slowly making my way to the bathroom. Every hard surface had been scrubbed; the carpet had been vacuumed, and the linens washed. The bottom line was this room had been stripped, sanitized, and sterilized to the point that nothing even resembling a clue survived.

On my way out, I stood in the open doorway and took a last look around. My eyes narrowed when they settled on the wall to my right. More specifically, the door.

Well, well. Mr. Locard might have gotten that principle right after all.

This was an adjoining room.

And that door was another way for a killer to enter.

36

I FOUND SHARON IN THE office lobby watering one of the giant spider plants that hung from the ceiling. The variegated green leaves of the mother plant and all the hanging spiderettes added a cheerful note to the otherwise drab interior.

She glanced at me when I entered. "Did you find what you were looking for?"

"That's an adjoining room," I blurted.

"Most of ours are."

"Is it possible for someone to have gotten through the door?"

"The cops asked the same question. I'll tell you what I told them. The adjoining rooms all have two doors. They both lock from the inside, and Esme is a fanatic about making sure those locks are secured each time a guest comes or goes. The bottom line is the person in the adjoining room couldn't have gotten in unless the dead man opened his door and let them in."

No. I couldn't be wrong. I just couldn't. "But it's possible, right? The doors aren't permanently sealed."

"Honey, I suppose anything's possible. I don't remember exactly, so I don't even know if the room was occupied that night."

"Can you check to see if you rented out the adjoining room the night of the murder?"

"Sure, give me a minute." She carried the watering can back to the desk, set it off to the side, then tapped on her keyboard. At first, she huffed, then a knowing smile spread across her face. "Oh. I'd forgotten about him. He was a handsome guy." Sharon laughed. Winked at me. "He paid in cash, too. It was one of those days when I started to wonder if maybe we were running a one-night-stand special or something."

If that was supposed to be some sort of motel-manager humor, I didn't get it. "If he was so good-looking, I'm surprised you didn't remember him."

Sharon laughed. "Honey, if I tried to remember every hot guy who came in here for a one-night stand, my brain would explode."

I rested my elbows on the counter and held Sharon's gaze. She was earnest enough. Most certainly telling the truth. But that didn't make her right. "What was the guy's name?"

"Will Smith."

It was my turn to laugh. "Seriously?"

"Not the actor," she said.

"No. I meant, another Smith?"

She smiled, revealing a set of slightly crooked teeth. "I know. Can you believe it? Doesn't anybody have any imagination?"

As I watched Sharon's face, I realized she probably thought the same thing about many of their guests. She'd most likely seen it all. Because she'd been so cooperative, perhaps I could press for one more favor. "Would you mind if I took a look at the room?" I asked. "Just so I can satisfy my curiosity."

"Why not? It's not like I'm going to rent it out tonight. Our business has dropped off to nothing since that poor man died." She plucked another key off the rack and handed it to me. "Like I said before, knock yourself out."

I hurried out the door and down the walkway. Standing before the door marked #12, the key in hand, I thought about how stuffy and oppressive Bert's room had been. This was a typical summer day—foggy morning, gorgeous afternoon. And with the fog long gone this late in the day, the sun hung low in the afternoon sky. It beat down on the front doors and windows. The thin walls radiated the heat, and the inside of this room was going to be just like #11, an over-sanitized sauna. If this place was so bad, why in the world had Gina rented a room here? To make Bert suffer? Or because the well was running dry?

My heart sank when I opened the door. More white walls. The same tired bedspread, dresser, and night stands. This room was a mirror image of Bert's, right down to the dingy, forest green carpet with worn traffic patterns around the bed and leading to the bath. The air felt close and warm, and the odor of cleaning products, though not as strong, still clung to the furniture and walls.

What had I expected to find? The killer's bags? A note? *Hi, I killed Bert Darlington.*

With a sigh, I did a thorough inspection. Nothing out of place. No damages. I even checked the door connecting this room with #11. The interior door for this room opened, but the handle for #11 didn't budge. I blew out a slow breath and wiped away the drop of sweat trickling down my neck. Esme had done her job. Again.

Sharon was right. The only way a killer could have gotten into #11 was if he…or she…had been invited. To my knowledge, only two people had been in that room—Bert and Gina. No, wait. Eric had brought Bert home from Fat Cat's.

I'd sat across the street watching his Mercedes for…how long? I looked back at my notes from that night. Thirty minutes. That's how long he'd been in the room with Bert. After Eric left, Zoe showed up. And then Gina. Which meant Bert had been alive long after Eric left. I let out a heavy sigh. Unless I could find a connection between Will Smith and Gina or Bert, this was pointless. I closed the door behind me and returned to the office.

Sharon was typing on the keyboard when I walked in. "Did you find what you were looking for?"

"I'm not sure. You told me the guy who rented the room said his name was Will Smith?"

"That's right. Nice guy. Good manners. Very polite."

"Is there any way to find out his real name?"

Sharon's lips parted; her eyes widened. "Do you think he had something to do with the murder?"

"Maybe."

"No, honey. I wish I could help you. But…wait. I do have a license number for him. Of course, sometimes people give us a wrong plate number. Not that we check." She shrugged and spread her hands wide. "Not much help, am I? Sometimes we see the car, but we certainly don't go look at it to verify the information they gave us. That would creep people out."

Whether or not the plate number was bogus was easy enough to check. The agency had access to online databases with all kinds of juicy personal information—not that I intended to abuse the resource for personal purposes, but I would definitely use it in this case. "I'll take whatever you've got. It's no problem for me to check out the plate number."

She pulled out a Sunny Days Inn notepad and pen. "Sure. I'll give you the make and model, too."

I read upside down as she carefully wrote out the information for a red Kia four-door sedan. Her letters were easily legible and, in some ways, reminded me of my mom's.

"Thanks," I said when she handed me the note. "Is there anything else you can tell me about this guy?"

There was a momentary pause while Sharon sighed and looked up at the ceiling. "Not much. I think he was married."

"What makes you say that?"

"Just a feeling. Had a certain look about him."

"What look?"

"The cheater."

My heartbeat ticked up a notch. If Eric had rented the room, he probably would have used a fake name. But unless he'd worn a disguise, Sharon just might be able to ID him. I pulled out my phone and scrolled through photos until I found the one of Eric, then held the screen so Sharon could see it. "Is that him?"

She pursed her lips and shook her head. "No. That is not him. This guy was much better looking." She then sighed and ran her tongue over her lips as she looked around the office. The upbeat facade she'd maintained throughout our conversations fell. She sighed. "I'd love to work in a better place. You know, someplace where the guests came in with more than just the clothes on their backs? But I've been here so long I don't think I could leave it now. It's kind of like my son—at times, I hate the things he does, but I love him anyway."

I waited, not sure what to say. What I wanted was for her to return to the point, but I didn't want to break the rapport we seemed to have. Apparently, she recognized my dilemma because she shook her head and made a face.

"Sorry. I didn't mean to put that on you. Anyway, we get a lot of one-night stands. You can always tell because two people show up without any luggage. Most of them come in after I leave, but I still hear about them. It usually goes in one ear and out the other."

"You mean you hear from the other staff about these people?"

228

"There's always some scuttlebutt. You know how it is. Wherever you work, there's always got to be something to gossip about. Anyway, this guy was my last customer of the day. He was unusual in that he came in alone, so I figured he would meet up with someone, then come back."

"Did you hear anything about him from the other staff?"

"Not him, but what he didn't do. Esme told me the bed hadn't been slept in. The seal on the toilet wasn't even broken. When Esme reported in, her sheet showed that the room went unused."

"Do you get very many people who walk in off the street to rent a room they don't intend to use?"

Sharon chuckled. "It doesn't happen often."

Often? How about probably never? "Did he have to check out in the morning?"

"Left the key in the room."

This was going nowhere. Fast. So far, all I had was a license plate number that was probably a fake, a generic handsome-man description, and a growing sense of impending doom. I stared at the countertop, massaging my temples with my fingertips. "This is just so frustrating," I said. "Please, Sharon. I need something to go on. How tall was he?"

"I'd say he was about six-foot. Black hair. He had one of those scruffy beards the guys like these days. And he wore a leather jacket. It looked expensive."

My mouth felt suddenly dry. I'd met a man who fit the description she'd given me right down to the jacket. I reached for my phone and brought up my photos. The one I wanted was very recent. "Do you think you'll recognize him if you see a picture?"

"Honey, a hunk like him? I'm sure I'll remember."

"Got it!" I turned the phone around so Sharon could see the screen. "Is that the man who rented the room?"

Her face lit up. She nodded enthusiastically. "That's him," she said. "Handsome devil, isn't he?"

Yes. He was.

37

WARMTH RADIATED THROUGHOUT MY CHEST, and for once it wasn't from embarrassment, but self-satisfaction. I knew something the cops didn't. Take that, Detective Des. I knew who had access to Bert Darlington's room on the night of the murder. She didn't.

My hopes still riding high, I pointed at the photo again. "You're sure that's him, Sharon?"

"Honey, I'm not going to forget a mug like his. I'm positive. Who is he?"

"Have you heard of the Amorous Assailant?"

"Who hasn't? It was on the news for months. That's not him, is it?"

"No. The man who was killed was the one who's been attacking women." My phone rang with a call from Gina.

Finally. She'd surfaced.

I positioned my finger over the button to answer and said hurriedly, "This man is the fiancé of a woman who was one of the victims. His real name is Armand Fraser. Excuse me, I have to take this."

Moving to the far side of the office, I listened as Gina talked, and quickly determined she was panicked. She didn't sound anything like the confident woman who'd hired me at the beginning of the week. I gestured to Sharon that I would be right back and stepped outside. Cars whizzed by on the busy city street, forcing me to plug my right ear and press the phone to my left. Despite my best attempts to block out the traffic mayhem, I had trouble making out the words.

"My accountant is telling me it will take everything I've got to fight this," Gina said. "I don't know if I'll be able to pay you."

Not good news for me, but at least she finally got it. "Hold on. Let's not get ahead of ourselves. I'm getting closer to finding answers."

"Aren't you listening? I can't pay you. I'm not an idiot, Jade. I know how this works. People don't work for free." A second later, she added, "I could lose my house."

Between the noise on the street and Gina's woe-is-me attitude, I had to do something. I took one step. Then another. Turned, went the other way. I'd never been one to pace, but then, I'd never owned a business before, either.

I could no more afford to work for Gina as a volunteer than Zoe could for me. The difference was, the agency had been in business too many years to simply give up. If I walked away now, I lost everything. As I reversed direction for the third time, I realized something elsc. I had to know the truth about who killed Bert Darlington. He deserved justice.

And I wanted answers. Especially that list of payments to Bert. The longer this went on, the bigger I suspected the problem might be. "Are you at home right now?" I asked.

"It's the only place I'm safe from the paparazzi. And even here I had to hire security that I can't afford to keep them away." She let out a little noise that sounded much like a growl, then hissed, "I hate them!"

In a perverse way, I found Gina's plight kind of funny. A week ago, she basked in the glow of celebrity. Now, she found herself trapped by the very aura she'd cultivated. "I'll be at your house in twenty minutes. Don't go near the windows and don't answer the phone."

I ended the call, went back inside to thank Sharon, and said goodbye. The closer I got to Gina's, the more the traffic thinned out. By the time I was climbing up the net-worth scale on the road up the Hills of Money, I no longer had to watch for oncoming traffic, but could sneak peeks at the elegant homes and massive remodeling projects. With each additional foot of elevation, the homes got bigger, the property values rose, and the smell of cold hard cash grew stronger.

The quiet aura changed when I got to Gina's block. She hadn't exaggerated. People with big-lens cameras hung out in force on her street. A security guard, a no-nonsense man with a perpetual scowl, stood at the gated entrance to her modest mansion. When I gave him my name, he passed me through without comment. Apparently, Gina had alerted him the cavalry was coming.

The house lacked the architectural opulence of its great southern cousins—it had no massive columns, more stone and stucco than white paint and masonry, and the driveway was short, albeit wide. I parked on the side closest to the front door and took the curving walkway. A fountain burbled in the courtyard while palm fronds overhead rustled in the gentle breeze.

Gina greeted me with a quick and subdued welcome. In her oversized tee and skinny jeans, she looked like any other fashionable twenty-something. The circular foyer had fifteen-foot walls on which large art déco paintings hung. A dolphin sculpture dominated the center. I followed Gina into a sunken living room, where she plopped down onto a corner of the massive sectional with her feet tucked under her. In front of the sectional was a glass coffee table with a large bouquet and a condolence card.

"I'm so screwed," she moaned. "Why are you wasting your time, Jade? You have a business to run."

I sat on the sectional about two feet away from her, positioning myself so we faced each other. It might seem silly, but I hoped the open body posture would make her more comfortable. "I won't abandon you, Gina. Friends don't abandon friends. That's my motto."

She eyed me closely, her brow crinkling with sudden interest. "You consider me a friend?"

Her reply caught me off-guard. Had I just committed a major faux pax in the Gina Rose world? Did she not use the 'F' word? "You don't have many friends, do you?"

She shook her head absently and gazed out the window. The Pacific Ocean stretched to the horizon, a sparkling canvas of dark blue beneath a clear azure sky, punctuated only by patches of white. "When you have money, everybody wants to be around you. But when the money's gone? They all scatter."

"I'm not scattering."

She watched me for a moment, almost as though she was searching my face for a lie, then pushed back a stray lock of blonde hair. Sitting on the corner of that massive couch, she looked afraid and lonely. "You're not? Really?"

I waited silently, allowing Gina—and perhaps myself—to absorb what I'd just promised. Friendship. Quite possibly, no more money. But it did mean she had an ally to help her fight whatever Detective Des threw at her. I was probably out of my mind, but I had to be true to myself, which meant I didn't abandon my friends, or my clients, and I fought to find the truth.

"Bert never had friends either," she said in a hoarse whisper.

"What about Eric?"

She laughed, but it sounded forced and almost sarcastic. "That's funny. Are you kidding me? He was never Bert's friend. They were always trying to outdo each other."

"How did they wind up in business together?"

"Eric had a setback. Bert decided he wanted to be magnanimous and give Eric a chance to make something of himself." She shrugged. "He made it sound so altruistic. I fell for it—all of it—and started loaning him money. Stupid me; I thought we were doing something together for a higher purpose."

I gave Gina a rueful smile. "And then the prince turned back into a toad."

"Something like that."

"They descended from frogs," I chuckled.

Gina craned her neck forward. "What?"

"Nothing. It's just something my friend Charlie told me after I found my boyfriend cheating on me."

After a few seconds, Gina nodded. Pulling on a stray tendril of blonde hair, she grimaced. "You don't have to do this, you know. I'll understand if you turn around and walk out the door." She suppressed a laugh and glanced toward the front of the house. "Last chance to save yourself."

I moved over until I was next to her. Placing my hand on hers, I shook my head. "That's where you're wrong. You need to stop feeling sorry for yourself. We need to prove you didn't kill Bert. And in order for us to succeed, we need to work together. The truth is, I need your help. There are things you know about your husband, his business dealings, and even his so-called friends that nobody else knows. So, this is me, holding up the mirror for you to look in. If I walk out, you lose your last chance. Truth time, Gina. Do you want to help me or would you rather just go down in flames feeling sorry for yourself?"

She stared out at the ocean, tears misting her eyes. I waited, my hand on hers, until she blinked back her tears and looked directly at me. "Wow. You know how to get real, don't you? You should have been a motivational speaker. I almost feel like I have a chance."

"You do. One. And I won't lie to you. The odds are not in your favor. But what is in your favor is the truth. If we can find it. Now, are you going to help me or not?"

Her forehead crinkled as she gazed out at the expansive view. She choked back a sob and faced me again after taking a deep breath. This time, determination—or at least a close facsimile—lined her face. "I don't want to lose my home."

"Then you'll help me?"

"Yes. What do you need?"

I told her what I'd learned at the motel and asked if she'd ever heard of Armand Fraser. She hadn't. "Is he the one who murdered Bert?"

"It's too soon to tell. I'm not saying he didn't kill Bert. I just don't know how he could have gotten into the room. What I need at this point is context. Let's go back to the beginning. Does Bert have a home office?"

"Of course. We both do."

"I need to see it."

She nodded, stood, and led the way to an open staircase. I gawked out the massive floor-to-ceiling windows as we climbed, and when we reached the second floor, I stopped and stared. If the view from the living room ranked as exceptional, the one from up here needed a few more superlatives. It was a hundred-and-eighty degrees of Pacific Ocean and California coastline.

"I know," Gina said.

I stopped gawking and hurried to catch up. "Sorry, it's just…"

"Don't worry. I did it the first time, too." She gestured at the open door behind her. "Bert's office. I've…never gone in there."

"Never? Didn't the police search the room?"

"I…just let them in. The only time I've been in there since Bert and I got married was when the furniture was delivered. After that, Bert always said it was his private domain." She quickly added, "He didn't come into mine, either."

"It's okay, Gina. Really. But now…I'm only saying you'll have to go through and clean it out sooner or later."

Her jaw tightened as she reached for my hand. I squeezed hers in response, amazed at how fragile she appeared in this moment.

"I'm glad you're here," she said. "Will you go in first?"

I nodded, then led the way.

38

THE INTERIOR OF BERT DARLINGTON'S office was a study in elegance. The oversized mahogany desk and filing cabinet matched perfectly. The in-office bar was stocked with bottles of Scotch that had been made before I was born. And the plush leather chairs and area rugs? They probably cost more than I would make this year.

The artwork on the walls included the same artist's rendering of the Carlsbad project I'd seen in Eric's office. There were also autographed photos from sports figures and one of four men dressed in soccer uniforms.

Gina pointed at one of the men. "That's Bert. I don't believe I've ever seen this particular photo before. He was a soccer player in college. He told me all the girls were always taking pictures. When I met him, I thought he was so sexy. Little did I know." She rolled her eyes.

Looking closer at the photo, my eyes widened. I recognized three of the men, but not the fourth. "Do you know all of them?"

"Eric Andrews is to Bert's left. I don't know the other two."

I pointed at the man on the end. "That's Armand Fraser."

"You mentioned him before." Gina blinked and took another, this time, closer, look. "I never…wait. Bert might have mentioned him once at a party when a bunch of us were talking about things we'd done in college."

"Who sent the flowers on the table downstairs?"

"Larry Lawson. I've never met him, either."

"Maybe he's the fourth man in this photo."

"I don't know. Bert didn't talk about him. Actually, the flowers came as a total surprise."

"How strange. I wonder how Mr. Lawson found out about Bert's death? I'll want to take a look at the card. In fact, I hope there's a phone number included."

"There is," Gina said. "It's on the inside."

"Good. If he's one of these four, maybe he can tell me more about the others in this little group. Did they hang out a lot together? That kind of thing. Maybe he's remained close to them." I scanned the room, checked the desk drawers while Gina stood to the side with her fingers pressed to her lips and a dazed expression on her face. I supposed this was another shock she hadn't prepared for.

There was nothing of any substance in the desk or the filing cabinet, which appeared to be used mostly for computer and printer supplies. There were no convenient, tell-all, computer printouts on the printer, either. I took a stab at printing out the last page from the printer's memory. The document was a copy of a receipt from a pharmacy for Norpramin. Great. Bert bought the drugs that killed him. I folded the paper until it was small enough to fit in my back pocket, then looked at Gina.

"This isn't helping much," I said. "I'm going to need to go to his work office."

"They close at five," Gina said. "You should get going."

I checked the time. There was almost an hour and the drive wouldn't take that long. "Let's call this Larry Lawson first. I can leave him a message if he's not available, and then I'll head out."

Gina led the way back downstairs, which offered me another opportunity to ogle the view and appreciate the major selling point of this home. As we crossed through the living room, I asked the question that had been in the back of my mind since I entered the front door.

"Gina, who paid for everything?"

"What do you mean?"

"Who paid for the house, the furnishings—all of it? Was it you?"

"Bert was putting his money into the business."

I locked my gaze onto hers. "You mean your money."

She glanced away and grimaced. "He took me for so much. I was so stupid."

"Was it more than the five-hundred-thousand you told me about?"

"I don't know exactly. Can't we just…move on?"

"The police have already looked into your finances. They intend to use the information against you. They'll call it part of your motive. We need to know how much we're talking about. You have to get me that accounting of what you gave him."

She blew out a slow breath and closed her eyes. "I'll see what I can do."

Really? Was that all I would ever get out of her? There was either something big she was hiding, or she was too ashamed to take action. I hoped that wasn't the case because what Gina didn't understand was that I would not let up until I found what she was keeping from me.

"Gina, just because Bert conned you doesn't mean you should try to keep it a secret."

"What will people think?"

The way she fidgeted, I wondered if her long, slender fingers might actually work themselves into a knot. I crossed the room to the coffee table and picked up the card, which was standing upright next to the flowers. The area code for the phone number wasn't one I recognized, which meant Lawrence Lawson wasn't local. Still, it was worth a try. To my surprise, he answered right away. His voice was upbeat—sounding like that of someone who enjoyed life.

"Mr. Lawson, my name is Jade Cavendish. I'm investigating the death of Bert Darlington. Right now, I'm at the home of Gina Rose, and we have a few questions for you. But she would also like you to know how much she appreciates the bouquet you sent."

"Thank you, but call me Larry. I hate formalities."

"Okay, Larry, how did you hear of Bert's death?"

"I read about it online. I use search engine alerts to follow a bunch of my old friends from college. It's a fun way to see what happens in their lives. It came as a tremendous shock when I read about it. Especially…under the circumstances."

"Are you referring to the homicide investigation?"

"And the arrest. Bert always was a thrill seeker."

"You knew him well?"

"I don't know that I'd say I ever knew him well. But we played soccer together. We hung out a little bit, but Bert had his other friends, and they weren't exactly focused on academics. My parents would have cut off my support if my GPA dropped. That's what saved me from becoming the fourth member of their little clique."

Four? The magic number. And what did he mean by a clique? "A few minutes ago, Gina and I came across a photo of four members of a soccer team. We can identify three of the men. Might you be the fourth?"

"Yes, there was a photo of the four of us. I'm surprised Bert kept that."

"So you hung out a lot back then?"

"We called Bert, Eric, and Armand the Three Inseparables. They were always doing things together. Actually, it was more like Eric and Bert were the ones doing, and Armand was hanging on. He never really fit in, although he certainly tried. And every time he didn't make it, he tried harder. I felt sorry for the guy."

"Go on," I coaxed.

"This is ancient history. I don't see why you're interested."

"The more background I have, the better I might be able to sort out how Bert died."

"You're trying to find out who murdered him," Larry said flatly.

If he was trying to shock me, he'd have to do better than that. Doing my best to convey no emotion, I said, "To be blunt, yes."

"Well, I'm probably in the clear. I'm a stockbroker in New York and I'm confined to a wheelchair, thanks to a drunk driver."

I didn't know the man, and yet I felt a pang of sympathy for him. "I'm sorry."

"No worries. I'm adjusting. So what else do you need to know?"

"Can you tell me more about the Three Inseparables?"

"Arc we on speaker?"

"No."

"Good. The truth is, Bert was not a nice man. And the way he treated women—I can understand how one of them would want to kill him."

"You mean the Amorous Assailant victims?"

"Not just them. All women. Bert was the player, always looking for his next free ride. He only dated rich girls, and he always found ways to get money out of them."

I glanced sideways at Gina. Never had I realized how difficult this part of the job could be. I took a deep breath and asked, "What about Gina?"

There was a long pause, then he cleared his throat. "Just between you and me, I hoped she might be the exception. But Bert..."

I listened, wondering if he might continue, but he didn't. "He didn't change. Did he?"

"No."

At least Gina hadn't been the first, though it probably wouldn't be much consolation to know her husband had been a professional at what he did. "When Bert got money out of these women, did he use it for something good? When I first met Eric, he told me Bert was big on paying things forward. Is that not true?"

"Bert was big on doing favors for others. It was his version of an admirable lifestyle. The difference was that for him, it always meant do something now so you can get paid back with interest later."

"You're saying he was more of a loan shark than he was an altruist?"

"You could call him that."

"What about Eric? Did he go along with that philosophy, too?"

"Eric's more of a take-what-you-want kind of guy. He could get very pushy when he didn't get what he wanted."

"His ex-wife claimed he was an unfit parent. Would you call him a bully?"

"That would be a good description."

"What about Armand?" I asked.

"He was the guy who was always in love. Armand was a one-woman man—until the woman got tired of him and broke up. Then he'd move on to the next great love affair. I guess you'd call him a serial monogamist."

Gina, who had been staring out the window while she chewed on the remnants of a perfectly manicured nail, turned back to gaze at me. I had mixed feelings about bringing her in. Hearing this kind of thing about her husband could be overwhelming and hurtful. But it was her life. Her husband. What the heck? Unless she'd been completely lost in thought, she'd probably picked up parts of it, anyway. She might as well have all the facts.

"They sound like quite a trio. Larry, Gina's pretty devastated over Bert's death. If you don't mind, could I put this on speaker so she can hear, too?"

Larry wasn't thrilled, but he agreed. We did another introduction. Another thanks for sending the flowers. Some small talk. And finally, he did the thing I'd been hoping he'd do. He lied.

39

THIS WAS ONE OF THOSE times when mercy mattered more than the truth—and I was willing to let Gina, who had moved closer, have her moment of solace—even if it was based on a lie. "Did you hear that, Gina? Bert settled down after he met you." I looked up at her from my spot on the couch and gave her a reassuring wink.

She turned away again, but this time there was a slight smile on her lips and I wondered if she was recalling some fond memory. Perhaps.

"Lately, I wasn't sure what he was up to," she said.

Her jaw tightened, and I leaned closer to the phone. If only I could undo the inevitable pain she'd feel for the foreseeable future. "You said you followed the others online, Larry. Did you ever have a reason to contact any of the Three Inseparables?"

"Bert and I talked a few times a year. It wasn't really the same with Armand. He was always busy with his latest love, so he just faded away. I cut Eric off after the Israel Castillo debacle."

"I read something about Israel Castillo filing complaints against Eric at Watson, Watson, and Oberdorf. Do you have any insight into what that was all about?"

"If it wasn't for Castillo, Eric might never have been fired and D&A Investments would never have existed."

"I don't understand something, Larry. Gina told me Bert took Eric on as a favor, but with these types of complaints hanging over his head, Eric was toxic. Why would Bert take him on?"

"Bert had his reasons."

Well, rats. Now I was regretting my decision to bring Gina into the conversation. Larry had provided the consolation I'd gambled on, but we'd gone from honesty to what might best be called guarded. "Please, Larry. That doesn't help us. I get that Eric probably couldn't have gotten on with another law firm, but why wouldn't he start his own? Why would Bert want that kind of partner?"

The silence, and the anticipation of what Larry might say, seemed to consume the oxygen in the room. About the time I was ready to prompt him for an answer, he said, "Gina."

"What?" From where she stood, Gina peered down at the phone as though Larry was speaking in tongues.

"Sorry. What I meant was that you were the reason Eric wanted to work with Bert. Eric always had a soft spot for you. He was smitten from the moment he saw you, but you only had eyes for Bert."

There was a long pause, during which Gina slowly lowered herself onto the couch next to me. She grabbed my hand and squeezed with a grip so strong it made my fingers ache. She stared at the hardwood floor and stammered, "I…I don't understand."

But, based on her reaction, I thought she understood perfectly. I looked right at her and asked, "When did you and Eric meet?"

She shook her head as if she was in shock. "Not until the wedding. He was at the dinner the night before."

"Did you know how he felt?"

She drew into herself, her frown deepening until I thought the furrows might never come out. After shooting a glance across the room, she rubbed her bare forearms with her hands and choked out a single-word response. "No."

I turned back to the phone. "That's sick, Larry. Are you positive? He never even met Gina until the wedding, so how would he…" I stopped, sat up straight, and sucked in a breath. Of course. He knew her the same way I had. "Was he following her online?"

Gina's eyes widened. She pulled out her phone and frantically tapped the screen. She swore once, swiped up, then tapped again and turned the screen so I could see it.

After a few moments of silence, Larry said, "I assume you have your answer."

"How did you know this?" I asked.

"Frankly, I follow Gina, too. She probably didn't even know it."

"What should I do?" Gina whispered.

I waved my hands in front of me. "Nothing. You will do nothing about it. Not yet. We need to see where this takes us."

Gina tossed the phone off to the side and stared at it. After a few seconds, she planted her elbows on her knees and pressed her palms against her eyes. She probably wanted to block out the world at this moment, but while she was busy letting herself feel devastated over her crumbling world, I was growing more curious. Larry's story had only raised more questions in my mind. I knew I could push; I just didn't know how far.

"I still don't get it," I said. "Even if Eric thought being in business with Bert would get him closer to Gina, why would Bert even want him?"

Larry uttered a quiet, 'um', then said, "Are you sure you want to hear this?"

"Absolutely."

"Yes!" Gina demanded. "I want to hear this."

I looked at her. Her devastation had apparently transformed itself into anger. I could tell by the fire in her eyes. How long it would last, I didn't know. "Gina wants the truth, Larry."

He let out an audible sigh, then said, "As Bert put it, if he bailed Eric out again and gave him a job, he owned him. I never asked what he meant by that, but I can tell you this. Bert was ruthless, even with his friends."

"Why would you stay friends with a man like that?" I asked.

"Better friends than enemies."

It had been a pure statement of fact. No emotion whatsoever. So Larry probably saw Bert as just another business transaction. Using that philosophy, I'd be having lunch with Jason once a week. Larry Lawson and I operated on completely different principles. "So that's why you talked to Bert a few times a year? Do you mind sharing what those conversations were about?"

"It was usually after he'd had a big row with Eric."

"That's a lot of arguments."

"They had a lot to disagree about. The last time was back in January. Middle of the month, I think. Bert was complaining about how much money Eric's settlement cost D&A."

"January?" Gina croaked. Her eyes narrowed; she leaned forward on the couch, and her cheeks colored. "January!" she exploded. "That was my money! Not his." As abruptly as it came, her anger receded, and she fell into quiet sobs.

Okay. Gina was definitely riding an emotional rollercoaster. I blocked her out to focus on the phone and getting what I could while I could. "What kind of settlement was this?"

"It wasn't just one. It was two. Look, I didn't realize the money Bert was shelling out so freely was Gina's and not his."

Another sigh came through the speaker, then Larry spoke slowly, as though he were carefully choosing his words. "You deserve to know the whole story."

"Which is?"

"Israel Castillo wasn't the first."

"The first what? Settlement?"

"These are not exactly court settlements," Larry said. "Bert was buying silence."

Where did I even begin? I had a million questions rushing through my head, yet I couldn't decide which one to ask first. "Can you explain?" I finally asked.

"The first incident I'm aware of was four years ago, but it started in college. Bert, Eric, and I were all part of a fraternity. Hazing was common."

"Hazing?" I blurted. Was that what the Amorous Assailant attacks were all about?

"Yes. Bert and Eric sold the others on the idea that pledges would be put in the trunk of a car and driven over a bumpy dirt road. It took the two of them to stuff this one kid into Eric's trunk. The poor kid kept crying that he was claustrophobic. He was screaming and kicking like a maniac. A few of us said we needed to do something different, but Eric got in the car and drove off. Somehow, he lost control while he was driving. The pledge wasn't killed, but suffered some very severe injuries."

A wave of anger rushed through me. I don't know what I would have done in a moment like that—would I have come to the kid's rescue? I would hope, but would never know. After several seconds, I asked, "Did the pledge sue the fraternity? What about Eric?"

"Not then. That came later."

"Did Eric show any remorse?"

"None."

"What about Bert?"

"He claimed he was sorry."

Once again, I wished this was an in-person interview and not over the phone. I really would have liked to have seen Larry's face when he'd said that. "What was this pledge's name?"

"Karl White."

"Any idea how I can contact him?"

"Sure. Just look in Bert's contacts. He's the one who stepped in and got Karl to drop his threat of a lawsuit against Eric and the fraternity."

"You're saying Eric traumatized and injured Karl White, never expressed any remorse, and he never faced any consequences?"

"Not until last year. That's when Karl White ran into some medical complications. He decided the deal he'd made with Bert wasn't to his advantage, so he tracked Eric down through their alumni association and showed up at his work. He made a very public scene and threatened to pursue civil and criminal remedies."

"So Karl wanted to go back on the agreement he'd made with Bert to stay silent?"

"That's my understanding. And that was a huge problem for Eric because when the partners heard the allegations, they decided they didn't need the baggage that came with Eric. They forced him out of his job. His chances of getting on with another law firm after that were in the toilet."

"When exactly did this happen?"

"One week before Bert's bachelor party."

"So the company blackballed Eric because of what he did to Karl White in college? Surely he could have gotten past that at some point."

Larry hesitated, then said, "That would have been possible, but Israel Castillo made sure that didn't happen."

I hadn't planned on needing a notepad to keep track of all this detail. My expectation had been that this would be a call charged with emotion for Gina and lacking in substance. Instead, I was struggling to absorb the details of Bert's dealings—and now we'd circled back to this Israel Castillo. No doubt. My brain was about to explode.

"What can you tell me about Castillo?" I asked.

"I told you. Castillo got Eric fired. His claims are public record. You should be able to find him easily. We're done. I've already said more than I should and have a meeting coming up in a few minutes. I will tell you this, though. If you really want to understand the relationship between Bert and Eric, follow the money."

He clicked off and left me staring at my phone.

40

THE WAY LARRY LAWSON ABRUPTLY ended our phone call left me momentarily stunned. Apparently, Gina felt the same. She stood, crossed her arms over her chest, and stomped to a spot in front of that massive floor-to-ceiling window with its million-dollar view. But I saw no joy in her eyes as she stared glumly out at an ocean of glinting diamonds.

Her voice quavered as she asked, "Do you think it's true? About that poor kid?"

"Gina…" I pleaded

She whirled around, her arms straight down at her sides, and demanded, "Do you?"

"Yes," I sighed. "It wouldn't be the first time that kind of ritual went too far."

Follow the money. How many times had my dad said that same thing? What I needed to focus on was how all these players, from Eric and Armand to Israel Castillo and Karl White, were all connected. And based on what little I had to go on, the one to start with was Armand.

"As much as I despise Bert for that kind of cruelty, I don't see what it has to do with his murder. Why does all this have to be connected?"

"I don't believe in coincidence, and the timing is just way too coincidental. Maybe it's nothing, but it sounds like if we find the money connection, we'll be one step closer to finding Bert's killer."

"So do you think one of them killed Bert?"

"Maybe. But it's too soon to be drawing any conclusions. It sounds like any of them could have had motive, but Armand Fraser is the one who rented the room next to Bert."

Gina lowered her gaze to the floor and squeezed her eyes shut tight. Her shoulders shook, and she moaned, "I don't want to be like Bert."

"I'm not following you, Gina. You're not like Bert at all."

She shook her head. "I lied to you. Back when I hired you. All along, too. I knew Bert was up to something, but I didn't know…." She looked at me and gave me a weak smile. "If I could trust you. I'm sorry, Jade. I was wrong."

I stood, went to her, and hugged her. She leaned against me and sobbed while I considered my next course of action. When I knew what it was, I gently pushed her away and held her at arm's length.

"We need to do what Larry suggested and follow the money. My dad once told me, 'people lie, money can't.' So let's follow the trail. I also need to track down Israel Castillo and Karl White."

I stared out the back windows of Gina's home at the ocean, contemplating the logic my dad, and now Larry Lawson, espoused. My dad had also told me I needed to prioritize. It was good advice, but which of the options came first?

"Gina, could I get a glass of water?"

Arms still folded in front of her, she glanced to her right and nodded. "Sure. Be right back."

With the weight of Gina's presence gone, I gazed out the back windows. Lazy ocean waves waltzed toward shore in a never-ending dance. The shoreline seemed to go on forever. It was just me, the California coast, and my thoughts. And in that moment, I realized Armand was the critical priority, but was dealing with him urgent? I didn't know. The money, however, was both important and urgent. And to get the story on Castillo would take a minimum of two hours.

I'd have to drive to the courthouse in San Diego to read the filing—unless I could kill two birds with one stone. Armand. Why did my thoughts keep returning to him? Because he was the one who rented the room. The third, the wannabe, member of the Inseparables. And he was the only one I could clearly link to that motel.

No coincidences, I thought. I crossed my fingers and whispered, "I hope you're right, Dad." I dialed the number for Jacqueline Brooks.

When she answered, her voice was tentative. "Hello?"

"Hi, Jacqueline. This is Jade Cavendish. I spoke with you and Armand a couple of nights ago at your work."

"I remember."

"How did Armand's business trip go?"

"What do you want?"

Ewww. Snippy. I took a breath and bit my tongue—I was looking for information, not a catfight. "That's what I like, a woman who gets straight to the point. I've come across some information about Armand's past. It appears he was friends with Bert Darlington, the man who was murdered. And yet, when we spoke, he acted like he'd never met him."

"Bert Darlington…that's the guy who attacked me. No. You have to be wrong. Armand would have told me."

"They were on the same soccer team in college. Bert and one of his teammates, a man named Eric Andrews, became business partners. A fourth member of the team told me Armand was a member of their little group, so I'm trying to determine if there was any kind of current relationship between Bert Darlington, Eric Andrews, and Armand. Have you ever heard the name Eric Andrews before?"

"What are you trying to pull? Is this some kind of sick joke?"

"It's no joke. I'd like to talk to Armand about this, but I thought you might want to be there, too."

"Leave me out of this. I don't want any part of it."

Wow. She was really in a mood. What if her anger wasn't directed at me at all? I tried to sound compassionate as I continued. "The truth is, I was hoping to get some straight answers before I started asking questions Armand might want to avoid or lie about. I remember all too well how convincingly my boyfriend lied to my face on too many occasions."

There was a long pause during which I expected to be cut off, but when Jacqueline spoke, she sounded resigned. "I wouldn't know much about what he's doing. He flew to San Francisco last night. He's not back yet. I need to get going."

"He does a lot of these out-of-town trips, doesn't he?"

"It's his job."

"Right. What about last Friday night?"

"He said he had some last-minute meetings that came up and he had to fly to Phoenix. He came back Sunday morning."

Maybe I was barking up the wrong tree. If Armand flew to Phoenix on the night of Bert's murder, how did he commit the crime? Better yet, if he was leaving town for the weekend, why would he rent a room in a dive motel he didn't intend to use? "We're talking about a week ago on Friday. You're positive he was in Phoenix that night?"

"He sent two selfies from the hotel he was staying at. I'll send them to you if you want." She paused, and her tone softened. "Your boyfriend lied to you? A lot?"

"About some very serious stuff. And those photos would help."

"Give me a sec."

Gina returned from the kitchen carrying a bamboo tray on top of which there were two coasters that matched the tray and two glasses filled with water. She placed the coasters on the tabletop, then handed me one of the glasses. I mouthed a silent thank you, took a sip, and set the glass on the coaster when my phone pinged.

"Did you get them? I sent them both."

"I did. Thanks."

In the first, Armand stood in front of Harrah's Ak-Chin Hotel and Casino. The second pictured him in front of a sign announcing the Serrano Chiles were playing that night. So much for him as a suspect. So why would he rent a motel room here… something still didn't make sense.

"Is he always gone for a few days on his business trips?" I asked.

"It's his job. It happens. Look, the more of these trips he makes, the harder it is to keep things on an even keel."

"Hey, I get it. When he leaves, you have a few days to yourself, then he comes back and you both have to readjust. Believe me, I've been there, too."

There was another uncomfortable pause, during which Gina sat at my side. She fussed with the tray, huffed a little, and fidgeted impatiently. I raised a finger to indicate the conversation would be over soon. She gave me a nod, but didn't look happy over the delay.

"Do you have any other questions?" Jacqueline asked.

"Only a few. You said he's still gone. When will he be back?"

"His flight should be landing anytime now."

"When Armand isn't traveling, does he follow the same routine?"

"He works from home for a couple hours, then goes into work at about ten."

"Ten? That's kind of late, isn't it?"

"He deals with clients on the east coast. Since he has to be on the phone super early, he usually starts his day here. There was one day a few weeks ago when he went to the office early. I remember it because he left at six, right after I got home from working a double. All I wanted to do was sleep, but he was running around the apartment like a madman trying to get out of here for some stupid meeting. I was pretty irritated at the time."

"And it's unusual for him to do that?"

"Very."

One of my favorite criminology professors once told me changes in pattern could be an investigator's best friend. It was worth a shot. "Do you remember the date?"

"I don't have a calendar in front of me, but it was a few weeks ago on a Wednesday."

The timeframe sounded familiar. Could that have been the week of Esther's attack? "Jacqueline, this could be important. Was that on Wednesday, April 12?"

There was a momentary pause, then a tentative, "Um…yeah. That's right. I pulled the double shift on the eleventh. Look, Armand just texted me. His plane has landed. I have to get going."

"Are you picking him up?"

She huffed. "You might as well know. I'm going to stay with a friend for a while. There are things I need to sort out."

I recalled Jacqueline's statement that Armand loved her unconditionally. "Jacqueline, are you sure you know what you're doing?"

"It's not what you think. I'm staying with a girlfriend. Things have just been too tense around here since Armand got back from Phoenix."

Since Phoenix? I mentally calculated how much time it would take for Armand to get his luggage and make that drive. "Do you think you're in jeopardy?"

"I don't…I don't know."

"If you're unsure, get out of there. I won't hold you up. If you think of anything else—or if you need help—just call."

Jacqueline stammered a quick thank you, and when we said our goodbyes, I had the feeling I might have finally broken through her defenses.

"That was victim number one," I said. "She's the fiancée of Armand Fraser."

Gina's lips parted, and she swallowed hard. "Bert attacked his friend's fiancée?"

"Twisted, right? Do you remember what Larry said about Armand? That he was a serial monogamist? I met this guy, and he just seemed like he was head-over-heels in love. If Bert attacked his girlfriend…who knows how he'd react? I can't imagine he'd take kindly to having his relationship torn apart."

"How did I get myself into this?" Gina asked, then bit her upper lip.

"If I could bottle that answer, I'd be rich."

Gina's brow furrowed, but she said nothing.

"Larry told us Armand didn't quite fit in with Eric and Bert," I said. "He must have had a lot of resentment over always feeling like the third wheel. It could be he decided he didn't like his status and wanted an upgrade."

"So now you think he's the killer?" She sounded more inquisitive than snarky, but maybe that was just me wishing for the best, because right now I was feeling very snarky. I wanted answers and couldn't seem to find them.

"The photos he sent Jacqueline contradict that theory," I said. "But I can't help feeling there's something creepy about the guy."

"Can I see the photos?"

I held out my phone and showed her the photo of Armand in front of the sign announcing The Serrano Chiles. Gina pointed at it.

"The sign says 'Tonight Only.' Does that help?"

"Of course. All I have to do is call the hotel to see if this is legit. If that band was playing on Friday night, it pretty much seals the deal."

It only took a moment to get the phone number for the hotel. The clerk I spoke to had to transfer me to his supervisor, but within a few minutes I had what I needed, confirmation that the Serrano Chiles had played on Friday, April 28. There was no other possible explanation—Armand Fraser had been in Phoenix on the night of Bert's murder.

It was a perfect alibi.

Too perfect.

41

THE LACK OF FINANCIAL RECORDS in Bert's home office made sense because this wasn't his actual place of business. The records would be there. That's what I told myself, anyway. As my available window of time to make it to Bert's office narrowed, I left Gina alone, instructed her to stay home, not answer the phone, and avoid standing in front of windows. Above all, avoid the cameras. She pointed out that the entire back end of the house was a wall of glass and that the paparazzi were out front, not in her backyard. We settled on not answering the phone.

With only twenty-five minutes left, I played the odds and took the side roads. The gamble paid off because I arrived with minutes to spare. Meghan was gone, but a lobby security guard gave me directions to Bert's office. When I walked in, a buxom brunette with shimmering blue eyes greeted me. She had a tissue in one hand, her mascara was mostly gone, and her eyes were rimmed in red.

"I'm sorry, but I was just on my way out," she said, her voice cracking with emotion.

I glanced at the clock; her gaze followed mine. Four-fifty-five. She looked back at me and winced. "How can I help you?"

"My name is Jade Cavendish. I'm looking into the death of Bert Darlington. Are you—were you—his assistant?"

She leaned against the desk, told me her name was Glenda, and said she missed Mr. Darlington terribly. Dabbing at the corner of her eye with a tissue, she wadded it up and tossed it into a trash can. Then, her lips pinched together in a thin line of sadness, she plucked another tissue from the box. "I don't know what I can tell you. I was only assigned to Mr. Darlington about a year ago. He was a good boss."

"Assigned? So you don't work directly for Mr. Darlington?"

"No. I work for an agency. I started right after he leased this office."

Glenda wore a conservative navy dress, matching pumps, and a gold necklace. Her attire gave her a professional appearance and conveyed the message she was a woman who expected to be taken seriously for what she could do, not what she would do. In contrast to that image, though, were her tears. They seemed over the top for someone who'd only worked with their boss for one year. It wasn't like they'd worked together for twenty. And what about the 'good boss' moniker? It was nothing like the Bert I'd been learning about—unless he operated under the philosophy of not making a mess in his own backyard.

Never having been part of the Corporate America workforce, I had no experience to draw on, but even with my limited experience, I was fairly certain that badmouthing a dead boss was a big no-no. Maybe the best option was to play along. "It sounds as though you liked him a lot."

"I didn't really know him. Not personally. He was my boss. I was his assistant. I set up his meetings, took notes, and handled his email."

Then why was she so upset? "I don't understand. You seem terribly distraught."

She choked out a sob, the sort of thing people do when they're trying to laugh and cry at the same time. "Oh." She sobbed again. "I'm sorry. Mr. Darlington was a good boss, but that's all he was. I have to put my dog down. Buddy's been my best friend since I was in tenth grade."

Oops. My bad. I nodded sympathetically. "You have nothing to be sorry about. I jumped to conclusions. I'm sorry for your loss."

"Oh…you thought. Oh, God no."

That was more like it. "Can I ask a couple of questions before you go? It will just take a moment."

"I guess."

"You said you handled his email?"

"The business account. He also had a personal account. I didn't have access to that." She glanced again at the clock. "Look, I really have to be going. I need to get to the vet—I don't want Buddy to suffer any more than he has to."

"Nice name for a dog," I said, then told her again I was sorry for her loss.

She sniffled, dabbed at her cheek absently, and shook her head. "Why does death always have to ruin things?"

I regarded her for a moment. Her eyes seemed to search mine for an answer to an impossible question. "I don't know. This has to be a terribly difficult time for you. Glenda, I know you have to get going, so I'll get right to the point. The truth is, Gina Rose, Bert's wife, is quite likely going to be charged with the murder of her husband unless I can find the real killer. I need your help."

"That's awful." She dabbed at her eyes again. "I've already said more than I should. I shouldn't be talking to you. He'll complain to the agency."

"Who will?"

"Mr. Andrews." She gritted her teeth, crossed the room to the entrance, then looked up and down the hall. When she returned, she whispered, "You can't repeat what I tell you."

I extended my hand. "Pinky swear."

For the first time since I'd entered the office, she gave me a genuine smile. "Oh God, what are we, twelve?"

"Things were easier then. Right?"

"I'm not so sure." She rolled her eyes and looked up at the ceiling.

"Me, either. Look, I know a little about Eric's background. He can be very volatile from what I've seen—especially when he drinks. He can be a bully."

She walked away, then spun on her heel to look at me with a renewed determination on her face. "Screw it. The man's an obnoxious Neanderthal. He tried to boss me around a few times. Once, he said I needed to meet him for drinks after work."

"We're talking about Eric Andrews?"

"Mr. Darlington must have told him to back off. Mr. Darlington really was nice to me. He had a way of complimenting you without making it sound like a come-on."

"Some guys are better at that than others," I said.

"The ones like Andrews don't even try."

I thought back to my dinner with Eric. Glenda didn't need to know the details, but Eric's volatility could provide the segue I needed. "You're right. When he asked you out, he made you feel uncomfortable?"

"He always made me feel that way. Until Mr. Darlington talked to him, I didn't think he knew how to turn it off. But he does, because he's kept things professional ever since."

"Glenda, have you ever heard the name Karl White?"

"Who's he?"

"He received a large sum of money from D&A."

"I've never heard the name."

"What about Israel Castillo?"

"I don't recognize that name, either."

"Does that mean you didn't handle the books?"

"You mean write the checks? Mr. Darlington handled that on his own. He was very particular and said there was a lot of money involved, so it required tight security." Her eyes lit up when she smiled. "But I have a key to the filing cabinet where he kept the register."

"He hand wrote the checks? Himself? He didn't use a computer program?"

"Mr. Darlington was old school as far as money went. He always handled it. He wouldn't even let Mr. Andrews sign checks. And then he shredded the statements when he balanced each month."

"Andrews can't sign checks? But they were partners. What happens now? Mr. Darlington is dead. Does Andrews inherit check-signing authority?"

"I don't know. There's probably something in their partnership agreement about it. That's way beyond my pay grade."

"Glenda, that register could tell us a tremendous amount about the motive behind Mr. Darlington's death."

She let out a little huff as she glanced away, then said, "Let me think about it."

"Sure. No problem." It appeared her anger with Eric had made her forget about Buddy for the moment. My pulse raced against a mental countdown of how many questions I could squeeze in before she rushed out. "How often did you see Eric Andrews?"

"Too often." She shook her head. "That's not right. He only came down every couple of weeks or so. He and Mr. Darlington had a private meeting the last time."

"Were you usually in on those meetings?"

"Not in the private ones, no. But this last time? They were both on edge, and Mr. Andrews was in an awful mood when he left. I could tell because he rushed out of here and never even looked at me."

"Did Mr. Darlington ever have a meeting or a phone call with a man named Armand Fraser?"

Again, I got the quizzical look. "Where are you coming up with these names? Did he get money, too?"

"To be honest, I'm not sure how they all tie together. Not yet, anyway."

Glenda winced and checked the time. "I really need to go."

Crap. "I understand. Just one last question. You've heard about Mr. Darlington confessing to being the Amorous Assailant, right?"

"Yes."

"I'm trying to find contacts from his schedule that might help me figure out who would have had a motive to kill him. That might even include Mr. Andrews. I really need to see his calendar."

Glenda's eyes widened, and she bit her lower lip, then a sly smile spread across her face. "I'm not sure how Mr. Andrews would feel about it, but he's not here to say no, is he?"

"He's also not here to stop you from letting me get a copy of that register. Who's going to know? I won't tell anyone where I got the information."

"Promise?"

"You want me to pinky swear again?"

"No. That's okay. You can have both. Just don't tell anyone. I'll have the agency transfer me, anyway. There's no way I even want to be alone in the same room with that man again."

A few minutes later, Glenda had copied Bert's calendar for the past two months and also made copies of the check register pages. When she handed me the calendar, I noticed an identical entry every Monday at six p.m.

I held it out so Glenda could see it and pointed to the entry. "Do you know what this is?"

"It was one of those things he would never discuss. I guess it's some kind of regular business meeting. That's the address."

"Are you sure? Garfield Street? I'm almost positive that's right near Magee Park."

"I live in Oceanside, so I don't really know this area that well. He never needed to prepare for the meeting, so I didn't worry about it." She glanced at the clock and winced. "Oh, God. I really have to go. Buddy needs me."

With a copy of the checkbook register and Bert's calendar in hand, I gave Glenda a tender hug and expressed my condolences one last time. I had just enough time to return to the office, gobble down whatever goodies Mom had packed, and make it to Bert's six o'clock meeting.

42

ON THE DRIVE TO THE agency, my stomach growled in anticipation of Mom's little care package. Those packages been a staple in my college days. In some ways, having one waiting for me was a reminder of how much I'd enjoyed academic life. With only a half hour before I had to leave for Bert's meeting, I found a spot close to the office and walked the two remaining blocks.

When I turned the corner, I saw a man wearing a leather bomber jacket pacing outside the Beachtown Detective Agency front door. It was Armand Fraser. What was he doing here? My nerve endings tingled as I closed the distance between us. When he spotted me, he stuffed his hands in his pockets and strode purposefully in my direction.

I did a quick survey of the area. It was mostly walkers and tourists, none of whom seemed to pay us much attention. I didn't expect trouble. That didn't mean I would let down my guard. Armand's face was a deep scarlet, up to and including his forehead. Anger etched itself into every line. He pointed an accusing finger at me and sputtered, "What have you done?"

I stopped just outside of striking distance, balanced my weight on the balls of my feet, and flexed my knees. "I don't know what you're talking about."

"You ruined everything with Jacqueline. We were fine when I left town. I come back and she's moved out. You and your stupid questions. You planted doubt and suspicion in her mind."

"Slow down, Armand. I did talk to Jacqueline, but all she said was she was going to stay with a friend. I thought her trip was temporary." Okay, it was a blatant lie, but he didn't need to know that, did he?

He grumbled something unintelligible, shook his head, and hissed, "She took all her stuff."

"Everything?"

"The apartment is empty."

Holy crap. I guess she hadn't needed my advice. She must have planned her escape well before I told her to leave.

"She left this." He pulled a piece of paper from his pocket and shoved it at me. It was a note telling him they were over. He pointed at a line that said she'd been thinking about their relationship a lot lately.

"I know how you women work. That's code for her talking to you and you making her doubt my love."

"This says nothing about me."

"Oh yeah? Your card was on the counter next to the note. Why are you out to ruin my life?"

He inched closer, slowly encroaching on what I considered a safe distance. Rather than backing away, I held my position and let my irritation surge. "Back off, Armand. Or I'll call the police."

A look of panic overcame him, and he slowly took a small step back. "Sorry, I didn't mean to scare you," he stammered. "We don't need the cops."

"I called Jacqueline to find out where you were the night Bert Darlington was killed. She told me you were in Phoenix."

"That's right."

Narrowed eyes. Hard swallow. I had him worried.

"Why'd you talk to her?" he blurted. "You should have come to me. In fact, why do you even care where I was that night?"

"Because you were friends with Bert Darlington. You pretended you didn't know him the night I spoke to you and Jacqueline. Why didn't you disclose your relationship when I asked about him?"

"I thought you were just talking to her, not me."

I heard the wheels of a skateboard about two seconds before Whistler zoomed by, nearly taking out me in the process. He called out an apology over his shoulder as he sped away. Armand had only avoided the near collision by taking a step to the side. This was one time I didn't mind Whistler's little games.

"That's right, Armand. He's a friend. And he can place you here if something happens."

It was total BS because Whistler probably hadn't been paying attention. Armand didn't know that, though. I stared at him until he looked away. The shift in power dynamics was almost as strong as the ocean's surf. Armand knew he was no longer in control, and I intended to make the most of his newfound uncertainty.

"Don't lie to me, Armand. I know you've been friends with Bert since college. I've seen the photo in Bert's office. You were all on the soccer team—you, Eric Andrews, and Bert. Now, maybe you want to level with me before I call Detective Martini and turn you into a murder suspect."

A man watched us closely as he approached. Not sure whether he was a gawker or a well-intentioned Good Samaritan, I made eye contact. "It's all under control," I said.

He nodded, quickened his pace, and avoided looking in our direction again.

Armand massaged his forehead with his fingertips. His breaths came fast now. I recognized the symptoms. Fear had taken hold. I pulled out my phone and held it up. "What's it going to be? Talk to me? Or the police?"

"Okay, okay." He threw his palms up. "I knew Bert. Eric, too. And I figured it would look bad if it came up, so I just didn't say anything. Sorry."

"It would look bad to who? Me? Or Jacqueline?"

"I didn't kill him. I swear." He locked his gaze on the sidewalk, wrapped his arms one over the other in front of him, and hunched forward.

"I'm not sure I believe you. Did you know what Bert was doing?"

"What do you mean?"

"The attacks. Did you know about them? A man fitting your description broke up the one on Esther Simpson. That's the day you left for work at six a.m. Don't lie, Armand. All I have to do is show her your photo and I'll know the truth."

"All right! I knew what Bert was doing. Okay? Eric told me. Me and Eric were worried. We kept thinking, what if he goes too far sometime?"

"Too far? What's too far? More than tying up a woman and kissing her?"

Armand's eyes darted off to the side. "Bert had to keep a low profile since he got married. The whole Amorous Assailant thing was a way for him to get back in the game. It was just innocent fun."

Heat surged through my veins. Fun? Even worse, both Eric and Armand had known about the attacks? I wanted to kick Armand where it counted so bad. After that, I could track down

Eric and do the same. Vigilante justice might not be legal, but at this moment it would feel immensely satisfying.

"There was nothing innocent about any of those attacks. How did you know where Esther's attack would be? Why did you stop it? Did you think he was going to go too far that time?"

"No! I don't know."

"So you're a caped crusader now? You roam the streets saving women? I don't buy that for one second." I stopped, stared at him, and felt my jaw go slack as a piece of the puzzle clunked into place. "Wait a minute. You knew what he was doing. That must mean breaking up the attack on Esther was a way to get back at Bert because he attacked Jacqueline. Was that it?"

The bright ribbons of anger that had been in Armand's face drained. I'd hit a chord. His role must have had something to do with Jacqueline.

"Yes," he whispered. "What he did to Jacqueline was wrong."

"Did Eric know in advance that her attack was coming?"

"No."

"Liar."

Armand's eyes widened. He bit his lower lip and pressed his fingers to his temples. "I never should have trusted him!"

"Trusted who?" I demanded.

"Bert," he whispered, then broke eye contact. "I told him about the problems me and Jacqueline were having. He's the one who said all we needed to do was scare her and she'd come around."

Scare her? My blood boiled at the very thought of what he meant. I looked back at Armand and caught the fear in his eyes. He knew on a deep level that what Bert had suggested was wrong, yet he'd gone along with it. Larry Lawson's comment now made perfect sense—Armand was always the third wheel.

Hanging on to be a part of the group. No matter how much I wanted to go for the jugular, I needed to keep my cool. I could always throat-punch him later.

"What problems?" I asked.

"Marriage. I've asked Jacqueline to set a date several times. We've been together so long now…it's time."

"I see…so you're the victim in all this? I thought you two met just over a year ago."

He resumed eye contact and gave me a smarmy grin. "When you're sure, why wait?"

He was smooth. I had to give him that. What I didn't know was if he'd lost his fear or had donned a mask to hide it. We were about to find out. I smiled at him and leaned closer. "Sure. I get it. You're ready. But maybe she's not. Is that why you wanted to scare her?"

"Me? No! I told you. It was Bert's idea. He's the one who wanted to…"

"What? Frighten her into marriage?"

The confident smile dropped away, and he stared at me with a classic deer-in-the-headlights image.

"You went along with it, Armand. You could have stopped it before it happened. And yet, you did nothing. And that makes you an accomplice to this whole perverse scheme."

"You're wrong. The Amorous Assailant was all Bert's idea."

I laughed at how ludicrous the statement sounded. "Are you serious? You're reaching, Armand. Why did Bert tie up your fiancée with red silk and kiss her on the cheek? Did you two come up with the idea all by yourselves—or was the third inseparable there when you two hatched this little plan?"

"What do you know?" he hissed.

"I know all about the Three Inseparables. The bullying. The payoffs."

His jaw dropped, and he stared at me. My pulse picked up. I leaned forward, forcing him to take another step away. I had him.

"You tell me what you know about Israel Castillo right now, or I'm calling the cops." I held up my phone, my finger poised over the emergency button.

He swallowed hard and shook his head. "I had nothing to do with that."

"You're lying to me again. I can see it on your face." I couldn't really, but it sounded so good.

Through gritted teeth, he snapped, "I don't have time for this. Thanks to you, I have to go see Jacqueline. Straighten this out."

"After you tell me about Castillo."

"Fine." He threw up his hands. Glanced at his watch. "He worked at the same law firm as Eric. It wasn't like they were friends or anything, but they attended some social functions. Eric didn't even like the guy."

"Why?"

Another huff. "Because he was always paying too much attention to Mary."

"Mary? Eric's wife?"

Crap! The moment I asked the question, I knew I'd lost ground. He now realized how little I knew about Eric. It was too late. The trace of a smile had already formed on Armand's face again.

"Yeah, his wife," he said confidently. The tightness in Armand's cheeks softened and the frantic undertones that had been in his voice earlier disappeared.

He thought he had me—little did he know.

43

ARMAND WATCHED A COUPLE STROLLING hand-in-hand. His jaw muscles tightened as he pulled his attention from them to me. "That's right. Eric didn't like Israel Castillo paying so much attention to his wife. It wasn't like he was a great husband or anything. I saw him with his daughter a couple times. Eric's a good dad, but a lousy husband." He stuffed his hands in his pockets and shrugged. "Not much more to tell. He's got his act together now."

"That's not even worth my time. We'll let the cops sort this out."

"Go ahead."

"How's Jacqueline going to feel when the cops start interrogating her about you?"

Armand jerked back as if he'd been slapped. The intensity of his stare intensified. "What's with you?" He threw up a hand and balled his fist, but rather than striking out, began to ramble. "When Mary filed for divorce, she and Israel started seeing each other. She said he was helping her deal with the divorce and that they were just friends. Eric didn't believe her and started threatening Israel at work. Eric told him to stay away from Mary and especially his daughter. He claimed his daughter wasn't safe with Israel around."

"Was that true?"

"It was all bogus. Eric doesn't like to lose."

"Did Israel retaliate by getting Eric fired?"

"Nobody knows for sure."

"That's a crock and you know it."

"How would I know what happened? I wasn't there."

Maybe he hadn't been there, but I was willing to bet he'd heard plenty. What else was he hiding? Bert's murder, perhaps? I raised the phone; his eyes followed. "Do I really have to tell you how much trouble you're in and what's about to happen? I'm sure once the cops talk to Israel, you'll have more explaining to do."

"Just leave the cops out of this. We don't need them." He took a deep breath and blurted, "Me and Eric…we kind of tried to change Israel's mind."

I stiffened as pins and needles coursed down my spine. Oh, no. What had they done? "How?" I demanded.

"Israel told Eric he was going to complain to the partners about him. You know? He thought Eric was creating a hostile work environment. That night, we sort of met up with him after work to make him see things differently."

Armand must have caught the look of outrage on my face because he quickly continued.

"We were only bluffing. We never meant to hurt him. So when Israel said he wasn't going to let up, Eric backed down. We never touched the guy."

My pulse raced. It was time. Armand was so off balance now. I could see he had little fight left in him. And I was so ready to do this. "I know you rented the room at the Sunny Days Inn."

"No…no. Now you're just making accusations to upset me. Why won't you leave me alone?"

"Stop whining, Armand. Nobody likes a whiner. The clerk positively identified you. She'll testify under oath if she has to."

"There's no crime in renting a room for the night," he shot back.

"I agree, but what doesn't make sense is why you rented a motel room when you were leaving for Phoenix."

"It was supposed to be a surprise for Jacqueline. But a last-minute meeting came up. I had to leave town and was in Phoenix the night Bert was killed."

The way he said the words, I was convinced he'd known Bert was going to die that night. He'd rented the room as his alibi. "You were going to take her to a cheap motel to surprise her? You're delusional—or still lying. I saw your alibi photos. You could have easily hopped the next flight back to San Diego, driven here, and killed Bert."

"No. I was in Phoenix. All night. You can check."

"It's a slick alibi, but it won't hold up for long. Not once the police put some resources on it. They'll check with your employer to see if you really did have a meeting in Phoenix."

"You're just intent on destroying my life, aren't you?"

"You seem to have quite a fixation on that, but I'd say you're the one who's doing a good job of it. And you're the one who destroyed your shot at marrying Jacqueline, not me."

He rubbed the back of his neck and slowly hunched forward. "I have to talk to her. I need to explain before she starts hearing all these lies." He took two steps backwards, then turned away and fled.

I watched until he rounded the corner. When he didn't reappear, I went into my office, locked the door behind me, and dialed Jacqueline. I explained that Armand might be trying to find her.

"There's something else you should know." I said. "I believe Armand is somehow connected to the Amorous Assailant attacks."

"What's that supposed to mean?"

"I don't have proof positive, but I think Armand had Bert Darlington attack you so you'd marry him."

She uttered a string of expletives, then said, "I hate that man! He'll pay for this."

The line went dead, and the image of another of Zoe's inflammatory headlines flashed before my eyes—*Crazed Fiancée goes on Shooting Rampage*. I dialed Jacqueline's number again. The call went to voicemail and the second-guessing began.

How was she going to make Armand pay? Would I get dragged into things? Maybe I should have kept my mouth shut until I had proof. Then again, why? Armand admitted he knew about the Amorous Assailant attacks. He hadn't stopped them. He might have even been involved in the planning of Jacqueline's attack. It seemed highly unlikely he was simply collateral damage in Bert's little game. Armand was right about one thing. I needed more information before I went around destroying lives. I groaned and tapped the screen to redial Jacqueline's number. No answer.

My email pinged. I checked to see who'd sent it. Gina. *My accountant told me how to get the list of payments super quick. See attached. G.*

I opened the attached document, a plain text file with rows for dates and amounts paid. My eyes crossed as I ran my finger down the amounts column. There were more payments than Gina had told me about at the start. What a nightmare. How was I going to make heads or tails of this? There weren't that many entries, but we'd gone from about a half million to…I scanned the list. Just eyeballing it, this easily totaled more like about

$700k. And it couldn't possibly include the house, furnishings, or other purchases.

I picked up my phone to call Gina, but changed my mind. It was nearly five-thirty. I had to leave for Bert's meeting in fifteen minutes. What was I going to do? Call her a foolish idiot and make things worse? I dialed Jacqueline's number again, got no answer, and turned back to the list.

My first step was to get a hard copy. I sent the document to the printer and numbered each line on the printout. There were fifteen payments altogether. I ran the total twice just to make sure. The grand total was $690,000. Gina had told me Bert's company lost money eight months in a row. Sure enough, there were eight payments in the amount of $10,000 identified as working capital. They began on July 3 and continued at regular intervals until recently. I highlighted each of the eight lines in yellow and labeled them as a monthly transfer.

Even with access to Bert's check register, I doubted if I'd be able to verify what those ten-thousand-dollar payments covered. Most of the register amounts jived with Gina's list, but there were some big transactions that weren't in both places. The first of those was the very first payment to Bert. Two full months before the wedding, Gina had given him ten-thousand dollars. It wasn't in Bert's records. What was the big mystery?

Six weeks after the mystery payment, Gina wrote a check to Bert for fifty-thousand dollars. Bert had written in the description, "startup capital." There was also a payment from Gina to Bert for the same amount on June 16. While the two payments for $50k were in Bert's register, that first one for ten thousand was nowhere to be found. What had Bert done with that first $10,000?

The mystery payment was before the business started. Before the wedding. It was enough money to—oh, gawd—I had a sick feeling I knew the answer. Closing my eyes, I whispered the mantra, "Please make me be wrong. Please make me be wrong."

But when I opened my eyes and looked again at the dates, only one thing made sense. Poor Gina. She'd been raised to be a financial wizard, but had been a fool in love. I made a note next to the payment—*when did Bert buy the rings?*

The remaining six payments were much larger and seemed to be spaced randomly. The first happened on August 1, 2016. Gina gave Bert $150,000; he made a corresponding deposit on the same day. The following day, he wrote a check to Israel Castillo. The queasiness I'd felt before deepened to outright disgust.

In January 2017, Israel was back. Sure enough, Gina gave Bert 200K. He made his deposit, but then split the money equally between Karl White and Israel. Each of them got one hundred thousand dollars. I wondered if either of them knew their cash cow was dead.

Another puzzling transaction was the one on November 18. I caught it for two reasons. First, it was another $200,000 infusion from Gina. Second, the money transaction took place three days before the first Amorous Assailant attack on November 21. Another coincidence? Probably not. So why were the transactions in such close proximity to the attack on Jacqueline?

Even more strange, however, was the person Bert had paid. It was Eric Andrews. On a hunch, I went to the public records database we used and searched for Eric's name. It took only a minute to see that one month after Mary Andrews filed for a temporary restraining order against her husband, she turned around and withdrew the order.

Maybe Bert gave Eric $200,000 in November to pay off his wife and convince her to drop the TRO. But why did that happen just one week before the first attack? What kind of twisted scheme was this? And what did it all have to do with Bert's Amorous Assailant persona?

I wanted to dig further into Bert's finances, but I was already running late for his meeting. It would be a week before I could get to the next one. I had so many questions. So few answers. Bert Darlington. The Amorous Assailant. The payoffs. It all had to be connected, and it was up to me to figure out how.

The most bizarre part of this whole mess was that despite her Ivy League education, Gina let herself be duped. Everybody around her had made tons of money at her expense. January must have been the point at which she realized she was being taken advantage of. Maybe her tax guy talked sense into her; maybe she just got tired of Bert's constant requests for money. Either way, it must have been the beginning of the end.

I locked the door behind me on my way out, but even as I hurried to my car, I kept coming back to the timing of that November payment, the Amorous Assailant attack, and Eric's divorce.

By the time I reached my car and was behind the driver's seat, I'd come up with a new, more troubling, question. What if the attacks were actually a smokescreen for something more sinister?

44

I CALLED GINA FROM THE car and told her I was on my way to a meeting I'd discovered on Bert's calendar. I didn't divulge my suspicion that it was at a local park, but did ask if she had any idea what this could be about.

"I'm clueless," she said. "Bert just told me he always had to work late on Mondays. I thought it was weird, but…I didn't want to seem naggy."

She then broached the subject I'd been hoping to avoid—had I made progress on tracking the money she'd given Bert? I'd already seen Jacqueline's reaction at the news about Armand and didn't particularly want to set Gina off, too. Doing my best to tread lightly, I explained how her money had been used, trying desperately to avoid using a hot-button word like payoff. My efforts were unsuccessful.

"So it's true? He wasn't using my money for investments, but to bribe people? Who were these people? I'll bet they were to women he'd had affairs with."

"I don't think so."

"This is Eric, then. When I gave Bert the two-hundred-thousand in November, I told him I wanted an explanation. I was tired of doling out all this cash. He said one of Eric's parents was sick and needed chemo. According to Bert, they didn't have insurance. You're telling me he lied to my face? What did Eric use the money for?"

Things went downhill from there, but at least Gina realized I was only the messenger. In the end, she confessed she now realized how little she knew about her husband. She finished off her tirade with a short, "He lied to me. And I never saw it."

"I don't know if this will make you feel any better, but it appears he lied to a lot of people."

I pulled into a parking space on Garfield Street, then took the sidewalk toward the main parking lot. As I walked, I surveyed the park. There was a beautiful little gazebo in the middle of a grassy area. To the right of the gazebo was Heritage Hall, one of three historic buildings in the park.

This evening, the usual crowd of dog walkers, joggers, and lovers dotted the park, but a small group sat around the gazebo in portable, white-plastic chairs. I wondered if that was Bert's regular meeting. An onshore breeze added a mild chill to the air. A few of the members of the group, I counted fourteen men and five women, wore light jackets. Others were dressed in typical SoCal style, sweatshirts and shorts. A lanky man standing at the north end of the gathering saw me approach and smiled. He was in the process of welcoming newcomers by asking their names and why they'd come. The woman he was talking to as I entered their meeting space spoke softly. I had difficulty making out her words, but the meaning was immediately clear—this was an Alcoholics Anonymous meeting.

When the woman finished, the leader faced me, introduced himself as Robert, and asked my first name. Of all the things I'd been prepared for, an AA meeting was not one of them. I felt the heat in my cheeks and wondered whether I should stay or go.

"My name is Jade. I'm just a visitor. I'm actually here about Bert Darlington."

"Welcome Jade," Robert and the others in the group said. Then Robert continued on his own. "We missed Bert at the last meeting. Do you have news about him? I hope he's okay."

Was that code for, did he start drinking again? Did he overdose? How did I politely tell him Bert wouldn't be attending meetings anymore? I couldn't. "Bert is…um…deceased. I was hoping to talk to someone who knew him." There were whispers around the group. All eyes now turned in my direction. "I'm sorry, I didn't mean to interrupt."

A hand went up to my right. An elderly man. Trim beard. Craggy face. He looked like the kind of man my mom would say had suffered a hard life.

"I knew Bert." The man who had raised his hand stood, bracing himself on the back of the chair in front of him. "Not well, but maybe enough to help you out."

I couldn't tell what the murmurs throughout the group meant. Had I breached the rules of the group? Committed a major faux pax? Or were they appreciative that someone else spoke up?

"We'll just continue while you two talk," Robert said.

The elderly man side-stepped himself between a pair of chairs. He limped toward me and motioned with a crook of his neck toward the walkway.

"What happened to your leg?" I asked.

"Auto accident." He smiled weakly and shrugged. "It was the beginning of the end for me. I'm Jerry." He gestured at a park bench on the other side of a small bed of roses. It was far enough away that we wouldn't disturb the group, but close enough for him to make the walk without difficulty. "Let's sit there."

We made our way to the bench in silence, then sat. Without waiting for a question, Jerry said, "I saw the news story. He really was murdered?"

"The police are convinced his wife killed him, but I believe her when she says she didn't do it."

"You're working for Gina Rose?"

"You've heard of her?"

"Of course. She's very…outgoing."

"Is my working for her a problem?"

"Not at all. I just like to know who I'm talking to. I spoke to Bert on several occasions. We went for coffee a few times. There are things he told me I know to be true, and some I can surmise based on the things he didn't say."

"Such as?"

Jerry stroked his grizzled chin. At one point, he'd been a handsome man. These days, he appeared broken and resigned. There was a sadness in his eyes, and I wondered how long ago his life had changed.

"Bert had been coming to these meetings for several months. I tried to befriend him—he seemed like he needed someone." Jerry paused, grimaced, then continued. "My sense is he was a very lonely—and troubled—young man. And I'm not just saying that because he was an alcoholic."

"Why do you say he was lonely?"

Jerry glanced back toward the group. "In some ways, all of us who are here are isolated. We've done things that have tested the patience of our loved ones. Bert wasn't yet ready to admit he caused his problems, though. He was going through the motions, but he didn't seem to have the strength to succeed. He was always looking for the easy way out."

Talk about a man with insight into the soul of Bert Darlington. It all tracked perfectly with the manipulator image and the lies he'd told to Gina and others. "How did you learn so much about him?"

"He opened up during one of our get-togethers. Basically, he was complaining about all the pressure he was under. He had a friend who was in trouble, his company was losing money, and his wife was calling him a failure. I don't know how much of it was true, but he seemed to think getting rid of his wife would solve all his problems."

I stared at Jerry, my mind reeling from the convoluted weaving together of fact and fiction—and from the way he'd phrased something. "Is that how he said it? He wanted to get rid of Gina? He didn't say divorce?"

"I think he intended to say his friend wanted to get rid of his wife, but slipped. He definitely said he needed to get rid of his wife. At the time, I assumed he meant divorce, but he never did say that word. It gave me a bad feeling."

"I can see why. If Gina died, Bert would get everything. But in a divorce, he'd have to negotiate for every penny."

Jerry pulled in a long breath, gazing at one of the rose bushes as he thought. When he blew out the breath, he said, "With the way he looked at life, marriage would have been difficult for both of them."

"I was never there to see the interactions between him and Gina, but according to her, she thought Bert was manipulating her for money. Stealing, basically. That's why she hired me."

"Yes. The news stories painted quite the sordid picture about the Amorous Assailant attacks when Bert was arrested. That's when I started connecting the dots. I'm not a shrink, but I have some background in dealing with people like him, and I believe Bert was a pathological liar. The signs were there—feeling like he had to be in the spotlight, inconsistencies in his story—you know, little things didn't add up."

"The attacks certainly put him in the spotlight."

"Yes, they did. It seemed odd at the time, but he never expressed disapproval about them, either. Everyone else I know did, but not Bert. Of course, his attitude made much more sense after his arrest. I must say, Bert seemed to relish setting people on edge." Jerry paused as a frail old woman pushed her husband's wheelchair by us on the walkway. When they were out of earshot, he continued. "You know, in looking back at it now, his behavior was even worse when he brought his business partner to one of the meetings."

"Excuse me? He brought Eric Andrews here?"

"We only knew him as Eric. They did say they were in business together. Actually, Bert joked about them being partners in crime."

"That's what they called themselves?"

"Yes. And the funny thing is the business partner was very uncomfortable in this type of setting. Just to be clear, I'm referring to the help group, not the park."

"So Eric never returned?"

"That's right. It happens—someone gets pushed into being here. I could see why he might not come back. What I don't understand is why Bert did. Unless this was a place where he could anonymously brag about his accomplishments."

"Wow," I said and let out a slow breath. A gust blew through the park, a reminder that we were only a couple of blocks from the coast. With the coming of evening, a band of gray clouds were marching onshore. "Do you see that kind of behavior often?"

"Not very."

"Jerry, did Bert ever mention women? Other than when he was complaining about Gina?"

"Bert never provided details about anything. Even when he was complaining about his wife, he didn't provide specifics. After listening to him a few times, I realized nothing he talked about could ever be proven. I stopped trying to be his friend when I realized he didn't come here to get sober."

He paused and looked back at the group. A heavyset man, his hair pulled back in a ponytail, leaned on a cane as he spoke to the group. A smile formed on Jerry's face and he said, "I really need to get back. Bill had a breakthrough this week, and I'd like to congratulate him."

"Of course. I'll let you go. Do you think anyone else will talk to me?"

"I doubt it. The only reason I did was because I've been in your shoes before. I was a cop for twenty-five years—and then one day I wasn't."

45

I THANKED JERRY FOR SPEAKING to me and watched him return to the group. A few expectant faces looked in his direction, then cast wary glances at me. Before returning to his seat, Jerry went to the heavyset man and shook his hand. Except for the few who had shown their obvious suspicion, the others made a point of ignoring me. Perhaps Jerry was right. They probably wouldn't be so forthcoming.

The sun was dropping fast now. Streamers of pink and purple laced the sky, interrupted here and there by fingers of gray fog that inched their way inland. The ringing of my cell phone jarred me back to the here-and-now. It was Jacqueline. Good. I hoped she'd finally come to her senses.

"Hey, Jacqueline. I'm glad you returned my call."

"He's here," she hissed.

"Who?"

"Armand. How did he find me? Did you tell him?"

"I don't have your address. He's at your apartment? Is he trying to get in? You should call 9-1-1, not me."

"He's in his car. Across the street. Watching. He's just sitting there watching the apartment."

My heart pounded in my chest. What had I triggered? "Tell me where you're at. I'd really like to talk to him again. But if he comes to the door, call the police immediately."

She gave me the address, which was in an older neighborhood near I-5. It was an area where the cheap apartments left over from the fifties and sixties were slowly giving way to newer, larger complexes. Cars filled the available parking spaces on both sides of the street. Armand sat in his car, the engine running, in front of a fire hydrant.

I texted Jacqueline to let her know the cavalry had arrived.

This neighborhood exemplified the problem of parking in many parts of San Diego—the number of cars had long ago outstripped the number of spaces. In this case, that was going to be my advantage. I double-parked next to Armand's car and turned on my flashers. The red-hot anger building within him clearly showed on his face. He looked ready to boil over as he watched me exit my car and approach.

No problem. I had a plan.

I pulled out my phone and held it so he could see my finger poised over the emergency key.

He shoved his door open and stood in the street a few feet away from me. Armand hissed, "What are you doing here?"

"The bigger question is, why are you here? Jacqueline called me because she saw you sitting in your car. How did you even know where she was?"

Without making eye contact, he stammered, "I found the address."

"Where?"

Still avoiding my gaze, he mumbled, "In her contacts."

How did he get into her contacts? Unless… "What did you do? Go into her phone and download everything when she wasn't paying attention?" When he didn't answer, I said, "You did, didn't you? So when she disappeared, you started calling all of them?"

"Why won't you let up? What do you have against me?"

"Other than you're a jealous, insecure man who has bad taste in friends and whines a lot? Unless you can prove you had nothing to do with Bert's death, you might be facing murder charges."

He slumped back against his car and crossed his arms over his chest. "I didn't do it!" he growled.

"I don't believe you, Armand. And I don't think Jacqueline's the kind of girl who will pine away while you rot in prison. Once I tell the police you're the one who rented the room next to Bert's, they'll figure out how you faked your alibi and you'll be spending the rest of your life in prison."

Armand looked like a man whose knees were ready to buckle. Still leaning against his car, he finally looked me in the eye. "It was Eric's idea to rent the room."

Oh, how I'd love to believe that. But I needed more than a baseless allegation from a man who blamed everyone else for his troubles. "Why would Eric Andrews have you rent a room you weren't going to use? You can't shift the blame that easily."

"It's true!"

"Seriously? What little game is this? Pointing the finger elsewhere isn't going to save you. You're still an accessory. And under California law, you might as well have been the one who drugged Bert and put that rope around his neck. Even if they don't get you on an accessory charge, there's always obstruction of justice. You're facing serious jail time no matter how this falls out."

Armand groaned and stared down the street. I followed his gaze. A black SUV pulled up behind my car. The driver glared at me as he pulled out and rolled past. Armand seemed not to notice any of it.

"There's another option," I said.

With a start, Armand peered at me. "What?"

"If you cooperate and tell us everything you know, you'll be in a much better position to strike a deal."

The only way I was going to get the truth was to let Armand tell his version of the story. I waited, letting the silence weigh on him and, as he stared off into space, I felt a growing certainty he was debating two ugly alternatives—be the rat or the one accused of murder.

"The Amorous Assailant was Bert's idea," he said, his voice shaking with emotion.

Dad was right. Self-preservation always won. "Go on," I coaxed.

"It was only supposed to be Jacqueline, and Bert promised he wouldn't hurt her, but then he got really jacked up during the attack. When he got all kinds of news coverage, he started talking about doing it again. I didn't know about the second victim until after it happened."

"It was because of your complaints about Jacqueline not being ready to marry that Bert got started?"

A nod. "I agreed because I thought she'd…need me more afterwards. I never expected him to get off on all the publicity. But he loved it. Couldn't get enough."

I deliberately kept my voice level as I asked, "Other than Jacqueline, how did Bert pick his victims?"

"He'd go to a coffee shop, hang out, and find one he thought would be fun."

"Fun? Do you even realize what you just said?"

"I know the whole idea was wrong."

"Wrong doesn't even come close." My anger was now on a full rolling boil. I had to level out and not let this moron get to me. As twilight settled in, the light softened. Purple and rose-colored clouds now dominated the sky. Lights glowed behind window coverings in most of the apartments. Taking a deep breath, I shifted my position and focused on my goal—getting information, not physical retribution. To save my client, I had to find Bert's killer, not seek justice for the Amorous Assailant's victims.

"It's done. Okay? Now that Bert's dead…" He winced and his voice trailed off.

"No, Armand. It's far from done. Mary Andrews took out a restraining order against her husband in November, but withdrew her complaint and filed for divorce two weeks later. At the same time, Bert gave Eric two-hundred-thousand dollars. I'm betting the money was a payoff."

Armand's jaw dropped, then he swallowed hard. In that moment, I think he realized he'd underestimated how much I knew.

"Yes," he said. "Eric said it was all bogus, but it was going to cost him a bundle either way, so he paid her off."

"So Bert gave him the money—and wanted something in return. That's a lot of cash, so it must have been a big favor."

"Eric didn't want to do it."

"What was the favor?"

"It didn't happen. Okay? Eric reneged."

"You do not get to pull that crap. If you lie, you won't get anything. The DA will take a very dim view of an uncooperative witness. What was the favor?"

Armand turned around, placed his forearms on the roof of his car, and laid his head down. He sighed once, then stood up straight. "Bert asked Eric to help him kill Gina."

Holy crap. Jerry had been right? "What? So he could get control of Gina's money?"

"Yes."

"So your story is that Bert decided the only way to get Gina's money was to kill her, and Eric didn't want to do it because he's in love with her? Is that what you're going with?"

"Yes. We had to stop him."

"And you couldn't turn him in because he'd take both of you down with him."

Armand hung his head. He muttered something unintelligible.

"Who's idea was it to get rid of Bert?" I demanded.

"Eric. He started talking about ending things with Bert back in November."

"Right after Bert bailed him out." Armand seemed to be an expert at pointing fingers everywhere but at himself. I resisted the urge to swat him like the insect he was. Or to tell him he was a fool if he thought he could lie his way out of his role in a murder conspiracy. "Do you have proof of this alleged plot?"

"No. Bert was very cautious. So was Eric."

"What happened Friday night?"

"I don't know. I really don't because I wasn't here. All I was supposed to do was rent the room, get the key to Eric, then fly to Phoenix."

"Whose idea were the selfies you sent?"

Armand glanced toward the apartment as though he were expecting to see Jacqueline. I did my own check just to be sure. There was no sign of her.

"She's not coming," I said, then repeated my question.

"The photos were Eric's idea. He said I needed a bulletproof alibi."

"Do you really expect people to believe Eric killed his best friend to win over his wife? That's pretty farfetched, Armand."

"It's the truth!"

"It sounds like a fairytale to me. The only proof you weren't here are those photos. But Phoenix is just an hour's flight. With time for commuting to the airport thrown in, you could still make the trip in less than three hours. And you could drive it in four. Do you really want to spend the rest of your life in jail?"

"I need a lawyer."

"More like a shrink. Where's Eric?"

"We were supposed to meet at Fat Cat's at eight. Be careful, he's probably been drinking."

I wasn't worried. I had a Taser, a gun, and a strong urge to bury my fist into Eric's face.

46

A TAN SUV WITH A bad case of oxidized paint on the hood inched by us. Just like the previous one, the driver gave me a dirty look as he passed. I waved him through, but recognized it as a sign this game was coming to a close.

Armand hadn't given me anything that, at least immediately, could land him in police custody. I could bluster and bully him the way I had for only so long. His statements were hearsay, pure and simple. Out of my presence, he could flip and turn me into the aggressor. And if he played his cards right, the cops might even commend him for breaking up the Amorous Assailant attack on Esther Simpson.

"I have a real problem, Armand. I don't know what to do with you. Letting you go is not an option. You'll either run straight to Eric or head for the border. I hate both of those options."

"I don't want anything to do with Eric. He'll have my head if he finds out I talked to you."

I needed help. Someone to watch Armand while I went to deal with Eric. I ran through the possibilities: my dad—not a good choice unless I wanted to arm wrestle him over who would stay here and who would go to Fat Cat's; Roger Lowe—given his relationship with Des, not likely; Zoe—seriously? Not even.

There was only one other person I could think of who could handle this immediately. I pulled out my phone, dialed Jacqueline's number, and explained what I wanted her to do. She showed up about two minutes later with her friend, both looking determined and fearless.

Jacqueline immediately started in on Armand. I had to force her to back off, then asked if either of them owned a Taser. They both shook their heads.

Crap. I had one, but I didn't want to leave it in untrained hands to guard a guy who could go ballistic at any moment. I ordered Armand to give me his keys and his cell phone, which he did. Handing over my Taser to Jacqueline made my skin crawl, but she needed protection, so I caved and gave her a quick lesson on how to use it.

Five minutes later, I was on my way to Fat Cat's, all the while praying that nothing would go wrong in a situation fraught with bad possibilities. I was two blocks away when my common sense kicked in. What was I thinking? Armand might be a killer. What if he overpowered Jacqueline? Or simply ran? Leaving two angry and frightened women in charge of a murder suspect was lunacy.

"Screw it," I said and made two quick right turns. On my way back to Armand's car, I called my dad. I needed to put results and safety first. Dad could easily keep Armand in place while I dealt with Eric. The question was, would I keep control of the situation or was I relinquishing it? Dad arrived within ten minutes and double parked directly behind me.

"What do you need me to do?" Dad asked as he approached.

"Keep this one here until I have a chance to deal with Eric Andrews."

"The guy from the restaurant? He's dangerous, Jade. Tell me where he's at. I'll deal with him."

"No," I said firmly. "This is my case. I know the facts. I know how to break this guy. You don't."

Despite his reservations, Dad went along with the program and agreed to keep Armand under wraps until he heard back from me. Jacqueline and her friend made a hasty retreat into their apartment, and I left for Fat Cat's. I arrived at eight-twenty. Meeting with Eric ranked right up there with having a pedicure done by a blind woman who spoke no English. But right now, what did I have? Not much. Certainly not enough to change the mind of a cop like Des Martini. But if I could break Eric, I could call the cops on both him and Armand.

Knowing this was a potentially dicey situation, I jammed my Taser into my crossbody bag and slipped it on. If things went sideways with Eric, I definitely wanted protection.

The bar at Fat Cat's was filled to capacity. Customers crowded every table, and several of the small two-tops had been pushed together by a large, rowdy group. Eric sat at the bar talking to an attractive twenty-something blonde, a half-finished bottle of beer in front of him. They both leaned in close to the other. Her body language, along with her skimpy tank top and call-girl makeup, left no questions—she was in the available-and-willing category.

I approached from Eric's blind side. The blonde glanced in my direction once, but her gaze flicked away from me and back to Eric without ever stopping to register that I was headed straight for them. She laughed at something he said, brushed at her bangs, then placed a hand on Eric's upper arm. These two were perfect for each other—a couple of barracudas each trying to out-flirt the other.

The blonde's smile fell the moment I inserted myself between her and Eric. "He's busy right now." I spun around and fixed Eric with an intense stare. "You and I need to talk."

He reached out to push me aside, but I grabbed his arm above the elbow and pressed beneath his bicep. His face contorted in pain and he leaned over onto the bar in an effort to get away.

"Hey!" the blonde yelled. "Stop that!"

I glared at her. "Back off. And believe me, I'm doing you a favor."

The blonde grabbed her glass of wine and scurried away, looking over her shoulder and cursing me as she went. Turning back to Eric, I released the pressure and smiled sweetly. "Looks like you're free now."

"I have nothing to say to you—Mandy, Jade, whatever your name is."

"That's where you're wrong. Armand told me everything."

His expression turned dark and serious. "Whatever he told you, it's a lie."

"I thought lies were your specialty, Romeo."

"What do you want?"

"The truth about what happened to Bert Darlington."

Eric snatched up his bottle, then straightened and licked his lips. "You want the truth? Fine. Armand killed Bert because he was being blackmailed. The guy's a sociopath who can't cut it in a long-term relationship, so he masks it with his whole always-in-love routine. Bert told Armand he was going to expose his past to Jacqueline if he didn't get what he wanted."

"Which was?"

"Armand was supposed to kill Gina." He looked over my shoulder, motioned at one of the servers, and said, "Is it okay if we sit over there?"

I stared straight back at him. This guy was about to be accused of murder and his big concern was getting a table? He was either pure crazy or completely innocent. I found it hard to believe the latter, but followed him to the table and sat, all the while keeping an eye on him. Once seated, I said, "Armand told me you were the one who was supposed to kill Gina."

"That's Armand. Always twisting things around. He's been that way since college. It's why he can never have a real relationship. They always find out he's a pathological liar."

"So now Armand is a sociopath and a pathological liar."

"That's right."

"I guess the Three Inseparables have separated."

Eric did a double take, then took a sip from his bottle. "You must've been talking to Larry Lawson. Another piece of work."

"What's that mean?"

"He was another one who always wanted to hang out with us. He never made the cut because he was too unreliable. Did he tell you about his auto accident?" Eric paused, nodded, then continued. "Yeah, he did. I'll bet he forgot to mention that he was the drunk driver. Him and Armand, they were always trying to turn me and Bert against each other with their lies. But I know the whole story. And while you might want to paint me as the bad guy in this whole deal, I'm just on the sidelines. Did you know Armand committed the first Amorous Assailant attack all on his own?"

"Bert confessed to those attacks. All of them."

"He did that to hide the deal with Armand because Armand told him if he didn't confess, he'd tell the cops about Bert's plan to kill Gina."

I felt a chill fill me from within. Had I been wrong? Which one of these two was the bigger liar? Or was this all just part of membership in their clique? Just as I'd done with Armand, I had to play Eric's game and hope I could sort truth from fiction. "I stopped the fourth attack. I know for a fact that Bert assaulted Belinda James."

"Because by then, Armand was pulling the strings. He had the leverage he needed on Bert. What do you think Gina would have done if Armand showed up with proof her husband had created a blueprint for murder? She'd have had a restraining order within an hour. Bert was screwed, so he committed the third and fourth attacks."

My breath caught. Criminals followed patterns. The Amorous Assailant used the same coffee shop for the first two attacks. My dad might be with the real killer.

Eric nodded again. "That's right. You figured it out. The change in location. Armand never intended to do more than a couple of those attacks. He staged the whole Good Samaritan thing on number three to set himself up as the reluctant white knight. It ratcheted up the pressure on Bert because Armand had a witness proving he wasn't the Amorous Assailant."

"Let's suppose for a moment that I believe your story. How did Bert ever convince Armand to participate? Was there any money exchanged for this supposed hit job?"

"No. It was all *quid pro quo*. Bert got tired of having to go to Gina every time he needed cash to do something."

"Do something? Like what? Bail out his friends? I've followed the money, Eric. I know Bert was paying off people for you."

He took a sip from his beer and shook his head. "There you go again, making accusations when you've only got half the story. I'm surprised you fell for that. Don't you remember? I was an attorney before I went into business with Bert. Well, I had to broker deals for my clients. Bert was one of those, but he needed to keep a low profile."

"You're blaming Karl White on Bert?"

"Me and Bert were young and stupid in college, and we made a big mistake with White."

"You're admitting you forced Karl White into the trunk of your car?"

"What of it? Statute of limitations has run out on the original incident. Nothing happened recently, even though Bert was ticked when the guy came back after he'd been paid off. Bert wanted to make White pay for going back on the deal they made originally, but that would have only made things worse. I met with White and got him to sign an NDA."

"You made the deal with White even though he cost you your job. Really? You expect me to believe that?"

The muscles in Eric's jaw tightened. Something told me he was done talking about Karl White. That was not a problem because I had another line of attack in mind.

"What about Castillo?"

He squinted at me and said, "You really know how to dig up the dirt. Don't you? Fine. Castillo was a danger to my daughter. My ex wasn't going to stay away from him, so I got Bert to loan me enough to make him break off the relationship."

"Bert was just being a good guy and doling out money to keep everyone happy? That's BS and you know it."

"Bert got greedy. He wanted everything Gina had, so he went to Armand and said he'd forgive the debts if Armand did this one thing for him."

"Why not just say no?" I asked. "Armand could have gone to the cops and told them what he knew."

Eric took a long pull from his glass. When he set it down, he leaned toward me and lowered his voice as if he were sharing a dark secret. "In which case, Bert would have gone to Jacqueline and told her everything. It was checkmate. But once Bert thought he had Armand where he wanted him, Armand went into planning mode. Didn't take him long to figure out how to turn things around. Bert was never much of a planner, but Armand, he was always scheming."

"So Armand committed the first two attacks, then blackmailed Bert to continue. Bert decided to get rid of Gina and tried to force Armand to do it, but Armand killed Bert to remove the threat."

"Pretty freaking brilliant. Right? I gotta hand it to Armand. He almost pulled off a major game reset. Too bad for him you came along and figured it all out." Eric sat back in his seat, smiled at me, and sipped his beer.

47

THE ROOM RUMBLED WITH THE sounds of a rowdy crowd fueled by alcohol and camaraderie. They talked in loud, boisterous voices. All around us, friends laughed freely. And across from me, Eric seemed very pleased with himself. For all I knew, this environment, or perhaps the beer he'd just polished off, bolstered his confidence. All it would take, though, was one phone call. With that, I could prove whether Eric was telling the truth or lying through his beer. I reached for my phone, showed it to him, and held his gaze.

Beneath his furrowed brow, his gaze narrowed. "What are you doing?" The honeyed tones that had laced his voice while ratting out Armand had given way to bitter suspicion.

"Phoning a friend. There's an easy way to get to the bottom of this. It's basically a coin toss. If Armand was here during those first two attacks, you win. If he wasn't here, you lose."

Eric's smile returned as he leaned forward. "The guy's probably faked his records. He's smart enough to put appointments on his calendar."

And Eric was smart enough to have faked his. But there was one record he couldn't touch. "He can't fool the airlines. He was either on his flights or he wasn't," I said.

"So he bought a ticket. That doesn't prove anything."

"No, but the manifest will show, and the cops can get those with a warrant. The detective in charge of the murder investigation can have the information in no time. What do you say? Shall I call her and have her get started on that warrant?" I opened my contacts and scrolled down until I found my dad. "Here she is," I said. "Detective Martini."

I dialed, waited, and when Dad answered, I said, "Detective, this is Jade Cavendish."

"Jade? What are you doing? Are you in trouble?"

Eric squirmed in his chair. He looked like he was getting ready to bolt. I couldn't use my Taser in this crowd. And I certainly couldn't use physical force. We needed the cops. And fast. I prayed Dad would understand the meaning of my call. "I'm with Eric Andrews at Fat Cat's. He's telling me Armand Fraser killed Bert Darlington. The only thing we need to verify his story is the manifest from the flight he took on November 21."

"I'm calling the police, Jade." The line went dead.

Thank goodness. Now, could I keep Eric here? He scanned the crowd, a crimson vein on his neck pulsing with anger. He stood and took a step, but I jumped up and blocked his way. "No. You don't get to leave."

The vein throbbed. His eyes widened. "Move!" He yelled and faked a lunge toward me.

I held my ground. But Eric wasn't done. He tried to grab my arm, but I swatted away his hand. Someone tapped me on the shoulder.

"I've got this," I snapped.

"This guy bothering you, Miss?" The guy behind the voice was large, hulking, and drunk. He had a half-filled schooner of beer in his hand and swayed on his feet. His gaze bounced between Eric and me in a slow-motion tennis match.

I tossed a glance at the drunk. Started to tell him everything was fine. To back off. Then caught Eric's movement. My self-defense training kicked in as Eric threw his punch.

My arm went up. Blocked Eric's blow. Wrong move.

The punch nailed the drunk. He went down easily, toppling sideways like an unbalanced stack of milk bottles at a carnival. He smashed into a woman who was pushing her way through the crowd. She screamed as they both went down. I tried to help, but she grabbed my hand and pulled me into a tangle of bodies, splashing beer, and scattered furniture.

I watched helplessly as Eric shoved his way through the melee toward the exit.

On the way down, I yanked my arm free. I landed hard, but absorbed the impact by rolling once before being caught in a forest of legs. My phone was gone, lost somewhere in the crowd and probably under someone's foot.

I jumped up and dove into the crowd. "Stop that man!"

Curses and angry warnings, first issued at Eric, then me, traveled in our wake. Eric burst through the front door at full speed. The door rebounded, then pushed open. When I got to the other side, I found a woman dressed in a tight tee, jeans, and stilettos sprawled in the bushes. The man standing over her spewed expletives at Eric as he helped the woman up.

Halfway down the parking lot, Eric was squeezing between his car and a large SUV. The guy wasn't stupid, which meant he most likely had an escape plan and, if he got away, might be almost impossible to find.

I looked around desperately for something, anything, to help me stop him. I pulled out my Taser, but it and my martial arts training were useless against a car. Behind me, a pair of headlights swung into the parking lot. I shielded my eyes from the blinding lights and recognized the outline of a light bar atop the vehicle. It was a police cruiser.

"Thank you, Dad," I whispered to myself and ran in the opposite direction. Right toward Eric's car.

The red-and-blue strobes kicked on, the siren wailed once, and the cruiser followed. I stopped behind the big SUV on the far side of Eric's car. The cruiser pulled to a stop in front of me. I smiled at my handiwork and raised my hands.

Both cruiser doors swung open, and two figures exited the vehicle.

"Put down the weapon, Miss," one of the officers said.

"I'm putting it down now." I bent down and placed the Taser on the asphalt in front of me. I pointed at Eric's car. "The man in that car is responsible for the disruption inside, but he's also involved in the murder of Bert Darlington. My name is Jade Cavendish and I'm the owner of the Beachtown Detective Agency."

Eric had apparently caught on. He was penned in until the cruiser moved. He got out of his car and stood with the door ajar. "Hey, Officer? Can you move? I'm late and need to get home."

"Step out here where I can see you, sir," said one of the cops as he approached Eric. Over Eric's innocent-sounding protests, the second officer got him out from between the cars and asked him what had happened while his partner approached me.

I read my guy's name tag. Remembered to keep my composure. Got straight to the point. "Officer Foster, my ID is in my purse. It will confirm who I am. That man's name is Eric Andrews. I believe he killed Bert Darlington. You should call Detective Martini. I'm sure she'll want to talk to Mr. Andrews."

"She's a lunatic!" Eric took two steps toward me, but was immediately blocked by the second cop. Eric jabbed a finger in my direction as he tried to make his case. "She was harassing me in the bar, and then she followed me out here. You need to lock her up."

"Calm down, sir. We'll get this all sorted out."

"You'd better," Eric snapped. "You two screw this up and I'll have your badges!"

The cop kept a wary eye on Eric. I had to admit, Eric's anger was so convincing that I almost believed he was the aggrieved party. While Eric's guy dealt with him, I produced my ID.

"Beachtown Detective Agency," Foster muttered when he glanced at the document. With one eyebrow raised, he regarded me and asked, "You said you owned it. Is Thomas Cavendish your dad?"

His tone had been so even I couldn't tell if him knowing my dad was a good thing or a bad one. I just hoped my answer wouldn't work to my disadvantage. "He is," I said.

Another cruiser pulled into the lot and parked behind Foster. One of the newcomers took over the job of directing traffic, which was in chaos thanks to a car that had pulled into the lot and apparently decided he couldn't pass a police car while there were red-and-blue lights flashing.

I looked at the parking lot entrance and the line of cars extending out into the street. "What a mess," I said.

Foster took one glance, then returned my ID and said, "I'll call Detective Martini." He exchanged a nod with the other officer, who took Eric's arm.

"Sir, I'm going to let you cool down in the car," the officer said. He guided Eric to the back of the cruiser, then eased him inside, all the while enduring a tirade fit for a king losing his throne.

Finally, with Eric secured, I felt like I could relax my guard. True, I was the center of attention and everybody watching probably thought I was just another troublemaker, but I knew better. And that was all that mattered.

After Foster spoke to Detective Martini, he smiled for the first time. "Most of us liked your dad, Ms. Cavendish. I was sad to see him retire, but he did a lot of good in his time. You've got a big pair of shoes to fill."

Great. Just what I needed—the bar set high before I even got started. "Don't worry. He's not gone completely. He's my… mentor."

"Good to know. I'll pass the word."

"Thanks," I said reluctantly. All I needed was for my dad to hear about this and he'd be itching to come back. "Officer Foster, can I have my Taser back now?"

"It hasn't been fired?"

"No, it hasn't. Although, it was very tempting."

Foster tried not to laugh, but his attempt to remain impassive failed, and he muttered, "I'll bet."

While Foster took my statement, the other cops got the traffic moving, funneled gawkers into the restaurant or, if they'd actually seen something, took their statements. The whole operation was beginning to look like a well-oiled machine, and then Detective Des showed up.

48

Detective Des wore a conservative white shirt and khaki pants. She'd topped it off with a blue blazer. What was it with this woman? We were pushing ten p.m. and she looked exactly the same as she had the morning I'd first met her. I wondered if maybe she had a much larger go bag than mine, maybe even an airline carryon.

I steeled myself for another grilling as she spoke with Foster far enough away so that I couldn't hear their voices. Detective Des looked at me a couple of times and even gave me the raised eyebrow once when she glanced up from reading my statement. When she finished, she dismissed Foster and approached.

"So, you caught yourself a real-life bad guy," she said.

My cheeks warmed at the hint of a compliment. "I did."

"Excellent work, Ms. Cavendish. You've given us everything we need to put this guy away."

I went into full blush mode. This was a whole different Detective Des than the one who had interviewed me at the Sunny Days Inn. "Look, about Roger…"

She shook her head. "Don't worry about Roger. We're fine.

Now, let's go through everything again."

By the time Detective Des finished grilling me, the adrenaline had taken its toll. I was done. But when she asked me to come in and sign my statement, I thought of Gina and how drained she'd looked earlier. I volunteered to do it right away if Detective Des would officially declare Gina no longer a suspect.

To my surprise, the detective agreed to my terms immediately. After I finished at the station and was on my way home, I called Gina and gave her the good news. She broke down in tears.

At five-thirty the following morning, my alarm went off. I dragged myself out of bed and, ignoring the beckoning of my warm and cozy covers, went downstairs for coffee. Mom was already in food-prep mode; Dad was reading on his laptop at the center island, and I had a severe case of sleep deprivation. When I leaned over Dad's shoulder to give him a kiss on the cheek, I caught a glimpse of his screen.

"You're reading Zoe's blog?" I asked.

"She did a really good job on that story," Mom said. "Didn't she, Thomas?"

"It doesn't seem like the same person wrote this." He laughed. "There are no wild accusations, no conjecture—it's no fun at all. It's actually decent journalism."

I gave the story a brief read through. It included much of the information I'd given her last night after I'd spoken with Gina. It laid out the Amorous Assailant plot—how it had started as a way to kick start Jacqueline's interest in marrying Armand, how it turned into a blackmail scheme, and ultimately had become a motive for murder. She must have stayed up until dawn working on the story.

When I finished reading, Dad looked at me from over the rim of his coffee mug. "Is what she said at the end true?"

"Only Bert Darlington knows for sure, but all indications are he never intended to help Eric out of the goodness of his heart. He always preached about how people should pay it forward, but the truth is he always wanted something in return. Because he had access to money, he could buy whatever he wanted."

Dad took a sip from his mug and grimaced. "Including people?"

"Uh-huh. Eric was easy. His aggression was catching up to him. The lawsuits were getting larger. And Bert decided if he could wipe the slate clean for his old buddy, he could get a huge quid pro quo. Eric would be freed of his past, and Bert could get what he really wanted—more money and power. All he needed to do was to eliminate Gina."

"The dark underbelly of human greed," Dad said. "It's what keeps people like us in business. From what I saw at Carlucci's, I'm surprised this Eric character didn't go along with the plan."

"Eric developed some sort of weird crush on Gina. The fact that she never slept with him made her all the more attractive. Eric's not stupid. He saw the prize Bert was after and decided it could be his. So he set Armand up to take the fall. Knowing Eric, he would have played the consoling friend for a while with Gina, then made his move. The bottom line is he had no interest in killing her, but he went along to make Bert's death look like a revenge killing. If he played his cards right, he figured he'd wind up with the girl and the money all to himself. Pretty twisted. Right?"

"Beats my Three Eggs story," Dad said.

"Your father's first case was nothing compared to this, honey." Mom handed me a mug filled with steaming coffee. "So now that you're friends with someone like Gina Rose, I suppose you're going to want to find your own place."

I shook my head. "Not really. I've learned a lot on this case. But it also taught me how much I don't know. So if you don't mind, don't rent out or remodel my room, I'm happy to stay here."

"Good," Dad said. "Because we like having you around. It's also a nice way for me to keep tabs on the agency without having to stop in all the time. Besides, you probably won't have a lot of time for your old man now that you've got important friends."

I sat across from Dad. "You don't have to worry. Now that I realize just how screwed up Gina's life is, I have no desire to be her friend. I'm happy to keep her on the same fashion-icon pedestal I've always had her on. She could be a good source for referrals, though. This morning she left me a message. Apparently, a friend of hers wants to hire me. Her friend's home has been burglarized three times recently. It happened again last night. She's convinced it's one of the help, and she wants me to find the culprit. I'm meeting with her this morning."

"A burglary? Why doesn't she just report it to the police?" Dad asked.

"Apparently, each theft has occurred when she was 'visiting a friend.'"

Mom, who'd been riveted in place since she'd handed me my coffee, rolled her eyes and laughed. "Code for having an affair. Right, Thomas?"

"In my experience." Dad bit his upper lip, but couldn't stop from smiling. "So what happens?"

"Each time, the burglar steals one piece of expensive jewelry. It's always been something the woman's husband gave her. What's weird is that the house looks like someone had a party."

Mom pointed at Dad's laptop and giggled. "Does your friend Zoe know about this?"

"Not yet. Why do you ask?"

"I was just thinking she might want to start another expose."

Dad, of course, had to add his two cents. "I can see the

headline now—cheating wife finds valuables missing after night on the town."

"No, Thomas. That has zero sex appeal. You have to think big—something more like…" Mom paused and spread her hands as though she were describing a movie marquee. "How about The Case of the Boisterous Burglar?"

Oh gawd. All I needed was Mom giving Zoe drama lessons.